The Very Special Dead

"A wonderful, haunting, atmospheric story that reinvents the Gothic novel for the modern world. Christian Livermore has achieved something quite unique and extraordinary in this tale of stolen lives and loves."

– Gerard Woodward, twice Booker-shortlisted author
of The Jones Trilogy

"Elegant and strange, studded with lore and loss, The Very Special Dead has something of a New England Under Milk Wood and Invasion of the Body Snatchers in its salty darkness. This is a vivid tale of abjection and possession, of missing truths and memories told with stylish irony and black humor. Christian Livermore has written a special book, indeed."

- James Reich, author of The Moth for the Star

"Written with the crustaceous eloquence of a ghastly sea-shanty, The Very Special Dead is a salt-soaked, brine-blasted fable that echoes with lean grief and life lost. You can nearly hear the voices of the dead lifting up from its haunted pages."

– Clay McLeod Chapman, author of Ghost Eaters

"Moving, profound, beautifully observed: here's a vital book by a vital new writer. You'll want to read everything she writes."

– Jacob Polley, T.S. Eliot Prize-winning author of Jackself

"Compelling, impossible, heartbreaking, wildly imaginative and at the same time grounded. Livermore writes with ease, her language fraught with homesickness and the pull of the sea, considers what it means to love and to be human. The narrative moves like poetry along the trajectory of one long breath. Even the most harrowing passages are beautifully written, allowing the light in. This book reminds us that sometimes we need to look beyond the darkest parts of ourselves to find the mystery of possibility."

– Lillian Nećakov, author of Midnight Glossolalia
and Duck Eats Yeast, Quacks, Explodes; Man Loses Eye

"In The Very Special Dead, Christian Livermore delivers a tale that is part domestic drama, part horror, all allegory. Through taut, timeless prose, she provides a window into the lives of the blue-collar denizens of a small New England town and their struggles: family, jobs, finances, gentrification, friendship, loneliness, and even existential dilemmas. Then, just when you think you know where this story is going, a bizarre supernatural occurrence delivers them from their humdrum existences. Sort of. Except death, as it turns out, is kind of humdrum too. Livermore beautifully illustrates the nameless longing we all feel, the nagging belief that there's always someone or something better, just out of reach, and how that belief robs us of genuine contentment. It's downright Dickensian – like A Christmas Carol, the dead instruct the living. Or at least, death throws reality into stark relief. A quiet, insightful tale about finding your place in the world, it's a fascinating, compelling read."

– *Lauren Scharhag, author of The Order of the Four Sons series*

"The Very Special Dead is a melting pot of ideas, a bubbling cauldron of genres overflowing with imagination. This is an exciting new slant on the undead, but much more than that it is a powerful commentary on the oppressive forces that face working families today. Like a potent blend of Steinbeck and Matheson, The Very Special Dead offers a clear denunciation of the modern world where some come to view death as a preferable alternative to a life with crushing debt, no healthcare and little hope for the future."

– *Iain Maloney, author of Life is Elsewhere/Burn Your Flags*

"Christian Livermore's crisp, clear prose will lead you into the afterlife and back again. Filled with humor and heartache, The Very Special Dead reminds us that the only thing that tethers us to this life are the relationships we make and the hearts we touch."

– *Jesi Bender, author of Kinderkrankenhaus*

"Christian Livermore's The Very Special Dead immerses its reader in a hard world of families scraping by, of once-good men ground down by living check-to-check, of grief and the lack of control that threatens to overwhelm those grieving. Like the best horror and literature, the desperation swells as the protagonists navigate a marriage fractured, an investment gone wrong, and a career lost to illness until they are willing to trade places with the dead. In the end, full of darkness and light, love, humor, and heart ache this is a book about agency and responsibility, of understanding what one means in the lives of those around them before they are lost forever."

– *Andrew Najberg, author of The Mobius Door*

"Clear-minded prose that tackles big issues is what we've come to expect from Christian Livermore, and her new novel The Very Special Dead is no exception. In a skillfully rendered seaside New England town, we see the modern world collide with tradition, as each character ponders the central question: 'How had he become a man on the outside of his own life?' Their answers lead to extreme consequences that will keep you turning the pages."

– *L.L. Kirchner, author of Blissful Thinking*

"Writing with literary verve and undeniable compassion for her subjects, Christian Livermore gives life, death, and the spiritual shallows between the two their full due in this off-beat, heart-wrenching tale of New England's working poor."

– Kurt Baumeister, author of Twilight of the Gods

For Jacob Polley and Ian Johnson

ISBN: 9798852079206

Copyright © 2023 Christian Livermore
Published in 2023 by Meat For Tea Press, Holyoke, Mass.
Editor-in-Chief: Elizabeth MacDuffie
Book Design: Mark Alan Miller
Front Cover Art: Steven Archer

The Very Special Dead

Christian Livermore

"What we essentially want is to draw something unknown to us in all its shadowiness, not something we know in all its illumination."
–*Orhan Pamuk, My Name Is Red*

~

Fair warning: it is a strange tale that will be told here,
and a preposterous one.
Who could be blamed for not believing it?
And yet believe, if you can, for in such marvels lie truths we dream of
but can find no other way to speak.

~

Much later, after the corpse had stolen his body, Bent Fiske understood the secret of death, but this morning he was just a man rising early to check the traps. The silver light faded and the moon dropped, the window showed naught but black, and he knew he had to rise. He braced himself against the cold and flung off the covers, shimmied quickly into his clothes, zipped his fleece high round his throat. Jean, daughter and sister of fishermen, didn't stir.

"Kip."

The dog jumped off the foot of the bed, stretched, and clattered into the hall after him.

The air bit. Kip sniffed the bare branches of the brown, dead forsythia and lifted his leg. Bent watched the steam rise. When the dog had finished they crossed the lawn, the ground still crunchy, and descended the hill.

Bent opened the shed door and stepped into his waders and took the bucket and boatswain's hook from behind the door. When he reached the sand Kip was following a scent around the beach. Bent mounted the jetty and Kip left off and followed. Bent moved slow and chose his footing, feeling the rockweed quivering beneath, but the dog could not be troubled to wait and clambered ahead, nosing the crevices for hermit crabs and whatever else would run.

Farther and farther out Bent went, rock to rock, stepping on barnacles for traction where he could, holding out the bucket on one side and the hook on the other for balance like a high-wire act.

At the head of the jetty he wedged the bucket in a gap in the rocks and reached with the hook beneath the black water and fished for the first rope. It was a job finding it, hidden in the rocks as the ropes were so Fish and Game wouldn't find them and make him buy a license. He found the rope and drew it in with the hook and caught hold and hauled hand over hand and brought up the trap. The crabs scrabbled over each other's backs and crackled and bubbled, and one angry sook raised her red claws at him like a prizefighter waiting for the bell. Bent opened the hatch and dumped them in the bucket. Their claws scraped the plastic and the sook clambered atop the pile and scratched at the sides for a way out. Kip poked his snout in and the sook snapped at it. Kip jerked back and blinked, shook it off and went back to sniffing amongst the rocks.

Bent pulled in the rest of the traps and stood and arched his back, felt his joints grind like crushed glass. He looked across the way to Mouse Island. The sky was a slash of blue-hot iron. He whistled for Kip, hanging off the edge of the jetty watching something slither by in the water. Bent turned to see what he was after, and the rockweed shifted under him and he went down and felt his head connect with a rock. He jerked up and grabbed for the bucket. He'd made a fist round the handle and managed to hold it but it had gone sideways. The pain was sharp and he worried maybe the elbow was broken, but still he snatched at the crabs that had been thrown free and were scrambling down the sides of the rocks. He caught one or two, and Kip snapped at the others, but they were down the sides like spiders and in the water and gone.

He sat up and put a hand to the back of his head and brought back blood. Kip sniffed at his face and at his hand. He pinned the bucket between his knees and worked his fingers around the elbow, flexed the joint. Not broken. He looked into the bucket. He'd lost about half.

"Shit."

Good job one of the fugitives was the sook, anyway. Less meat. Don't bring as much. He'd still get thirty for the rest, maybe thirty-five, if he could sell to Norm. Grocery money, anyway. He tore loose a couple fistfuls of rockweed and dropped them in amongst the blues and snapped the cover on. The crabs crackled through the air holes and Kip snuffled at them.

He stood, more carefully this time. As he rose, something skittered by along the sand to his left. He turned but it was gone. He watched a moment but saw nothing more. A shiver ran through him but he shook it off. *Just your imagination.*

Back at the shed Bent hung his waders on the hook and put the bucket in the back of his truck, then he let Kip into the house and went upstairs to wash. Before the bathroom mirror he dabbed at the wound with a rag, rinsed it and squeezed, watched the pink water spiral down the drain, then dabbed and rinsed again, and again, till the water ran clear. He squeezed the sticky unguent onto two fingers, found the tender spot and smeared it on.

He stepped out under a grey woolen sky and climbed the hill toward Little's and sang for company.

> Come list to me, and I will tell
> of a lad so brave and strong
> I'll tell you of Olav Åsteson
> Who slept a sleep so long.

> He laid him down on Christmas Eve
> And fell asleep full fast,
> And he woke not till Epiphany,
> When folk to church did pass.

At the top of the hill he turned left and passed the park. Not a soul in the place, none living anyway. There was an uncanny feel to it, like something lurked, he didn't know what. The inlet black, water flat as a dime. Wraiths of fog like hag's fingers clutched trees, water, stubbly yellow grass. Leafless branches plucked at the air. It felt like the moment before something happens, something wonderful or something awful maybe, Bent couldn't say which. Something broke the water's surface and he turned in time to see a flash of grey, then circles rippling out, and then the water sealed over the spot and turned to glass. Sturgeon breaching, probably. Bent scanned the water, waiting, and soon it surfaced again, a splash, a flash of olive-green, prehistoric, arcing and rolling, and then it slipped under and the water swallowed it once more. Bent watched awhile but didn't see it again. It would probably surface farther out next. Bent walked on. At old St Mary's he turned right, looked up at the stained glass left in place by the family who had bought the church and converted it into a house and crossed himself. He shook his head. Still following the old superstitions.

Easterly used to be a proper working town, home of fishermen and lobstermen and glazers. Houses were clapboard and two-storey, what a man needed to keep his family decently, and families were large in those days. They weren't rich but they owned their homes and had quarters to give the little ones for ice cream at Little's and even to treat their pals.

Then a few New Yorkers stopped through on their way to Block Island or the Cape or Provincetown or somewhere, and word got out, leaked back to the city, about the pretty little town set high on a bluff on the Sound. Real New England. Lobsters big as your forearm. And these New Yorkers came with real estate agents, and offered money for houses occupied by widows, the last of their name, good money, and the widows took it. What else could they do? They could barely keep themselves anymore, never mind a drafty old saltbox. And slowly the New Yorkers moved in and the old families moved out, to who-knows-where, Florida maybe, with their big fat profits. And the families left behind watched as New Yorkers moved in to the left of them and New Yorkers moved in to the right and planted high hedges and held garden parties for more New Yorkers. Watched as home values shot through the roof and their property taxes with them. And had to take second jobs to pay them. Or couldn't pay them and watched the family home for three generations and more auctioned on the courthouse steps. Bent was one who swore he wouldn't sell and would keep up with his taxes, wouldn't see his home sold away to out-of-towners who didn't know this place and cared nothing for it.

They were Norwegians mostly, in the old days, anyway, when the town was settled. Descendants of berserkers, the historian in Bent liked to reflect. They came across the sea and liked what they found, liked the salt air and the high protected bluff, and traded the battle-axes and dragonships of their ancestors for skiffs and trawlers. They married Portuguese and Italians and Irish and abandoned their own religions and became Roman Catholic like their spouses. A few grandmothers, like Bent's, had remembered the old songs, but they were gone now, and all that was left of those people and those ways were the ropy arms and the sense of the sea and a faint a-yut in the accent.

Bent reached the playground and saw the warm yellow light in Little's window. The steam from his breath billowed and he stepped up his pace. The lobster pots were in for the season and the boats hauled out. There was winter work to be done, scraping and painting and repairs, but that needn't be done at dawn, and yet a man doesn't break the habit of rising in the dark so easily. So, at half past four every morning the men who worked the sea woke and, after a while, when the time they allowed for daydreaming was filled with debts owed and things needed, they rose, pulled on their jeans and their wellies and wandered up to Little's for coffee and talk.

Bent climbed the steps, his boots thrumming on the wooden porch slats. The big window sweated and inside it was like Christmas morning, though it wasn't yet Thanksgiving. Steam rose off the coffee cups and the grill smoked, colorful penny candy sparkled in row after row of big glass apothecary jars, red fireballs and Swedish fish, orange and green and purple jellybeans, black and red rope licorice wound around old wooden spools like boat line. Sometimes Bent was numb to it, but other times, this morning, it struck him, the smells, the colors, the look of the place, all just as it had been for a hundred years and more, and his breath caught in his chest.

He paused at the counter and took the mug of coffee Sandy had poured when she saw him through the window, the porcelain stinging as it thawed his icy hands. She made a note on her order pad and tucked the pencil behind her ear.

"Can I have an orange juice, too?"

She wrinkled her nose, drawing its red freckles closer together. "With your stomach? No, orange juice is too acidic. I'll bring you apple juice."

"I don't like apple juice."

"Tough."

Sandy filled a glass with apple juice and slid it across the counter. Bent dutifully accepted it and took his place in the booth with his buddies. He cupped his elbow briefly in one hand, but it wasn't too bad now. Just the arthritis making it seem worse than it was. Tell Holland reached for his flask and spiked Bent's coffee with whisky and finished telling of the man from the gas company who'd called to dun him at supper.

"I said, whadja do with the money I gave you last month?"

The men laughed. The story probably wasn't true, Tell's stories hardly ever were, but they liked the bravado, what they hoped Tell had said to the bill collector, what they wished they could say themselves.

Sandy came round with the pot and topped everybody up and Tell tipped the flask over each man's cup and sighed his heavy sigh.

"Tell me something, can ya? Why're we all made to suffer?"

The others groaned. They'd heard this saw before, but Tell was off and there wasn't any stopping him, nor Gravel either who'd be starting next with his talk.

"Original sin, boy." There was Gravel off and running. "Eve ate of the tree of knowledge and made her old man do it too, and now we're all forever sunk in sin and condemned to toil in vain for our own redemption. Bitch."

Sandy shouted from behind the counter. "Gravel, what did I tell you?"

Gravel was chastened. "Sorry, Sandy."

"All that's nothing but a hoax, anyway," said Tell. "Oddments of Roman Catholic bullshit, meant to keep the kiddies in train. Stop em playin with theirselves when the old folks shut the lights for the night. Nope, this, my friends, is all there is."

"Christ help us if that's the truth."

"It's a ball-ache," said Tell.

"Why'nt ya kill yerself then?" said Gravel.

"In this weather? Not on yer life."

"What's the fuckin weather got to do with it?"

"Nothin, if you do it right," said Tell. "If you've kilt yourself, sure, it makes no difference if you're lying dead on the frozen tundra. Weather's a help to you then, ain't it? Keep your body preserved, lookin all spiffy for the wake, for your ma to say her fare-thee-wells. It's if you make a hash of it, that's where you got problems, right? If you slip with the gun, blow yourself only partways to hell. Then there's you, lying in the bitter fuckin cold, two three days maybe if you done it like a man, way off in the woods somewhere so your family don't have to find you, your blood oozin out the hole you blew in yourself and nobody around to help you and you slowly freezin to death."

"And then you turn into a ghost."

Sandy was wiping down the counter. Everyone turned to look at her.

Tell cocked his head. "A *ghost*?"

Sandy nodded. "That's what my grandmother always said. You kill yourself you leave unfinished business, so you come back as a ghost."

"Your grandmother was one witchy broad," Tell said.

"Go ahead, scoff," Sandy said. "Kill yourself and see if it's not true. But don't come haunting me cause I got a bad heart."

The men laughed and returned to their conversation.

Machlon was quiet, hadn't said a word since Bent had sat, wasn't even listening, seemed like. Tell spiked his coffee some more, and shouldered him silently, and Machlon drank. Bent watched. *What's this?* But he said nothing. They didn't seem to be like that anymore, him and Machlon.

"Fifteen hundred dollars a month," Tell was saying. Eddie, the cook, had come out from behind the grill and was leaning against the counter, wiping his hands on his apron. "And that's just to turn the key in the lock. Then there's the mortgage, taxes. Already you're more than twice the cost of a reasonable rent. Now what if the furnace breaks? Five hundred dollars. What if the basement floods? Two thousand dollars. New roof? Fifteen thousand. Garbage collection, utilities, yard work. You're a young guy, why d'ya want to saddle yourself with that kind of debt?"

"But then I own my own house," Eddie said.

"You don't own your house, the bank owns your house. You'll never own your house. All you'll have is a bunch of bills and agita."

"A young guy coming on the market now?" Gravel said. "Two-hundred-thousand-dollar mortgage at six percent? Twenty years it'll be paid. Then he owns the house."

"Two-hundred-thousand? Where's he buying? Appalachia?" Tell turned back to Eddie. "This is Easterly, boy. You're looking at four-fifty at the least. And that's just the mortgage. You gonna pay that on a cook's wages?"

The door opened, and one of the new people came in. He didn't look at them. He was talking on his cell phone and went straight to the counter.

"Morning," Sandy said.

The man tipped the mouthpiece beneath his chin to order. "Coffee, please. Black." The man returned to his phone call. "Yep. Uh huh."

Sandy nodded and poured his coffee and attempted no more conversation. The man took a *New York Times* from the stack Sandy had begun to stock for the new people, paid and left.

"So, anyway." Tell turned back to Eddie. "What about the home equity loans?"

"What home equity loans?"

"Unexpected repairs. College for the kids. Vacation to Disney World."

"I won't."

"You will. Everybody does. So you borrow the original four-fifty on a 30-year mortgage, pay three-hundred-twenty-thousand in interest plus the principle, and by the time you make your last payment, you've given the bank seven-hundred-seventy-five-thousand. Or you die, the bank sells your house to recoup the unpaid balance, and your wife and kids are left with nothing. Why not stick with nothing? It's more realistic. I'm telling you, *home ownership* is the biggest swindle perpetrated on working people since...work."

"Oh my god," said Gravel.

"What?"

"You're a communist."

The men all laughed.

"I don't think I'm a communist. Capitalism sucks, communism sucks, every system ever invented by man sucks."

While they were talking, Marshall came in and stopped at the counter. He reached in his pocket with chubby, hairy fingers and deposited some coins before Sandy and stood raking a hand across his shorn hair.

"Coffee, Marshall?"

Marshall pointed to one of the breakfast sandwiches Eddie had on the go on the grill. Sandy tallied up the change.

"I'm sorry, Marshall, you don't have enough." Marshall looked at her, plucking at the wild gray hairs of his eyebrows. The social services lady kept his hair in a buzzcut so he couldn't pull it out, but she hadn't done his eyebrows in a while. "I can't do it all the time, Marshall. Wish I could, but I can't afford it."

Bent caught Sandy's eye and raised a finger. Sandy nodded and signaled to Eddie to wrap up a sandwich for Marshall. Eddie flipped an egg to do it over easy the way Marshall liked.

At the table bodies began to shift and feet to tap as they do in men unused to sitting idle, whose muscles begin to seize and notice they're wearing out unless they're always stretched, renewed. So the men rose and arched their backs and Bent waited to pay his check.

Sandy wrapped a breakfast sandwich and poured coffee into a Styrofoam cup. Marshall took them and turned in one motion like he did without moving his neck. He stopped beside Bent without looking at him.

"They're coming," he said.

Bent was stunned. Marshall had never spoken to him before. As far as he knew, he'd never spoken to anybody, not since he was a boy.

He watched as Marshall shuffled to the door, opened it and walked out, then he paid his bill and Marshall's.

Outside they split into parties, one group down the hill to tend their vessels, Machlon toward the cottage on Church Street which had been left him by his mother, and Bent and Tell along the high road that traced the spine of the bluff through the village.

How strange life is. They played together as kids, the way most children will, becoming friends with anybody who would have them. In their teens Tell became obnoxious, a braggart and a bully, and then Bent went away to college and they didn't see each other so it didn't matter. When he returned here still was Tell, operating his father's old fishing boat, a bit milder, the way a hard life can rub the sharp edges off a person. And here they were still, just as when they were boys, but older, a bit slower, less sure-footed, age and rough work and disappointment leaving their marks. The forty years in between had nearly wrecked them both.

"What's with Machlon?" Bent said after a while.

Tell shook his head as if to say how bad it was before he said it. "Cancer."

"Oh Christ..." Bent stopped in the road.

Tell nodded. "Pancreas. He started gettin fevers and pukin, and we all seen how skinny he's got. Looks like God didn't breathe into him hard enough. Other day in the mirror he looked yellow, so he went to the doc and that's when they found it. Yellow's bad. You don't go yellow unless you're far gone."

Bent couldn't breathe, and he stood listening to Tell and trying to catch his breath while he looked off down the road at nothing. Used to be he and Machlon were like a pair of crossed fingers, shaking apples from the trees at Haley Farm and hiking to the end of Bluff Point to eat them and taste the sweet juice mingle with the salt from the sea.

Riding their bikes far out of calling distance and staying gone till dusk, playing freeze tag in the road till it was so dark they couldn't see each other till they collided in the blackness and collapsed and lay laughing and out of breath. And when Machlon hid himself away in the grove, in long sleeves and turtlenecks to cover his bruises, Bent sat with him and together they plotted revenge against his father. Bent used to stop Tell chasing down the skinny runt for his lunch money, now here was him getting such news from Tell in the street. He understood why, but it didn't bother him any less. It had been Bent who'd sat on the floor that terrible day while Machlon wept on his shoulder. But nothing can stay the same forever.

"Can they treat it?"

Tell shrugged. "He's to see a specialist next week. If the insurance company don't find a reason to drop him before. They're goin through his paperwork for sure, seein if the least little thing ain't right."

Bent nodded. He wanted to ask what they could do, but every way he said it in his head sounded stupid, empty. So they stood in the salty fog, listening to the buoys clang and the gulls call. One banked overhead and alighted on the playground blacktop where its mates had already gathered.

"Storm coming," Bent said.

Tell nodded. "A-yut."

Tell went still then, his gaze fixed on something in the middle distance behind Bent. Watching Tell's eyes, Bent felt the same shiver he'd felt earlier on the jetty.

"What?" he said.

Tell looked a moment longer, frowning, then turned back to Bent. "Nothing," he said finally. "Thought I saw something."

"What was it?"

Tell seemed on the verge of saying something, then shook his head. "Nothing. Never mind."

Bent watched Tell a second, thought of asking a second time, then decided against it. Fog playing tricks this morning.

"We'll talk more on Machlon," he said. "See what's to be done."

Tell nodded, and went his way, and Bent his. He passed the old grocery store, windows soaped over and sign advertising a new coffeehouse coming soon, one of the chain stores. The new people would prefer it, and Bent worried it would take business from Little's. Some people would stick with Sandy, the older ones, but the kids would be drawn to the sugary frothy coffee drinks at the new café and would spend their allowances and paper route money there instead.

Up ahead the Bentson boys burst through their gate and out onto the ashen road toward the school bus stop, their rucksacks looking light. They weren't much for the books. The eldest, Chris, set the pace, reaching far ahead on the road with his long spidery limbs like a cranefly and his little brothers scrambled to keep up. At the crossroads the puny Anderson boy dashed out from the side street and leapt onto the giant's back, and they all went their way, the giant toting the little one like a potato sack and the other two romping like puppies, all fussing and laughing and happy to be alive. Bent tried to remember when last he felt that way. And he wondered if these boys would continue to have the childhood he'd had in this town, this place till now almost outside time, untouched by the slick new world.

The boys crystallized beneath the white light of the streetlamp then dissolved into the fog and were gone. Bent continued his way alone, thinking on Machlon, and began to sing again.

> I have been up to the clouds above
> And down to the dyke full dark.
> Both have I seen the flames of hell
> And of heaven likewise a part.
> The moon it shines, and the roads do stretch so wide.

He sang quiet, as if devils might hear, or maybe like singing would keep them away. He sang it like his grandmother used to.

The light was up properly now and even through the mist he could see the last of how the trees had set themselves on fire, the reds and oranges and golds, curling in on themselves like dying beetles. The wind lifted and brown leaves skidded across the road. Bent looked at the piles raked together in yards and longed to smell them burning, but that was banned now. He passed the old Kelley place, sold off last spring. A dumpster on the lawn was piled high with boards, wiring and the other detritus of construction. A sign by the front door posted courtesy of the Historical Society read, "John Morgan, 1842." It was listed on the National Register but they didn't care anymore if you renovated or even pulled a place down. It didn't look like they were planning to, but they did seem to be gutting it within.

Almost at his road the yellow grass sloped up the hill to where the Willettes' house stood, crumpled, on the rise facing the western bay. It was haunted, people said, as they always do of such houses, broken down and wanting paint, and each had their tale they told of why. Some told of a spurned lover who came to kill her man and his rightful wife in their beds then hung herself from the balcony, others of a widow who threw herself from the widow's walk to the rocks below when she learned her husband's whaler had gone to the bottom of the sea off Narragansett. Bent and his friends had sprinted past the place as boys and so the young ones did still. Bent stopped and looked up at the windows of the widow's walk and tried to see the woman in white he used to think he spied as a boy. He looked hard but saw nothing, only dull glass and blackness behind, and he moved off down the road and bore right down the hill home.

Inside, the morning chaos was underway. Adelaide, for reasons only a child could understand, was running back and forth in the kitchen. When she heard Bent she turned briefly in the doorway as she ran past.

"Momma had a baby and its head popped off."

Bent laughed and turned to the living room. Jack looked up from where he sat cross-legged on the floor, rolled his eyes and returned to his comic book.

"Can you please get her dressed?" Jean was standing on the stairs toweling her hair. "I can't get her out of her nightgown."

Ada ran toward Bent and hurled herself at him and he caught her and perched her on his hip.

"Daddy, guess what?"

"I couldn't possibly."

"My tooth fell out. See?" She grinned grotesquely, flashing the empty space where her front tooth used to be. "I'm going to put it under my pillow and the tooth fairy will leave me money."

"I thought you didn't believe in the tooth fairy."

Ada grew serious and wrinkled her brow carefully. "Well, I'm not sure if there's a tooth fairy or not, but basically, it doesn't pay to take chances."

"I see. Very sensible.' Bent mounted the steps, Ada scrambling from his hip to his back. "How much do you think the Tooth Fairy will give you?"

Ada thought. "Um, three dollars."

"Pretty good money. Hey, can I borrow three dollars?"

"No!"

"You know, if you had a job, you wouldn't need to depend on the Tooth Fairy for spending money, or your mother and me, either."

Ada giggled and swatted him. "Daddy…"

On the landing Bent set her down and she ran off like a wind-up doll.

"Go brush your teeth, you little freeloader."

The truck bit gravel and Bent pulled past the front door of Norm's Seafood to the side. The kitchen door stood open. Pete was hosing down delivery crates.

Shit.

Bent killed the engine and climbed out. Pete looked up, then back to his work.

"Your dad around?"

"Out with deliveries," Pete said.

He finished the hosing off then cut the water, made Bent wait while he coiled the hose. The crates dripped and looked as dirty as before. Pete walked around to the truck bed. He pulled the cover off the bucket and rummaged among the blues, evading snapping claws, and when he'd finished, wiped his hands on his jeans.

"Twenty-five."

Bent felt his guts jump. "Pete, you know how it is, you've got kids."

"A-yut, I do. So I can't afford to worry about nobody else's."

Bent looked out at the rising chop on the bay and ran through the list of buyers. Wouldn't do any better with any of them, maybe do worse. He looked back at Pete and nodded.

Pete whisked the bucket from the truck and dashed up the steps into the kitchen. Bent calculated, struck items from the grocery list he had made in his head. Pete emerged with the empty bucket, tossed it back in the truck, handed Bent a twenty and a five.

~

Tell pulled into the marina and parked and crossed the gravel to the dry stack. He'd finished the sanding, a week of scraping until his hands cramped and his shoulders and neck ached then burned then went numb, all the time with an eighteen-inch sanding board. Couldn't use a belt sander on a boat such as this. Now he had to stain. So he gathered the stain and brushes from the dry box and approached the boat. He set the stain on the floor and popped the can. Beauty, this boat. Forty-two-foot gaff-rigged yawl, Columbian pine hollow mast, bronze-fastened cedar on oak, Sitka spruce spars. A boat such as he had never had and never would have. His plan was to stain one side today, then finish the rest tomorrow. It'd need three or four days to dry, more maybe as the air was so damp, then he still had to seal and varnish. Dumb bastard should have had this done two months ago, but Tell didn't care. More coin for him.

Behind him he heard footsteps and he turned. Hayes, come to check up on him, see he was getting his money's worth. Or maybe just to gaze at his boat. That could be it. If it were Tell's boat he'd be here all the time. Hayes hadn't acknowledged Tell at Little's that morning and Tell hadn't acknowledged him. Good. Didn't want the others to know he was hard up enough to take on extra work, and for one of the out-of-towners into the bargain.

"Beauty, isn't she?" Hayes ran his hand over the raw hull, its wood like scraped skin.

"That she is. You're a lucky man."

"It's not luck. Well," Hayes flashed a self-deprecating smile, "some of it is. I place my bets and spin the wheel, just like everybody else. But it's where I place them that has paid off. You ever play?"

"Stocks? Me?" Tell practically laughed. "Nah."

"Why not?"

"Haven't got the coin."

"I hear you. But, you know, you don't need that much. I started off with just a small stake from my father. I bought some stock, it split. I bought some more, that split, too. Pretty soon I had enough to buy a few bigger, riskier stocks. After that I was off to the races."

Same old story. Another rich guy thinks he made it on his own because his daddy only gave him half a million dollars.

"My old man left me a ten-year-old Ford and a house in hock to the bank." Tell returned to his staining.

"I hear you. But hey, if you're ever able to free up a little cash, come see me. I'll put you in something good. Pharmaceuticals are paying off big these days. Something like that."

Hayes slapped the hull and jogged back to his sports car with the energy of a man whose whole life was possibility. Tell dipped the brush and swept it firmly across the wood.

Bent nosed into a space on the side of the museum to leave the front free for visitors. As he stepped from his car a school bus passed. Someone had painted out the "o" in "County" so the school district name on the side read "Cunty Consolidated Schools." Surely it was an Easterly boy who did it and not some boy from one of the new families. Bent fought a smile.

Inside he switched on the lights and checked that the automatic timer had cranked the heat, for Mrs. Rutherford was ancient, her skin papery as dead moth's wings. His footsteps cracked the air as he walked the length of the museum, one long room lined with glass cases full of remnants of the town's shipping past: figureheads, galley plateware, candelabra, a Congreve rocket fired on the town when the British attacked in the War of 1812, artifacts from the China trade brought home by sea captains. The center of the room was given over to an exhibit on the old Easterly Shipyard, the largest shipbuilder on the East

Coast in the nineteenth century. It told how in its heyday three hundred men wrought schooners and sloops, of its failure on the death of its owner at the turn of the century on account of bad management by his sons, then of its revival during the world wars and its conversion to a marina for pleasure boats and small fishing boats as it was now.

A school group was expected at eleven. These were the days he liked least, when he had to find ways to make the unremarkable history of this small town interesting to children. How could he express to them the value of the quotidian possessions of people whose names they didn't know, who had won no great battles, occupied no public office, founded no countries or even towns, yet were as important as those great and public figures. Old doll houses and hairbrushes, Valentine's Day cards given by kindergartners to a teacher long dead and the students too. How could he make them see that each item connected those who saw it, those who touched it, to the person who had seen and touched it one hundred or two hundred years ago? As though that person was reaching out from that time to take your hand. That to understand who you are you must understand who your people are, and were, and how you came to be born on this high bluff overlooking the Atlantic? The summer before, they'd splurged on an overnight trip to Philadelphia as part of a project to interest Jack and Ada in history. In line for Independence Hall he'd told about John Adams and Jack had asked, "Didn't he invent beer?'

In his tiny office he picked his way through the piles of folders stacked like plates after a party. He'd been cataloguing. He removed the stack of archival folders from his chair and sat it on the floor and set to work finishing his plan for the talk he would give the students.

At nine, when the reading room opened to the public, he went out to find Mrs. Rutherford reliably at her desk. Now she would tell him of her evening.

"I had baked flounder, which I'd breaded and wrapped in foil with lemon. It was very nice, and fresh, though not strictly fresh. Then I read."

She was reading a history of Canterbury Cathedral and told him of a bishop buried there.

"He was, if you understand me perfectly, the natural son of John of Gaunt."

Bent thought for a moment. That would be Cardinal Henry Beaufort she meant. Then she told of a cook at the cathedral who fell in love with a priest there.

"She was, as it were, very attracted to him."

She did for him, apparently, by poisoning a cake when he brought in a cleaning woman she viewed as a rival.

Mrs. Rutherford had worked fifty years for the post office and was a spy during World War II. He longed to know more about exactly what she had done but to this day she maintained perfect secrecy on the subject, and what little was known was known only because her late husband Harold couldn't keep a secret and let out all the bits and pieces she told him, so she stopped telling anything even to him.

"Oh of course it's not true," she'd say, batting away questions with her hand, but then she'd turn and give you a sidelong glance and arch her eyebrows conspiratorially.

"Missus Rutherford," he tried now, "just tell me one thing you did in the war."

"Oh that's all a lot of nonsense Harold made up to make me sound more interesting than I am," she said, waving the question away. Then she turned her head and arched her eyebrows twice.

Bent laughed. "What am I to tell these kids today about why their history is important?'

"Well *of course* it's important. These are our stories. Who doesn't like a good story? And you know, many of the things we have here belonged to women. Wouldn't these children want them remembered if they were their mothers? Their grandmothers?"

Bent thought about that, nodding. Even if Harold had been lying about Mrs. Rutherford's spying, and he didn't think he had, he was glad of it, for it meant that people would remember her. Mrs. Rutherford should be remembered. He returned to his office and collapsed into his squeaky chair with a heavy sigh and returned to preparing for his talk to the children.

Bent had abandoned all ideas of the seagoing life for himself the day the police came to the house and told them his father had fallen overboard and drowned. Couldn't find the body. Currents probably took it out to sea. His grandmother muttered darkly that the *draugr* had carried him off, or they'd angered the *nisse*, forgot the old ways. His mother told her to leave off, that it was old wives' tales. It's all horseshit, his mother said, and she drank and took little blue pills.

"Fallen overboard; that's a load of horseshit right there." She put a little blueish pill on her tongue, took a slug of whisky and threw her head back to wash it down. "Your old man been on the water his whole life. There ain't no way he would fall overboard."

"The police said he drowned," Bent said. "Everybody says it."

"What the hell do they know? If he drowned, where's the body? Huh?"

Bent shrugged.

"He's gone all right, but he ain't dead." She looked at Bent darkly. "He left."

"Left? Why would he leave?"

"Are you stupid, boy? Think about it. It was hard enough to feed ourselves. Then you came along."

"He would never leave us."

His mother snorted and took another drink. "Do you have any idea what it's like? Having you around, every single day? You couldn't ride a bike, you couldn't play a sport. You couldn't jump, for Chrissake. He tried to love you, we all did, but..." She shook her head. It was impossible.

I can too jump.

Not long afterwards she decided he had a calling, and as soon as he was old enough she packed him off to the seminary on Enders Island. Sure she has, Bent thought. She's seen her chance and she's seized it. No father around to stop her getting rid of me now. A mother can fear a boy, fear his wildness, his boy-ness. She's sending me away in the hope that they'll tame it. And she said it: I'm impossible to love. *Honor thy father and thy mother, that the days may be long upon the land which the Lord thy God giveth thee.* All that was a fairy story to him now, but in the old days he held it true, and he obeyed. And anyway, he was glad to be gone from that house, gone from her.

He stayed at the seminary till he was fifteen years old, and studied his scripture and his Latin with the young priest Father Fintan, their own new parish priest, who traveled from Easterly three times a week to teach the boys, and the whole time Bent wished he were elsewhere. When the priest delivered the Eucharist and they recited the Creed, the seminarians chanted, "We believe in one God, the Father, the Almighty, maker of heaven and earth,' and Bent thought, *betrayer of his servants.* And when the priest held the Eucharist aloft and said, "Lamb of God, you take away the sins of the world,' Bent thought, *Bastard. You took my father. You let him leave me.* The priest said, "Take this all of you and eat of it. This is my body,' and the rest, and knelt. Bent rang the bells and the sound filled the church as the host became the body of Christ, but the only body Bent thought of was his father's, and whether it really was at the bottom of the sea or roaming the earth somewhere, fled as his mother had said.

He began to make mischief. He broke into the sacristy and drank the communion wine. He set a visiting priest's chasuble on fire while lighting a candle. They all stood listening while the priest recited in Latin, but then people began to smell smoke, and then puffs of white began to gather in the air, and then the chasuble was in flames and the priest began waving his arms madly. Bent and the other altar boys rushed forward to pull it off him, and they threw it to the floor and stamped it out. The priest was unhurt, and it was an accident, but the priest didn't believe it. Father Fintan took up for him, but the visiting priest never liked Bent after that. One day before class Bent stole a cast iron pipe from the janitor's supply room and put it in the locker of an older boy and ran off to chapel. The first bell rang, and the boy went to his locker to retrieve a book, and when he opened the metal door the pipe tumbled out and clanged onto his head and he hit the floor, out cold. He required fifteen stitches. After that they said Bent was not suited to take holy orders and they returned him to his mother. He told her he had wanted to leave because he wished one day to marry and raise a family, but the truth was he got himself expelled because he didn't believe a word of it. Drowned or fled, Bent had lost his faith the day his father vanished from his life.

So he entered the public school, and went to college and studied history, then returned home and got a job at the Easterly Library and Historical Society, first as curator and archivist for its small museum then later as director, which amounted to the same job as there was only him and Mrs. Rutherford, who had volunteered at the museum and looked after the books and reading room since she'd retired from the post office twenty years ago. And so it was that he could meet his friends on those mornings at Little's and talk about the old times, tell the tales of their shared childhood on the bluff, and brood together over their misfortunes.

At ten-thirty he rose stiffly from his chair. Only fifty and he was developing that old man walk. He gave his joints a few seconds to unclench, then straightened, arched his back, bent low, then drew himself up to his full height and went to arrange the room for the class.

The talk went as well as could be expected. He found it strange that he knew exactly how to interact with his own children but with others he was completely hopeless. Afraid, even.

Outside, Bent limped toward his car. Sometime during the day his hip had begun to hurt. He reckoned he'd landed hard on it in the fall at the jetty and been so keen on saving the crabs, then so focused on his elbow, he'd not noticed till later. Or it was age, maybe. Age and sitting all day save the hour before dawn he spent crawling amongst rocks tending the traps. Just out of bed a man his age oughtn't exert himself. He'd read in the paper once of a man, fiftyish, rose to shovel the drive first thing, clutched his chest and died there in the snow. His kids found him on their way out to school. The article quoted a cardiologist saying if a man's forty-six or older he mustn't exert himself so soon after waking. The spike in activity was too much for the heart.

Fiskes lived long, but it was labor that kept them young. His grandfather died in bed, ninety-nine and limbs like rebar. Tell, Gravel, the work kept their backs hard and their wind good. Bent had gone wrong, maybe, parting from that life. He was out of place with white-collar types, anyone could see, he was sure they could. A pleb amongst the respectable middle classes. They were comfortable in their own skins and spoke easily, certain, it seemed, that someone cared to hear what they had to say. But he had vowed he would never be like his father, never do anything his father had done. It had to be said, too, Bent liked what he did, liked reading on things that mattered and cherishing them and making others cherish them as well. Liked today.

He pulled into the city hall lot and found a space as near the entrance as possible. At Dieckerhoff's office he knocked briefly then entered. He was early but that was just as well. He could reach Abby sooner.

Dieckerhoff gestured Bent to a chair. Not a bad guy, the mayor. But a practical man, a man who had long ago reckoned up the wages of principles and the wages of compromise and saw compromise paid better. Dieckerhoff crossed his legs and flipped his tie nervously. Didn't want to say what he had to say.

"The thing of it is, Bent." Dieckerhoff stopped and worried his tie some more.

The city had a number of little villages like Easterly within its borders, and when he wasn't running his law practice Dieckerhoff was always attending a Chamber of Commerce meeting or a ribbon-cutting or fulfilling some other civic duty. Bent wondered why he was taking the time to meet with him in person. He reflected on this, and then it struck him.

"You're cutting my hours?"

"We're cutting the museum's hours, yes." Dieckerhoff cleared his throat.

"By how much?"

"Just over twenty."

"Over twenty? I'll lose my health insurance. And I can barely pay my bills as it is. Frank, I've got kids."

"The city's got a half-a-million-dollar budget gap, and the state won't make it up."

"So draw down on the general fund."

"The rainy day fund is for emergencies."

"What about all the extra property taxes you're raking in? Christ knows I'm paying more. All these out-of-towners with their weekend houses?"

"More people mean more services," Dieckerhoff said. "They aren't all weekenders. The school district has had to hire new teachers, buy more textbooks. They're driving, that's road improvements needed. Parks, playgrounds, it all adds up. If there were any other way, Bent."

"And if I leave?"

"I asked the Council that."

"What did they say?"

Dieckerhoff looked down, then back at Bent. "We'd miss you, but we would understand."

Dieckerhoff banged on with his explanations and apologies but his voice shrank to nothing, like Bent was inside a seashell. His hip burned as if somebody were sawing the bone with a blade.

At the tax office across the road he asked for a little more time to pay his bill, but after studying his record the clerk told him a payment extension was impossible as he was so far behind. Bent returned to his truck, slid in and wondered how he would break the news to Jean, though it was no different than they both expected. The hours, though. How would he tell her about that?

At least before he had to face her there would be Abby. Tuesday was their regular day. Jean had her book club, Jack had Boy Scouts and Ada had Brownies with her little friend Caitlin Olsen, so every week the Olsens picked them all up and kept them till nine. Bent circled the lot to the exit and drove the ten minutes into New Hope. He pulled into a space on Water Street and walked the block to Abby's house. He checked to make sure her husband's car wasn't in the driveway, then walked around back and let himself in by the kitchen door. Abby was bent toward the floor, a mason jar in one hand and a paper plate in the other.

He moved toward her, looking down to where she was looking. "What are you doing?"

"There's a spider."

"Where is it? I'll mash it."

"You will not."

"I know, I know."

"In front of the stove. There, see?"

Bent took the jar and plate. He and Abby had been friends at school. They'd gone sledding, and when they got older, lay on the rug in his room listening to Beatles albums. Once, as they sat on the sofa watching a movie, he worked up the courage to hold her hand. A few nights he snuck out and climbed the trellis into her bedroom window, and once she snuck into his. They shared a single bed, their arms draped over each other playfully, and talked into the night. But he could never work up the nerve to do more. Eventually she got tired of waiting, wasn't even sure anymore if he liked her, and then an older boy asked her out and soon she had less time for Bent, and eventually no time at all. After high school she went off to college and eventually moved away for good, married a banker in Greenwich, and Bent felt his life had ended.

When he heard she'd moved back, her husband to be president of the savings bank in New Hope, he spent weeks working up his courage. Finally, last spring, he found an excuse to patronize the nursery he learned she'd bought. *I didn't know you were back. Is it you who owns this place now?* She slid the crocus bulbs he'd just bought across the counter and handed over his change and their hands brushed and his stomach flipped. And Bent, who loved his children more than his life, never missed work, returned money when clerks gave too much change, Bent Fiske had an affair.

He felt guilty all the time, but he could never stop himself seeing her. When their day came, he had trouble breathing. When it came time to meet up, he broke the speed limit to get to her. He was a terrible husband, a terrible person, he knew, but he also knew that apart from when he was with his children, the hours he spent with Abby were the only times in his life when he was happy. He didn't know if he was entitled to such happiness, but he knew that without it, he could not endure. Afterwards, he would think of Jean, feel guilt, then irrational anger. Anger at Jean for not being Abby. He had tried to love her, thought he did for a while, and when he found he couldn't, tried to hate her, but he couldn't do that, either, for it was he who was being false. So he decided he would honor her. It wasn't love, but it was all he could give her, and if a person gives all he can to someone, that's something like love, isn't it?

Bent crouched at the base of the stove. The spider retracted its legs, then jumped.

Abby vaulted backwards. "He jumped. Oh God, he jumped."

"If you hate them so much, why don't you just kill them?"

"I don't hate them. I'm afraid of them."

Bent centered the mason jar above the spider, lowered it slowly, then when he was close enough brought it down fast. The spider ran but wasn't fast enough and, trapped inside the glass, drew in its legs again. Bent slid the paper plate slowly under the jar and beneath the spider.

"What kind of spider jumps?"

"I don't know, you should let me mash it."

"Let's look it up."

Abby took her phone from the coffee table and brought up a page about spiders. She scrolled, looking from the screen to the jar and back again. "Wolf spider?"

She held the phone to Bent. He looked at the photo, then at the spider. "Don't think so. This one's less stripey."

Abby frowned and scrolled some more. "Wait, here it is. Dark fishing spider."

Bent looked. "That's it."

"Oh God, it says they don't spin webs, they simply overpower their victims."

"There you go, it's a monster. We should kill it."

Abby went to the garden door and opened it. Bent walked slowly, supporting the plate with one hand and stabilizing the jar with the other.

"Spiders are your friend," she said, "and I'll tell you something else."

"Spiders hate me?"

"Spiders hate you. You know why?"

"Because I kill their brethren."

"You kill their brethren. And bees and wasps as well."

"Bees I'll concede I shouldn't kill, but wasps do nothing for anybody. They're just vindictive little bastards."

"You're assigning human traits to insects."

Outside Bent walked to the far corner of the garden and released the spider beneath a hosta. He stood and arched his back.

"When am I vindictive?"

"You're not. I just meant human traits in general."

He looked about. Abby had been cultivating a bee garden all spring and summer. She'd put in coneflowers and black-eyed Susans and the Queen Anne's lace and milkweed had spread and the garden had popped with color. They were done for the season now, their orange and pink and white pigments gone, the petals an ossified brown. All that remained of the green was the ivy that climbed the high stone walls that ringed the garden and shielded them from her neighbors.

"What are the grasses again?"

"Those are big bluestem, and those are Indiangrass, and over there are prairie dropseed." She pointed at each in turn.

The grasses riffled in the wind, and the garden looked wild, beckoning.

"It's still so beautiful," he said, feeling her arms wrap around him from behind. "I'll hate to see it weeded."

"I won't weed till spring."

"I thought weeding was done at the end of the season."

Abby shook her head. "People do that, but they shouldn't. Queen bees hibernate in the old growth, and it provides birds with warm places to shelter through the winter."

"I thought birds flew south for the winter."

"Not all of them, and not if they have a place to shelter and a food supply, which they have here." She nodded at the birdfeeder. "Don't you want to just lie back in the grass and watch the wind in the trees?"

"It's a bit cold …"

"I meant in general. Don't you feel the desire to be close to nature? To be creaturely? To creep through the tall grass?"

"The tall grass is where predators hide."

Abby pulled away and headed for the door. "Let's go back inside."

Bent felt as though he'd failed some test, and he knew it was a test of not being so negative about everything. He vowed to try harder.

The room was chilly because the door had been left open, and Abby shivered and rubbed her arms. Her physical discomfort somehow gave her the courage to endure emotional discomfort so she began to say what she had to say.

"We need to talk."

A chill went through him. He closed the door and turned to her. "Uh oh."

"It doesn't have to be 'uh oh,' but...well, sit down."

They moved to the couch and sat, both perched on the edge as if ready to run. Bent clasped his hands together between his knees and braced himself.

"I can't do this anymore, Bent."

His heart began to hammer in his chest. "Are you breaking up with me?"

"No. Not yet."

"Not *yet*?"

"Something has to change."

Bent sighed. "Why? We love each other, we spend time together. You know my situation. Why does it have to change?"

"I have you but I don't have you. There's always this empty place where you were a minute ago, an hour ago, a day ago. I can't do it anymore. It's too painful."

Bent reached out for her, but she pulled away.

"Maybe you don't really love me," she said.

"Of course I love you."

"It's not an accusation. Just think about it a minute. Maybe you love the *idea* of me, some idea you got when we were kids, when I was the rich girl down the river road. It's okay if you don't. I'd rather know than keep on this way."

"I do love you, I loved you in high school. But you started dating Chas, then you went away to college, and...you know all this. Let's not go over it again."

"But I'm back now," she said. "For good. I understood before, and I stayed away. But you're not happy with Jean, you say it all the time."

He held his arms up vaguely, then let them drop in his lap.

Abby fell back on the sofa. "What do you *want*, Bent?"

"I want you. And I want my kids. And I don't want to hurt Jean."

Abby laughed bitterly. "Pick two."

Bent sighed.

"I doubt Jean is any happier with you if you want to know the truth. You can work out a joint custody arrangement for Jack and Ada, half the time with us, half the time with Jean."

"I am not going to be one of those fathers who leaves his kids."

"Your father didn't leave you, Bent. Your mother was a bitter woman and a drunk. Your father drowned. You have to stop using it as an excuse for doing everything that's going to keep you unhappy because you think you deserve it."

Bent just sat, clasping his hands, staring at the floor.

"You have to make a decision, Bent. I don't want to be this woman, forcing your hand, but I can't keep doing this."

"I really don't need this right now, Abby."

Abby sighed. "Always a reason not to talk about it."

"Yeah, well, today is a *really* bad day."

He told her about his meeting with Dieckerhoff, the cuts, losing the family's health insurance, the tax bill, how behind they were.

Abby looked down and shook her head. "I'm sorry." She looked up at him. "What are you going to do?"

"I don't know."

"You could teach."

"I had a class of third graders this morning. I had to explain to them why it mattered, the museum, the exhibits."

"I'm sure you did a great job."

"That's the thing. Maybe I did, maybe I didn't. But then I went to see Dieckerhoff. So even if those third graders understood, does anybody else? Maybe I'm kidding myself. Maybe none of it matters as much as I think it does. Anyway, I couldn't teach. I never know what to say to little kids."

"I meant college."

"I wouldn't have the first idea how to teach college."

"Why do you always say 'I can't'?"

Eventually they agreed to talk about it when things had settled down a bit, and they had make-up sex. He moved inside her, and forgot his meeting with Dieckerhoff, forgot his tax bill, forgot everything outside that room. They clung desperately to each other but it wasn't enough, and they tried to get closer. When they had finished, she cried a bit as she sometimes did, and he kissed her eyelids and ached with love. After a while he started to draw away but she tightened her legs around him.

"Stay in me."

So they lay still and quiet, and he thought, *this is how I thought my life would be.*

~

Machlon knocked on the door and heard a voice bidding him come in. He swallowed and went inside. His line manager sat behind the desk, waiting for him. He knew what it was about. The manager gestured to a chair.

"Have a seat, Machlon."

Machlon sat.

"How are you feeling?"

"Okay. Fine." Machlon sat up straighter. He felt sweat in his armpits and hoped it hadn't soaked through his lab coat.

"Good. Good."

The manager looked around the surface of his desk, cleared his throat. His discomfort made Machlon even more uncomfortable. He wanted him to do it and get it over with and at the same time hoped it wasn't what he feared.

"The thing of it is, Machlon." The manager had found his voice. "I'm glad you're feeling okay, but, you know, that could change at any moment, and we want you to focus on getting better."

Machlon felt a rush of heat engulf his head. "Well, I'm taking the medications the doctor gave me, and I've started on vitamin supplements."

"Good."

"Getting lots of rest."

"Great. That's great. Still, though, we think it might be best … if you take some time off."

Machlon felt tickling in his throat. "How long?"

"You know, until you feel better."

"Well, but it's pancreatic cancer, so I don't know – I mean I don't think it's a matter of feeling better. I don't think that's how it goes."

"Right."

"I think it's a matter of managing it for as long as possible."

"Right."

"Seeing the doctors …"

"Right."

"Taking the treatments. Chemo, whatever."

"Right. Well, that's the thing. When you're on chemo, you're not going to really want to come to work."

"Well, but I need to come to work. I need to eat."

"Of course, we understand, and that's why we're giving you six months' pay."

"Severance pay."

"Six months' pay to keep you going while you heal."

"But without the job I'll lose my insurance, and I won't be able to get treatment."

"You could buy private insurance. COBRA rates are good."

Machlon's heart was pounding in his ears. "I won't be able to afford COBRA. I'll barely be able to pay my bills."

The manager looked down at his desk again. "I really am sorry, Machlon. I wish there was something I could do."

"There is something you can do. You can keep me on the books so I can keep my health insurance."

The manager stared at a pencil on his desk.

Machlon removed his hands from the chair arms, held them in his lap, put them back. "Maybe I could go part-time. Just enough to keep the insurance."

The manager just looked at him. "Like I say, I wish there was something we could do."

"I don't have much time," Machlon said. "I just want the time I have."

The manager looked down, and then his face went impassive. "Like I say, I wish there was something I could do, but it's … well, it is what it is."

Machlon was tired. Exhausted. There was never enough sleep. He tried to summon the strength to argue, but it wouldn't do any good anyway. He felt himself sinking.

"My secretary has some paperwork for you to sign. If you just see her on your way out, we'll have the money in your account by the end of the week."

The manager rose, so Machlon rose, too, and he felt himself reaching out and shaking the hand that was offered. He turned and stumbled to the door. He didn't remember later whether he'd signed the paperwork, but he must have. He didn't remember going to his car or driving home, either, but here he was, in his bed, soaked in sweat, staring at the drawn and yellowing shade. He tried to stop himself from thinking about the day, tried to think about something else, but then the goddamn memory came to him. He tried to stop himself from remembering, but on it came.

Blows like a ball connecting with a bat. Not him this time, his mother. He edges open the bedroom door. His father rushes forward, looms in the space, the door open just wide enough that he looks like he is standing in a coffin. Shoves Machlon back hard.

"Get out of here, boy, this don't concern you. Unless you want the same."

After that Machlon told his mother he wouldn't go away to school. He'd get a job, stay home. Stay with her.

"You'll not stay here, boy. Think I want this for you? You'll go. You'll get out."

Not a month after Machlon left for school neighbors heard screaming, called the police. By the time they arrived, Machlon's father was gone and his mother was splayed out on the kitchen floor. The police called paramedics, but they could see she was already gone.

The news travelled quickly and soon made its way to Tell. They hadn't found the father yet, hadn't properly started looking. No police in Easterly. Out of town guys, didn't know their way around and had enough to deal with at the scene. Tell knew where he'd be.

He opened the door to the Sea Witch, and there was Mr. Machlon sitting alone at the bar with a shot and a beer. Before anyone knew what had happened, Tell was on him. He slammed him to the floor like a rag doll and rained down blows.

"You hit a woman? Huh? You fucking coward."

The men pulled Tell off.

"He's killed Mrs. Machlon. Go see for yerself."

A posse of men piled into a pickup and drove to the Machlons' place. They returned a few minutes later, and with them the police, who rolled Mr. Machlon onto his belly and cuffed him roughly.

One of the men nodded to the rest in the pub. "House is surrounded in police tape."

Machlon was called, caught the next train home and went straight to the undertaker's to identify the body.

"Is there no one else who could do this, son?"

Machlon liked the man for trying to spare him. "There's just me."

The undertaker nodded. Machlon wondered if he was thinking about what that meant, a boy, alone. Probably he had seen it before. Probably he had seen much worse.

After the funeral, after the mourners had stowed the casseroles and cakes and other dishes they'd brought to keep the bereaved nourished and taken their leave, Machlon huddled on the linoleum like a child, head buried in his folded arms. Bent sat beside him, an arm hooked around his neck.

"I should have done something," Machlon wept. "Why didn't I do something?"

"How many times did you get battered trying to stop him?"

Machlon shook his head. "I shouldn't have gone away to school. I should have stayed."

"He's a giant, Machlon. He would have just killed you, too."

"That would feel better than this."

What else could he do? He rented the house out and went back to school.

He turned over, away from the memory, and closed his eyes, listening to the clock on the nightstand tick.

~

Bent took the river road home, drove slowly. He glanced from the road to the cove on his left, watched buoys bob on water the color of blue garnet. Above it the sky was already dark, but to his right the sky was pink as the last of the sun sank. The starlings whipped in tight circles above the graveyard in their nightly murmuration. Bent swiveled in the driver's seat to watch, craning as the road curved, then turned back to the road and made a left over the railroad trestle into Easterly.

The house smelled of roast and Bent bristled. Jean had been to her father's. He pictured her tucking her hair behind her ear and making excuses for him in her sing-song voice, talk of low wages and extra work taken on to make ends meet, a life her father understood himself, having taken on a job at the butcher's in the off season to pay the bills through the winter and then buying the place outright when he no longer had the strength for work on board the boat. He pictured her father waving it away, wrapping the meat in butcher paper and tying the string with his plump fingers. *Times are tough all over, things'll get better.* Bent reckoned up the cost of the roast and added it to the mental sum he intended to repay his father-in-law when he'd caught up, if he ever did.

Jean was stirring a pot on the hob and turned as Bent loped into the kitchen and set the groceries on the counter. He stowed the tax bill in the bill drawer and looked up. Jean was looking at him, waiting to hear of the outcome, and he shook his head. She sighed and turned back to her cooking.

"Did you get bread?"

Bent began putting the groceries away. "Wasn't enough. Be more crabs tomorrow. I'll pick it up then."

Jean reached into the cabinet for flour. "I'll make rolls. They're nicer with roast anyway. Better for sopping."

She really did try to be cheerful. So why did he want so strongly to heave the goddamned pot through the window? He stuffed the shopping bag into the closet and pulled out a chair from the table and sank. He drew a breath and told her about his meeting with Dieckerhoff.

Jean listened gravely, then put the spoon on the spoon rest and crossed her arms and shook her head. "Well, I don't see that we've got a choice anymore."

"Don't start."

The kitchen door swung wide and Ada tore in and flung herself at Bent.

"Daddy! Did you get ice cream?"

He gathered her up and tucked her under his chin. Her hair smelled of freshly cut grass. She was rangy like him and hugging her was like trying to contain the limbs of a colt.

"No, baby, not tonight."

"You promised."

"Later this week, I swear."

"O-kay."

She pulled free, the only punishment available to a six-year-old, and scuffed her way across the room to the counter. She stood there, brushing her lovely golden hair from her eyes with a clumsy child's hand, her knees bony and her limbs thin as saplings in her wellies, and Bent's heart ached. All the terrible things that could happen to her flashed through his mind, to her and Jack both, and he fought the urge to fold her in his arms and weep.

"Where's your brother?" Bent said.

"Still at Olsens."

"Run fetch him home for supper."

"Can Caitlin come over?"

"Not tonight, sweetie."

Ada huffed and stomped out arms crossed. Bent rose to shut the door she'd left standing open and called after her.

"Go nowhere else, only next door and back. And go by the back yard, not the road."

"She could've had her friend to supper," Jean said.

"I don't want people over tonight."

"Fine." She kneaded the dough, trying to resist the urge to stoke the argument. "I didn't have a great day either, you know. They've added another school to my rounds, and I treated a little girl who's so malnourished she has angular cheilitis. The corners of her mouth are red and cracked and crusty."

"I'm sorry."

"Before you go thinking that Jack and Ada are Victorian street urchins, that's all. They're better off than a lot of kids."

"I know."

Jean pounded the dough and shaped it into a ball.

"They have food, they have clothes, they have a roof over their heads."

"You're right."

Jean set the dough in a bowl to rest and stirred the pot angrily, wanting still to yell but having nothing to yell about as Bent had conceded the point. Bent looked around the kitchen, not knowing what to do. Jean stopped stirring and turned to him.

"Let's just sell."

"I said I didn't want to talk about it."

"We've tried, all right? *You've* tried. You've done everything you could. There's no shame. It might be better, even. We could get a good price, pay the back taxes and have money left over. Buy something smaller."

"We've been over this and over this."

"I know we have, but now with your hours being cut. We just don't have the money."

"And that's my fault."

"I didn't say it was your fault."

"I work my tail off for that museum."

"I know you do."

"Bureaucrats. They don't know what matters."

Jean sighed, started again. "Why are you putting so much

pressure on yourself? I know you're trying to keep the family together because your father died when you were so young. But this house doesn't make us a family. You spend so much time being distracted with problems and blaming yourself for everything, it's stopping us from being one."

"There are things you don't understand."

"Then tell me. What things?"

Bent shoved himself away from the counter. "I'm going to wash."

He left Jean standing in the kitchen. She sighed again and returned to cooking. Bent disappeared down the hall and up the stairs.

Jean tried to remember how it was when they'd first married, how it felt, the frisson of each new discovery about each other, personal details, interests and peccadillos, memories. To wake to early-morning sex, the intimate happiness stolen in the liminal hours before daylight, in the dark when you could pretend no problems waited outside. They'd married too quickly maybe, Jack came along and there was this momentum and everything happened in a big rush, but still, things were good for awhile. But soon worry began to snuffle at the door, the sex became rote and tapered off, and eventually stopped altogether. She'd always thought sex wasn't important, not very, not compared with companionship, a shared life, but she realized they didn't have those things. She knew now that, at least for couples who weren't perfectly matched, as they weren't, sex was a way to access the elusive place where you could connect. It was a way to stay open to each other, to face toward each other instead of away. When your interests or needs diverged, or your fears grated, you could think of those intimate moments you'd shared that morning or the night before and smile secretly together. Bent'd told her of Abby when they were dating, described her as his first love, but the more they grew apart the more she *felt* her, Abby's perfection, untested in Bent's mind by the challenges of marriage, the quotidian disagreements, the hardships of child-rearing, of lack. The more she and Bent drifted apart the larger Abby loomed over their marriage, and eventually she began to understand that when Bent said *first* love, he'd meant *true* love. *Only* love.

She removed the roast from the oven and basted it with the drippings. She wondered if she'd ever loved Bent. She'd thought she did. He'd been charming, and intelligent, and he cared about things. And he was tall. She towered above many men but could wear heels around Bent and still look up to see him, no longer the gangly beanpole clomping through the school corridors. She wondered if Bent knew she knew about Abby, about Bent and Abby now.

Bent had gone upstairs to the bathroom, to wash, yes, but mostly to avoid an argument. For they'd argue first about not allowing Ada's friend to supper, then about other things, for the argument was not about supper at all, or about the tax bill, or about selling the house. It was about why he couldn't provide the money to pay the tax bill and buy a hundred other needful things. They'd shout until the children returned and then endure a sullen supper. Or Jean would say nothing, and the silence would be worse, for Bent feared that in the silence was what they truly thought and dared not speak, for it would undo them both.

That night he ran the tap and cupped his hands, let them fill with warm water, and doused his face. In the mirror he saw his chin had started in again. Lately it did this from time to time, twitched of its own accord, on the left side where chin and cheek met. It throbbed rhythmically. He watched it cave in and recover like a heartbeat. Finally it stopped. He switched off the light.

In the bedroom he climbed in next to Jean. She'd already curled up, her back to him, but she was awake. He adjusted his pillow and faced the other way.

"You know you can leave if you want, right?"

She said it so quietly, he almost didn't hear.

"What? Why would I leave?"

Jean was quiet for a moment, trying to find the best way to say it, say it so it didn't sound like an accusation, so it sounded like permission. "If you aren't happy. With me, I mean. You could leave. No blame."

"I'm staying." *For the kids*, was the bit he didn't say, for they both knew and there was no need.

Jean thought carefully before she spoke again, then turned to him. "We could see somebody. A therapist."

Bent turned halfway, looking up at the ceiling. "What? No."

Jean thought carefully again. "Then you could. It's no shame, you know. It might help you. I think you need some help."

Bent turned away again. "I don't need help. I'm just under a lot of stress."

Jean knew there was no point in pushing it.

Bent fell asleep thinking the loneliest feeling in the world is to lie next to someone and still feel alone. Jean did, too.

~

Machlon did not appear at Little's on Wednesday, so after work Bent turned left instead of re-tracing the spine road home. The road dead-ended at the boat launch and it would be difficult turning around so he parked at the top of the hill and walked. He crested the rise and fought gravity down the plunging hill to the north bank of the village, his knees aching. He passed Fred's and its giant red lobster posted as sentry, rubbed pink by years of salt and wind, waving to the summer tourists, those who came, for the village had no proper beach, only the small one at the bottom of Bent's hill and the tiny town beach, the width of an SUV, and otherwise only this seafood shack where you ate lobster and oysters rough at wooden picnic tables. No fried clams or calamari, no fries or onion rings, none of the things tourists thought was seafood. But the New Yorkers had discovered it. The dearth of fried food suited their figure-conscious diets, and some of them were there now. Fred had tented in the seating area for winter, brought in patio heaters and set candles on the tables, and a few parties sat, smudges behind the cloudy plastic sheeting. A couple passed Bent, the man holding the woman's elbow to steady her in her heels as they descended the hill, and entered the restaurant.

The road dived into the bay at the boat launch. Bent turned in at the gate just shy of that drop-off and knocked on the wooden storm door. The door vibrated against the frame, loose hinges needing replacing. Machlon didn't come so Bent knocked again, and when still there was no answer he turned the knob and entered.

"Machlon …"

Straight back the bathroom door was half shut. Behind it Bent saw Machlon's shins on tile, toes dug in, and he heard retching, so he pulled up and turned right through the doorway into the kitchen.

Bent heard wet throaty sounds, like vowels caught in a stammer, and he knew Machlon had brought up all there was but still heaved, his body trying to rid itself of poison. Bent thought that there must also be shitting, and Christ knew what else. He knew nothing of this particular curse, and he tried to think on other things. Though what else could he think of while his friend knelt heaving down the toilet what precious little food he'd managed to eat. The house smelled, and Bent tried to place the odor, and then it came to him. It was like the stench of dirty diapers.

Bent looked around the house. It was much as Machlon's mother had left it the day she took her leave of the world. What had worn out beyond use had been discarded, the rest left as it was, except the linoleum, which had been scrubbed clean by some neighbor ladies the day after it happened. It should have been replaced, but Machlon had neither the funds nor the energy. Old scratchy brown sofa, faded flower pattern and threads loose at the arms, scuffed wood floors in need of refinishing, family photos, hung by his mother and not moved since. All arranged carelessly, no sense of order or eye for beauty. Machlon had never married and Bent had never heard him talk of anyone special. He wondered how he could still know so little of Machlon's private world.

The toilet flushed and Bent heard the tap.

"I'm in the kitchen," he called. He stood stupidly in the center of the room, not feeling it right to sit, him taking his ease in Machlon's kitchen, uninvited, while Machlon puked his guts out in the bathroom. A cluster of prescription bottles sat in the center of the table. Bent shuffled around then leaned against the counter. Open on the countertop was a letter, fluttering at its folds like a dying sparrow, and Bent noticed the letterhead of the pharmaceutical company Machlon worked for. Or had worked for, as Bent saw, for the letter was a dismissal.

"They say I'm too sick to do the job."

Machlon had grown so slight his feet made no sound when he walked and Bent was startled at the sound of his voice. He turned to see Machlon standing in the doorway, leaning unsteadily against the frame. Machlon padded to the table and opened one of dozens of prescription bottles stacked in a large plastic tub, popped a giant oblong yellow pill and swallowed.

"Antibiotic," he said. "With cancer you get fungal infections in places you can't imagine."

Bent contemplated the horror of this, imagined horrible growths, itching in private places a man doesn't want to touch even on himself. Machlon slumped in a chair and kicked another out for Bent. There was a smell to Machlon's breath, a stench really, but Bent couldn't place it. Like sweet shit it smelled, but that made no sense. Bent blushed at having such thoughts about his friend.

"You'll lose your health insurance?"

Machlon nodded. "I can get private insurance, but it's seven hundred dollars a month. I don't have that. I just put a new roof on this place. That's my savings gone."

"Medicaid?"

"I don't qualify. They say 'I worked last year.' That's how they reckon who's eligible."

"That makes no sense."

"No it doesn't."

They looked at each other, neither knowing what to think, or do, then out the window, seeking answers there maybe, or an escape from the need to find them.

"You should come to the house tomorrow," Bent said finally. "It'll be pretty simple, but we've managed a big turkey. We'd like for you to come."

Machlon scraped at a gouge in the tabletop, then looked out the window, smiled softly. "Think I'll have a quiet day at home this year."

"I don't want pie, I want ice cream."

"We have pumpkin pie on Thanksgiving."

Tell's wife cut a wedge of pie from the tin plate, cursing as the knife sliced through the aluminum and into her countertop.

"Dammit."

She slid the knife under the wedge and, balancing it, transferred it to one of her dessert plates with the violet design. She set it before the younger boy, who frowned and swung his legs.

"It's good. Eat it."

"I don't want pie!" the boy shouted, then turned the protest into a song, repeating it in time with the swinging of his legs, punctuated with a little soft shoe every time his legs scraped the tile in their revolutions. "I don't want pie! I don't want pie! I don't want pie!"

"Aw for chrissakes, Louise, it's Thanksgiving. Let the boy have ice cream if he wants it."

Louise cut the other slices as though she didn't hear him, or her son carrying on either, but when she turned and thrust a slice of pie each before her husband and older son she turned on her youngest, scooped the plate from his place and slammed it on the counter. She yanked the freezer door and grabbed for one of the pre-packaged ice cream sundaes from the supermarket, tossed it in front of him and collapsed into her chair.

"Happy goddamned Thanksgiving," Tell said.

"Dad, I need a new game for my Xbox."

"You don't need every damn new thing comes out, you know."

"You and Mom keep getting new cars."

Tell levelled a finger at the boy. "Watch your mouth."

But his son ignored him, course he did, for there was never any follow-through and the boy knew it, and knew he'd get his game as well. Tell'd been so excited to have kids he'd given them any damn thing they wanted just to see the looks on their faces, and now was tired and had no stomach for saying no.

"Can I get the game?"

Tell forked the last of his pie, pretending he hadn't heard.

"'It's just one game."

Tell pushed his plate away. "What is it, zombies, or what? Crime-fighting vampires?"

"Dad ..."

"We'll see."

The boys pushed their chairs back and Tell called after their receding forms.

"No Xbox."

Louise rose and began clearing with delicate movements, like a mouse on carpet, and Tell wondered how she stacked the plates without making a sound. The plates bore chips and nicks, scars from when Tell cleared, and maybe why Louise always insisted now that he needn't help. From the living room a crescendo of one note, like an orchestra tuning up.

"No Xbox!" Tell yelled.

"Just till you and Mom come in."

"It is Thanksgiving, and we are gonna watch TV as a family, now turn it off!"

"Just let them play with the damn Xbox," Louise said. "It's not like you ever play with them anyway."

"Hey, I work, you know."

Louise flipped him off behind his back and returned to the dishes. The living room was quiet and Tell wondered if they were playing with the sound off. Louise was rinsing plates and bowls and loading the dishwasher.

"Louise, you don't have to rinse first. That's why I got the expensive model. So you wouldn't have to."

"Oh, they say that but it always comes out with dried food caked on everything. Besides, even if it does work you get clumps of food all over the bottom of the thing. You pay the mortgage?"

"Mmm hmmm."

Louise hit the switch and the dishwasher began to hum. She glanced round, looking for something else to do, to clean, to store, but there was nothing. She turned to Tell. "Wanna watch a movie?"

Tell rose. "Later."

"You just told the boys …"

"Gotta check on Machlon. Back in a bit."

He walked through to the hall and plucked his coat from the rack. He pulled it on and felt in the pocket for the mortgage bill, worried maybe that was why she'd asked, but she hadn't found it. In the living room, the boys were playing the Xbox.

"Louise! Tell them to turn that damn thing off!"

He went out the front door and heard the Xbox sound turn on in his wake.

Tell rapped on Machlon's front door and went in without waiting for an answer. Machlon lay on the sofa, shivering beneath a tattered patchwork quilt, the television tuned to something he paid no attention to. Tell sat in a chair opposite.

"Just came to see how you're doing."

"How do I look?"

Tell looked at Machlon, then glanced around the room. "You need anything?"

Machlon shook his head and drew the quilt up around his ears and trembled. Tell rose to the thermostat.

"Leave it, I can't afford it."

"They can't turn you off, you've got cancer. Bent or I will call them."

Tell cranked the heat and returned to his seat.

Machlon sat up and wrapped himself in the quilt. "Sons of bitches."

"A-yut."

"I worked there twenty-eight years. Twenty-eight years." He yanked the quilt like he was fighting it. "You know, I could have done a lot of damage to them if I wanted. Made a lot of money. Development. Formulas. There's people who would pay top dollar for that kind of information. Some guys sold out. Didn't show up for work one day and pretty soon, big announcement. Rival drug company beats us to a patent. I never did. I stayed loyal. Now they're about to make another pile of cash and I'm here running out of pain pills and shivering half to death."

"That's how it is," Tell said. "These bastards make all the money and we get screwed."

"It's not just the money. This thing, I worked on it. Not like the scientists, but I played a part. I contributed. And it's really promising. Shows a lot of potential in treating Alzheimer's. It's a monoclonal antibody –"

"Machlon, you know I don't understand any of this shit."

"It's meant to clear plaque in the brains of people with Alzheimer's, basically. And it works. We just finished phase two clinical trials, and the results were really positive. The drug appears to slow cognitive decline in patients. This could be huge for people's quality of life. I wanted to see this through. They don't care about the people, all they care about is the money. When this is announced next month their stock value is going to double, maybe even triple. That's all they care about."

Tell leaned forward in his chair. "Triple?"

The glass rattled like it might clatter to the floor. Bent turned. Tell was peering through the windows of the back door, rapping on a pane with the knuckle of his middle finger, his bulk hunched to fit under the low ceiling of the tiny mudroom. Bent went to him and opened the door.

"Happy Thanksgiving, Tell." Jean's sing-song voice tried to mask that they'd been arguing. "Come in. There's coffee."

She plucked two mugs from the cupboard and set them on the counter, and then she was off to see to the children's bathing and tucking in. Bent stood away from the door but Tell hung back. He glanced at the leavings of Thanksgiving dinner still on the table, the carcass of the bird, leaned his hands against the doorframe and spoke quietly.

"Can you walk?"

Bent felt sick and stepped in close. "Is it Machlon ...?"

Tell shook his head. "No, no. Not that. Come out."

Bent pulled on his jacket and followed Tell out, shut the door quiet so as not to disturb the glass.

Tell stayed quiet all the way down the hill so Bent did too, at first because Tell was quiet but then because the silence began to feel holy, their walk processional. Monks to Compline. Bent matched Tell's stride, the part of him that remembered childhood worries that falling out of step would break some charm. The night was all sky, bruisy blue and pressing down on the earth, and Bent and Tell were tiny beneath it, miniature men in a child's toy town. The tide rode high on the dock pilings and almost reached the deck itself. The water was black and bottomless and lapped the ragged wood, and Bent pictured sea monsters gliding below and almost believed that at any moment one would thrust its head from beneath the waves and take him.

Tell walked to the end as though he planned to go off the edge, then stopped, and let his gaze drift toward the jetty. He stood in oily boots, hands in the pockets of his good trousers, still smelling of work, of brine and black rubber and turpentine.

"Remember when we used to catch crabs and sell 'em to old Norm for ice creams?"

Bent smiled thinly, more a wince really, and saw Tell register his embarrassment and silently repent.

"Sometimes the world don't let a man get by." Tell looked out at the water. "Don't want any of us to, seems like."

Bent felt the cold cut into him. "What's up, Tell? It's freezing."

Tell squared up then, his face grim. "You said we'd talk more on Machlon, about what's to be done. But there ain't no talk to help him. Or you. Or me. Poor bastards like us been talkin since time began about how to make a fuckin nickel. Never works."

He was right, Bent knew, but that wasn't the kind of thing you had to say. Why rub salt? He studied Tell and wanted to shove him, like his failure to provide for his family was Tell's fault. He didn't know what to do with it, couldn't shake the feeling, wanted badly to hit Tell, so he jammed his hands into his pockets.

"There's a drug," Tell said. "Machlon's company is working on it."

"A cancer drug? Will it help Machlon?"

"No. Listen to me. They just finished some clinical trials and it did real well. They're going to announce it in a few weeks. It's gonna be a big deal. Gonna double their stock price, maybe triple it."

Bent couldn't understand why Tell should be talking to him of drug trials and stocks, and then he realized. "That's insider trading. You could go to prison."

"How are they gonna know? I'm a fisherman. What do I know about drug companies? I go to a guy, he's a trader, this guy –"

"What guy?"

"Just somebody I know a little. I'll take all the risk, we split the money three ways."

"You don't have money to buy stocks."

"You're right, I don't. My part, I'm takin all the risk. I buy the stocks in my name. I never mention you and Machlon. That's my part.

Machlon gave me the information about the drug trials, that's his part."

"You want me to put up the money? I don't have any money. I sell blue crabs for groceries."

"You have a 401k, right?"

Bent took a step back. Tell had gone mad, and he told him so.

"Maybe I have," Tell said. "Maybe that's what it takes for a man to make it nowadays. Rich men they rip these companies off all the time, only the way they do it it's legal. And who are they robbing? Us. That's our money they're stealin. We bring it in the front door and they carry it out the rear. Well, I need a little of mine back. So do you. And Christ knows so does Machlon."

Bent shoved his hands in his pockets and executed a right turn toward the center of the bay to turn his back on the idea. But Tell had said it now, that idea that spoke of desperation but also of hope and the possibility of relief, and he could feel it in his skin and taste it on his tongue, but still he resisted.

"People like us don't do insider trading. They don't stand outside in the freezing cold talking about insider trading, like mobsters."

Tell stepped in front of him now, squeezed into the narrow space between Bent and the edge of the dock so tight that with one slip he would fall backwards into the water.

"Bent. I am at the end of my rope. If I don't get some money soon, and a sum of it ..."

He shook his head and left off, the unfinished sentence hanging in the air like an ax. He turned and stepped aside and rested his big cracked red hand on the painted white top of a piling.

The tide was still rising, and the water boiled beneath the boards of the dock. A wave rolled in and washed over the deck and licked Bent's boots.

"You're crazy," Bent told him, shaking his head. "You're crazy."

Friday broke cloudless and fine, a last taste of Indian summer his mother would have called it, though the season was late and the expression no longer acceptable. Climate change, is what it was. One more problem to worry about. It made Bent nervous. When Bent had finished with the traps and returned from Norm's, he hosed down the truck while the kids had their breakfast, giddy with their day off, and tried to plot for himself a day of chores, of maybe fixing the window in their bedroom, which shook in its casement on the rare occasions when he and Jean lay together. But the sun was warm, and by eleven windows stood open to let in the day, the last good day of the year, dogs barked, and people went about in shirt sleeves, and Bent proposed a trip to Block Island.

Jean argued they couldn't afford it and she was right, and yet Bent bargained, and told how the blue crabs had been plentiful that morning, though they hadn't. He knew Block Island wasn't his goal, only the means, it was the road there that he wanted, and he marveled at how he could fool himself so. But then wasn't that how half the world got by? In the end, Jean bundled the children up in layers while Bent warmed up the truck and Kip ran from one side of the front seat to the other, standing on Bent's knees one moment, pawing at the other window to urge the kids along the next, and Bent laughed when Jack stood as he often did before the ancient vehicle calling to his father behind the wheel and gesticulating, "Open the hood, I have to fix your car! Stand back, she's gonna blow!" Then the children climbed in and Jean waved from the porch as Bent backed into the road and pointed the truck up the steep hill.

Crowded together on the torn leather seat, Ada's knee bumping the gear shift, the children squabbled, Jack striving to remain nobly above it all till Ada tried to brush his hair with her doll's brush. Then he pinched her arm and twisted and Bent yelled at them to settle down. Ada was weepy after that and sullen, expelling and then sucking in little gasps to show how bravely she was bearing her pain. Jack kicked the underside of the dash rhythmically till Bent shot him a look, then left off and found a place to stare out the window where he would have to look at neither his father nor his sister. They ended the mood themselves when Ada shouted at an ice cream shack as they passed, re-opened for the day in light of the good weather, and they resumed the drive working at their cones with the single-mindedness of archaeologists brushing the sand from a delicate artifact.

At the ferry exit Bent turned off and made a right onto Woodruff. He slowed down where the road spilled onto the roundabout. The pharmaceutical plant rose, a series of grey brutalist buildings, thick white vapor gushing from smokestacks, the foul smell of chemicals seeping into the air. He drove casually past as though he didn't care, didn't see it, even. But he imagined labs inside where the drug was tested and retested. Imagined offices where the press release was being written and rewritten. Imagined executives buying stock through shell companies, for they knew what was coming. Imagined the money that would flood into bank accounts. He cursed himself for these thoughts and drove on toward the ferry docks.

The next morning, Tell snatched the credit card bills from the seat and slid out. At the cash machine he tore the envelopes in pieces and stuffed them through the trash window, then slipped his card into the machine and punched in his PIN. He withdrew the last of his cash and counted it out, then jammed the wad into his wallet.

Louise had almost found the bills that morning. He'd stayed past his time at Little's and when he'd got home the postman had already come. When he turned the corner Louise was coming down the walk to the mailbox but he'd upped pace and beaten her there, and distracted her with the glossy country decorating magazine that came weekly. He'd been racking his brain, but borrowing from one card to pay another only worked so long and here was the mortgage past due and he could think of no other way. If Bent agreed and it worked he'd get caught up on his mortgage and pay off all his credit cards and cut them all up.

But Bent said no.

"I can't do it," Bent said. "I'd climb into hell for you both. It's been us always through thick and thin. But this I cannot do."

Tell gripped the clothesline bar with one hand, and was rapping at it now, his wedding band pinging the metal in the dark like a buoy. He stalked off a few yards, then spun about.

"Goddamnit, Bent, you need money as much as I do."

"Not enough to do this."

"We got a chance here, Bent. Machlon has this information, right now. When will we ever get a chance like this again?"

"It's not a chance, Tell. Either you'll get caught and spend the next ten years in prison or you'll spend the rest of your life looking over your shoulder waiting for the feds to come knocking on your door. It's not worth it."

"It is to me."

"I've a family to think of."

"And so've I."

"Oh yes? And where were your thoughts of family when you racked up so much debt you can't make your mortgage payments?"

Tell stalked off to the edge of the yard. He stood just inside the line of light the kitchen window threw across the grass, and his face blended with the shadows beyond so that Bent could see only his outline. Tell tried to let things cool a bit, but instead of dissolving, the tension hardened like ice. Tell slipped out of the line of light into the dark beyond.

"Tell, don't do this. It's a huge mistake.'

But all Bent heard was Tell's step recede on the gravel drive and fade to nothing.

~

Abby knelt in the kitchen and tied the laces of her running shoes. She'd spent the morning in the greenhouse preparing seedlings and spring bulbs for the customers who wanted to plant before the ground hardened, and she decided to go for a run before showering.

Everybody's lives would be better with plants. She had an asparagus setaceus on the window ledge in her bathroom, and it drank the water as she poured it into the saucer beneath it. The water level dropped as it drank.

A scientist in India had placed plants in dark rooms, and in one of the rooms he played classical music, and those plants grew more robustly than the plants in the quiet room. Trees in the forest fuse their roots together to share nutrients. They keep ailing trees alive by feeding them a sugary liquid.

Her grandmother had known the names of everything and had made sure she learned them, too, as well as when to plant and what grew well with what. Cucumbers thrive near nasturtiums. Plant alyssum near lettuce to attract helpful insects and basil with tomatoes to keep pests away. And the Three Sisters – corn, pole beans and squash – are good together because the beans climb the corn stalks, then convert nitrogen to nutrients for the corn and squash, and the squash leaves spread to create mulch to choke out weeds. When she had a stomachache, her grandmother used to peel ginger and slice it thin, then boil it with lemon and a pinch of brown sugar. It tasted sweet and rich and felt warm and soothing in her belly.

She caught sight of her reflection in the glass of the patio doors, shocked as she always was by the sight of her skinny, almost bird-like frame. She compared herself unfavorably to an egret. She had never developed hips as other women had. Maybe it was the running. As a teenager she ran marathons and was on the school track team. The training kept her skinny, and she didn't get her period until she was 14. She worried that it made her look less feminine. She looked at her belly, undistorted by any fetus, her body devoid of the stretch marks of childbirth. She was able to bear a child, she just never had. She saw to it. It wasn't that she was worried she wouldn't be a good mother, or because she fretted over bringing children into the world in its current state. She just didn't want them. She liked children, loved them even, but she'd never had the urge to have children that so many women talk about. She worried that made her less feminine, too.

She looked at the clock. She had just enough time for a run along the river road and a shower before Bent arrived. Today he would have to decide. She would tell him. Yes or no. If it's no, as she suspected it would be, then it was over. It had to be.

It had been a beautiful day, and Bent left the museum feeling fine, for it was his day with Abby.

He drove to New Hope, parked his car around the corner and walked the rest of the way to her house. He climbed the back steps and stepped inside. The house was quiet.

"I'm here," he called.

There was no reply.

"Abby?"

Still nothing. He went through into the bedroom, then the bathroom. No Abby. Back in the living room, he stopped. Her purse sat on the couch. He looked at the hooks by the door. Her house key was gone, the one she kept on a wristband for when she went running. He took out his phone and called her cell, and from the bedroom he heard a buzzing. He went in and saw her cell sitting on the bed. He went back to the living room, plucked a book from the shelf and sat down to wait for her to return from her run.

He looked at his watch. Fifteen minutes gone. He went back to his book. He looked up, stood and walked to the window, looked out at the garden. She was thirty minutes late. Was she not coming? She had never stood him up before. Maybe she was still angry with him over last time. Or maybe something had happened? He pushed the thought from his mind. He always worried, and it was always nothing. After an hour he left. She had stood him up.

He walked to his car and pulled out. He didn't feel like going home. He had been waiting all week to see Abby and the kids wouldn't be home until nine anyway. So he turned north on Route 1 and drove toward Stonington, glancing over at the marsh and the houses of Lord's Point, jacked up on stilts to shield them from the high water in storms. He turned off at the road into the Historic District and cruised along, looking at the library, the colonial homes, the news agent where Truman Capote used to buy the morning papers when he came to town to write. He drove all the way to the end and parked at the Point and sat gazing out at the water. He checked his phone. Nothing from Abby. Not even a text. She must be really angry.

The sky turned orange and then pink and then crimson as the sun dipped into the sea and the moon rose. Bent started the engine and headed east toward home.

He thought about checking on Machlon, but he was worried he would bring up the stock business and he didn't want to get into it right then. Machlon had less and less energy for company these days anyway. The market in Easterly closed at seven, so he stopped at the New Hope market to pick up milk.

The woman at the till spoke in hushed tones as she rang him up. "Isn't it terrible about the accident?"

Bent took his change. "What accident?"

"Oh, you didn't hear? A jogger got hit by a drunk driver on the river road. A couple of hours ago. She died, poor thing."

Bent went cold and felt his body instantly soaked in sweat. He struggled to breathe and all the sounds around him faded. He turned, pushed open the door and left without quite feeling himself move, ran to his car and pointed it toward the river road.

About a mile down the road, he saw a cruiser with flashing lights blocking the road and beyond it an ambulance. A few more cruisers and an unmarked car lined the side of the road. He stopped the car and ran toward the front of the scrum where he knew the accident scene was, but the cop stepped from his cruiser and stopped him. Bent strained to see past him as the ambulance pulled away. There was a long smear of blood on the asphalt. He looked at the cop, who was saying something to him, but his heartbeat was pounding in his ears and he couldn't hear a word of it. He stared at him, uncomprehending, then his eye caught something on the front seat of the cruiser: an evidence bag, and in it, a wristband with a single key.

No. No. Just because it was a wristband like hers, it doesn't mean it was hers. He stumbled to his truck, threw it into gear and drove back to New Hope and pulled up across the street from Abby's house. A cruiser was parked in front, and behind it an unmarked car. A uniformed officer stood on the front steps. Bent felt sick. He looked in the front window. Abby's husband sat on the couch, his face in his hands, two plainclothes detectives comforting him. Bent began to hyperventilate. He opened the car door and vomited onto the asphalt. He wiped his mouth on his sleeve and closed the door, put the car in gear and pulled away.

The road was blurred by tears that burned his eyes. He wiped at them with his sleeve and the wheel slipped and the truck hit the verge. He regained the blacktop and choked on his cries, and he pulled in at a closed seafood shack and stopped.

He clutched the steering wheel, his forehead pressed against it, and gasped for air between sobs. He shook the wheel and howled.

"Bastard!" he screamed.

Maybe he did believe in God after all. Maybe he just hated him.

An hour later he crossed into Easterly. He had stopped crying, but he was broken and couldn't go home. Not yet. He was too restless to drive anymore but he needed to move, to stalk the road and feel landscapes vanish behind him, pretend maybe he would keep walking, past Little's, past the boatyard, to the edge of town, and cross the border and keep going, south maybe, or west, through nameless towns full of people he did not know, eat how he could and lie on a bed of pine needles to sleep. Walk through forests and deserts, all the way to the Pacific. To walk was a dream of his, to walk and never stop, and tonight he felt he could do it. Oh he could. If he didn't look back, he could just keep going. Take nothing. Just go.

So he parked near the house and walked west along the narrow back of Easterly, past saltboxes beaten by wind and sea where neighbors sat inert before the flickering blue of television while he stormed by outside, a creature that did not belong indoors, something feral. Abby was gone. But as he approached the railroad bridge he thought of Ada, her hair the color of honeysuckle, and Jack's way of holding his chin that made him look old and wise, and a little sad. Bent slowed. He knew he would not act on his urge to walk, and he turned and went back to his truck.

When he got home, Ada ran to him with a book. "Want to listen to me read, Daddy?"

He let her lead him by the hand into the sitting room and sat in the rocker, and she crawled into his lap. The wood stove was burning but he shivered. Ada lay back against his chest, tracing words with her finger as she read. She looked up at him. He hadn't heard a word.

"That's good, honey."

Does the world care at all if you lose the things you love, or does it give them precisely so it can tear them away?

"What's wrong, Daddy?"

"Nothing, baby. Keep reading."

Ada carried on. Bent wrapped his arms around her. He dropped his chin to her head and held her to him and tried to keep from shaking as he cried.

~

Tell thought for days about another way to get the money, until he realized he had something of value. So at the stroke of nine he walked into the bank, his house deed in hand.

He thought it would be harder, thought they'd laugh in his face. Behind on his mortgage payments and coming hat in hand for more? But he filled in some paperwork and spoke to the agent, and he reckoned they'd totted up the increased value of his house and decided that if this didn't help him catch up they could repossess it and make their money back and then some. When he stepped out of the bank an hour later into white late November light, he'd been approved for a second mortgage.

The money landed in his account two days later, and he called Hayes and arranged to meet. At the set time Tell drove into New Hope, crossed the drawbridge, turned right onto Water Street and right again onto the river frontage. He pulled into a space in front of the bar. No one would know Hayes here. Not the kind of place he would go. He waited in the truck, not wanting to be the first to arrive. Didn't want to seem too eager, or too desperate. So he sat, pretending to look at his phone, wondering if Hayes would even go for this. He seemed like a typical Wall Street dirtbag, but insider trading was a whole different story, and he doubted he could convince him he'd all of a sudden developed market expertise. He'd have to explain how he knew what he knew.

"I was a little surprised to hear from you," Hayes said, after he'd arrived and they'd found a booth in the back. "After our conversation the other day."

Through an archway in a small anteroom guys in Carhartt hats played pool, but Tell didn't think they could hear.

"Yeah, well, I figured out a way to move some things around."

"Yeah, I know how that is. That's great," Hayes said. He took a drink of his beer and set it on the coaster. "But are you sure you want this particular company? They're not that robust at the moment. A number of patents are about to expire and their R & D isn't what it used to be."

Tell shrugged. "I've got a good feeling about them."

"Tell, I admire you diving in with both feet, but this is a lot of money you're laying out, and you've never done this before. Maybe I got you all fired up the other day, but this might be too far too fast. This level of risk isn't for everyone."

Tell sat back in his chair. There was an extra coaster on the table, and he set it on end and tapped it against the tabletop, wanting to whip it at Hayes' head like a Ninja star, cocky bastard. He flipped it and tapped it again.

"Next month a pharmaceutical company is gonna announce a successful phase-two drug trial on a new Alzheimer's drug," he said.

Now Hayes sat back.

"How do you know this?" he asked.

"Can't tell you that." Tell leaned forward. "You're right, I never done this before. But I done some reading. A drug like this will change people's lives. And nobody else has one. News like this? Their stock price is gonna double," Tell said.

Hayes nodded. "Or triple."

Tell sat back. "So you want my business or not?"

Tell hadn't misjudged Hayes. He wanted it, and the speed with which he set things in motion left Tell dizzy. The day after they met, Hayes opened a trading account. Tell transferred his money into the account, and Hayes spent every cent of it on the pharmaceutical shares and bought a large tranche for himself, too.

Then Tell waited. He read the papers every day, watched the nightly news. One week went by, then two, and there was nothing, and Tell wondered if maybe Machlon had been wrong. This was still a risk, even with inside information. What if it didn't happen? Tell would be completely fucked. And then it happened. Tell was in the dry stack working on Hayes' boat with the radio playing when he heard the pharma's name spoken by the announcer. He ran to the radio and turned it up. It was a report about the successful drug trial. They had a medical consultant on to talk about the implications for Alzheimer's patients, and then a stock consultant to talk about the implications for the company's share prices. Tell listened to it all. The next morning Tell sat up in bed and checked his phone, and the pharmaceutical's share price had risen overnight from $7.42 to $19.21 a share. Tell texted Hayes one word: *Sell*. Then he went into the bathroom and turned on the shower so Louise, still asleep, couldn't hear him, and he sat on the toilet seat and wept.

Tell went downstairs and made coffee. He poured a cup and took it outside and climbed into his truck and sat. He thought of the money that was about to flow into his bank account and laughed and then let out a cry, which turned into tears again. He wiped his eyes. Jesus.

Jesus.

He drove straight to Machlon's to tell him the news. He wouldn't wake him, it was still early, but he saw a light on so he went in.

Machlon wasn't as excited as he thought he'd be.

"That's it?" Tell asked. "You're not happy?"

Machlon shrugged. "My share's all going to the cancer."

Tell nodded, and then he shook his head. "What kind of God."

Machlon looked out the window. "Bent know?"

Tell shook his head. "And we ain't gonna tell him."

"You're still mad? He was just worried about the risk, that's all."

Tell waved a hand.

"No, I ain't mad. But that's just it. The poor bastard worries about everything. What he don't know won't hurt him." He scratched his stubble. "I feel bad, though. Lotta money."

"We could share it with him."

"I don't feel that bad." Tell sniffed. "Anyway, he made his choice."

He told Machlon to keep it quiet and Machlon agreed.

Two days later Tell checked his bank account and for a moment he thought he might pass out. He'd never had that much money in his entire life. He had enough to pay off the second mortgage and the credit cards, plus a tidy sum left over. He thought about a new truck for him and a shopping spree for Louise. All new clothes, plus video games for the boys. No. No, that was the same shit got them in this mess in the first place. Pay off debt. That was why he had done this.

But maybe he would get himself a little yawl.

~

How do you learn to grieve? Bent had learned to tie knots, taught by his father with tricks to help him remember. Bowline (the eel comes out of the cave), clove hitch, sheep shank. He'd learned the books of the Bible and won goldfish. But where does a man turn for how to live with loss? He saw Abby in his mind day and night, and he ached for death. He couldn't tell Jean, of course, or Tell or Machlon. They had heard of the nursery owner who was killed in a hit and run, of course, but this meant nothing to them beyond the basic tragedy of death. They didn't know what she and Bent had been to each other. He thought then of the one person he could tell, and thought how sad it was, what a coward he must be, how false, that the one man to whom he could tell his secret was the one who offered a kind of comfort he did not believe in.

At the church he climbed the stone steps and passed from the moonless night into the candlelit cavern of the nave. He ignored the font and pressed on but with each step his legs slowed and stiffened like he was wading knee deep through hardening cement, and finally he turned back cursing his weakness, dipped his fingers in the well and crossed himself. He tried and failed also to stop himself genuflecting at the altar. Safely past, he sought a door behind the choir stalls and knocked. He heard a brittle throat clear and then the call to enter.

The priest looked up from his desk, saw who it was and turned his eyes heavenward. "Am I dead?"

Bent smiled thinly. Father Fintan hooked a chair with his foot and drew it up and bade Bent sit.

"When I am paid a visit by a prodigal son there has usually been a … life-changing event. Has something happened?"

"No, no," Bent lied. "I just …"

The priest waited but Bent said nothing and the priest saw he couldn't speak and rose.

"Help me put out the candles for the night."

Bent followed the priest into the nave. Father Fintan reached behind the altar and drew out a pair of candle snuffers, and they processed down the church's south aisle, pausing at each small shrine to cup the guttering candles.

"You've come to pick up where you left off with your Latin, perhaps. *Agricola* ..."

Bent tried to smile. "It's been ages."

"Humor me. Just to see if you remember. *Agricola* ..."

"*Agricolae, agricolae* ..."

"*Agricolam*," the priest helped.

"*Agricolam, agricola, agricola.*"

"Well done."

"That was an easy one. And you drilled us to death on it."

When they finished snuffing the candles the priest lowered himself onto a pew, his old back hunched. "Oh me."

Bent sat behind him and the priest rested an elbow on the back of the pew.

"Is it as you remember?"

Bent looked around. "Do churches ever change?"

"True enough."

Bent rested his wrists on the back of the pew in front. The wood had roughened with age. Bent felt scratches and gouges against his skin.

"How are you?" said the priest.

"Fit enough," Bent said, "though maybe a bit ... I don't know."

"Tired?" the priest said.

Bent looked over and saw the priest did not simply mean he needed sleep, that he saw the depth of Bent's thoughts. He was relieved to no longer have to pretend, and he hung his head and let his hands hang loose over the pew.

"Tired," Bent said. "I am so tired."

The priest nodded, and rubbed his own temple, and leaned his head on his hand. "Life can be a trial."

Bent looked up. "Then why bother?"

"Because that is what we do."

"Do you believe in Heaven?"

He just blurted it out. It wasn't the question he'd meant to ask. What had he meant to ask? It had to do with Abby, something about sin, and love, and living in a world in which we must endure such tensions, such pain. He'd come here so sure of what he would say, but now he couldn't remember.

"I do," the priest answered.

"What is it?"

"It is the presence of God."

"What about Hell?"

"Hell is the absence of God."

"Bit Presbyterian, isn't it?"

The priest shrugged. "The Presbyterians have some very good ideas."

Bent shook his head. "I hear people speak of knowing God, of having a personal relationship with God, and I have no idea what they're talking about."

"I don't, either."

"How can you say that?"

Father Fintan shrugged. "Some mystical traditions say we don't know anything. They couldn't care less if you believe in God because you can't know anything anyway." He thought for a moment. "Maybe we talk about God because we're looking for a way to talk about ourselves, what we wish we were, wish we could be. For myself, I simply hope."

"You're a priest. I thought you were meant to have answers."

"A priest is just the head idiot."

"This is some theology."

The priest shrugged again. "What is theology? It is a work of the imagination. It is a story we tell to comfort ourselves in the night."

"Strange priest you are."

"Is it so bad, to be comforted by stories? When you get right down to it, what else do we have?"

"I'd have thought you'd say God."

"God is what we say he is, no? We can never know Him, so we imagine Him as something we can comprehend. Christ was the Logos, the son of God, created or begotten. He was fully human and fully divine, both at once, or half each. He was oil and water or water and wine. When people couldn't agree, each went their way and he became something different to each of them. And so it went. And here we are, in this beautiful church, and we huddle together and light candles against the darkness."

Bent shook his head. "A very strange priest."

Father Fintan smiled. "A very strange world."

Bent stroked his stubble, enjoying the scraping sound. For all that he had rejected this place and its teachings, he had not rejected this man. He had always felt safe with him. And so the question slipped out.

"Did my father really die?"

The priest frowned, not understanding the question. "He fell overboard and drowned. You remember."

Bent shook his head. "I remember that's what people said, but..." He had said it now, and he wasn't going to let it go until he'd got his answer. "My mother used to tell me he left. That he didn't die. That he left us. Because of me. She said I was impossible to love."

The priest winced, as if in physical pain, and laid his hand on Bent's. "Oh, Bent."

"You'd know, wouldn't you?" Bent said. "If he'd left. If the drowning was just a cover story. If you know something, please tell me. I just need to know the truth."

The priest shook his head. "You already know it. There was blood on the starboard trawler beam. It must have come loose and hit him in the head and knocked him overboard. Your father drowned, Bent."

"Then why did they not find his body?"

"You know these currents. He was way out in the Sound. In these waters? He could have been carried anywhere."

"Then why did my mother say that? She said it all the time."

Father Fintan paused to think of how to say what he had to say. "Your mother was not well, Bent. You know that, don't you? The drinking? The pills? She was an angry woman. Bitter. Her life didn't turn out the way she'd hoped and she wanted someone to blame for it. I guess she blamed you. I'm sorry."

Bent wanted to believe him. Father Fintan had never lied to him before. But he'd lived with this for so long. How could it not be true? Why would she have said this to him? Why would she have given him this to live with all these years?

"I wish I'd known about this sooner," the priest said. "I could have reassured you. Your father wasn't a churchgoing man, as we all know, but he was a good man, and he loved you. Oh, how he loved you. He always talked about his boy, and he always beamed when he said it. 'My boy,' he said. 'My boy.'"

Bent was shivering. He didn't know what to think or say. Father Fintan seemed so sure. How could she have said such a thing to her child if it wasn't true? It was because she didn't love him. That's why. He'd always known it, somewhere down deep. Now it was out in the open. Now he had to live with why. How could a mother not love her own son?

Father Fintan, seeming to read Bent's thoughts, laid a hand on his shoulder and rested it there, and they just sat gazing at the statue of St Andrew, the patron saint of fishermen.

~

Tell was finishing up for the day on Hayes' boat. He had just finished replacing the gear oil and now he was lubricating the grease fittings. Nearly finished now. All that would be left after this would be to give it a fresh coat of wax, let that dry, and then cover it and move it into the dry dock.

When Tell was finished he washed up and climbed into the truck. He brought up his bank account on his phone. The second mortgage had come out, and one, two, three, all four credit cards. Paid off.

He switched on the radio and caught the end of the seventies classics set, and he drummed the steering wheel and thought of the tow package he had picked out for the truck when the stock paid out. On the radio, bells chimed and the news ticker sound effect started and kicked off the news break. He was only half listening, still thinking of what he would do with the rest of the money, the college funds he would start for the boys, so he only half heard when the announcer began the segment. Then the words began seeping in. He heard "arrested" and "securities fraud" and "Hayes." Then the announcer was on to the next story. Tell pulled over and grabbed his phone from the seat and searched the local news site. They had it right up top under "Breaking News." He read it all the way through, searching for his name or Machlon's, his own pulse throbbing in his ears.

He reached the museum as Bent was on his way to his car. Bent waved and walked over and climbed in. They sat in Tell's truck and Bent felt weak as Tell told him.

"Jesus, Tell." Bent ran his hands over his head. "They didn't say your name, or Machlon's?"

Tell shook his head. "FBI spent the day interviewing him. He made bail, and he's to report for questioning again tomorrow."

"So it's only a matter of time."

"Yeah."

"Maybe he won't say who tipped him?"

"He's a swindler. They all are, these guys. He'll want to save his own skin. They won't be able to find a connection to anybody at the company, they'll want to know who he knows that has one, they'll offer him a deal, and they'll follow the trail from him to me to Machlon. We're done."

Bent's breath left him like he'd been sucker punched. "Jesus ..."

Tell pounded his hand on the steering wheel. Bent didn't know what to say. He wanted words that would suggest maybe it would be all right, maybe they wouldn't find out, or maybe they would but wouldn't be able to prove anything. In his mind he launched a dozen scenarios and followed their paths, but each one ended with Tell and Machlon in prison. If Machlon lived that long. He knew it, and he knew Tell knew it, so he stayed quiet. Next to him he saw Tell nodding in the dark, and then Tell spoke.

"I'm gonna kill that son of a bitch."

Bent looked over, and Tell was looking at him, a look of terror and violence and madness all at once.

"I am. I'm gonna kill him."

"You're not going to kill anybody. Now let's think about this."

"Can't talk if he's dead, can he? Get out."

"Tell."

"Get outta the truck, Bent."

"Tell, stop, just think a minute."

Tell reached over him and opened the door. "Get the fuck out."

He pushed and Bent tumbled to the blacktop. Tell pulled the door closed and roared out of the lot.

~

Machlon was curled up under a comforter on the couch when he saw headlights and heard tires skidding. He looked out the window and saw Bent's truck fishtailing onto the grassy verge in front of his house, then saw Bent jump up and run up the drive. He already knew what it was about, he'd read the news, so when Bent burst through the door Machlon held up a hand.

"I know. I've read the papers."

Bent panted, out of breath. "Not just that. Tell's going to kill Hayes."

Machlon sat forward. "What?"

"He's going to find him right now."

"Shit."

"Does he know where he lives?"

Machlon held up his hands helplessly. "I mean, probably."

"Do you?"

"He mentioned that Hayes bought on the low road Missus Waldron used to live on, but that's all I know."

"I'm really sorry to ask you, Machlon, but you have to help me find him."

But Machlon was already up. He pulled on a pair of sneakers and grabbed a coat at the door and they went to Bent's truck and jumped in.

They drove to Cutler Street first where Mrs. Waldron used to live, but they didn't know which house was Hayes', so they drove all along the street, Bent looking out the left and Machlon looking out the right, but they spotted neither Tell's truck nor any car that looked like it might belong to Hayes. Just old beaters, all belonging to locals, obviously. They went to Tell's house, but he wasn't there, either. They drove across Easterly then, blindly, from one road to the next, seeking Tell or his truck. It occurred to them after a while that he might be at the marina, so they drove the marsh road and pulled in. Eventually, they spotted Tell's truck near his boat, so Bent pulled up. At the water's edge nearby, Tell stood staring out at the bay.

Machlon went to stand with him. "Tell."

"You didn't have to get him out of bed," Tell said to Bent.

"I didn't know what to do," Bent said.

"He thought I could talk some sense into you."

Tell shook his head almost imperceptibly. "I wasn't gonna do it."

Bent breathed then. It felt like the first time he had breathed all night.

"We can't do anything, men like us," Tell continued. "We can never do a damn thing."

Bent approached and laid a hand on Tell's shoulder. "What now?"

"My time's nearly up, anyway," Machlon said. "At least in a prison hospital I'll get morphine. What'll you do, Tell?"

Tell just shook his head. He didn't know. He didn't know.

They stood there a long while, no solution but to wait and no words that could help.

"Fuck it," Tell said finally. "Let's get drunk."

They crossed the gravel lot to the Sea Witch, an old double-wide cemented in place. The owner had fitted it with a wooden deck but then couldn't afford tables. Christmas lights and neon brightened it some, but not much. Inside, the floors were sticky and the lights low and everything smelled of beer. They sat at a table in the corner. They didn't talk, just watched others. Watched two guys in grimy jeans playing pool for pints, an old man at the bar feeding quarters into video poker. On the tiny dance floor a middle-aged couple swayed, drawing back to gaze at each other in a way that said to everybody who cared to observe, this is love. Bent watched them and his heart ached for Abby. The door opened and a couple stood in the open doorway. New people, easy to tell by their clothes, his blazer, polo shirt and narrow trousers, her printed dress and heels. They looked around, decided this was not a place for them and left, off to one of the tony restaurants in New Hope, no doubt. Bent rose unsteadily for another round and slid a twenty across the bar. As the bartender pulled the pints, Bent looked at himself in the mirror. *Idiot. Worthless piece of shit.* The insults came in his head one after the other, and he gave them rein. *What good are you? Why don't you just …* But something made him stop. It passed by the mirror quickly, and he turned to the window where it had been. But it was gone, and surely it must never have been. He was drunk. That was all.

At closing time they spilled out into the lot. Bent made for the road and Tell grabbed his elbow.

"Where you going?"

"I can't drive."

Tell waggled his fingers. "Give me the keys."

"You can't, either."

Tell lunged for the keys and Bent yanked them back and dropped them. He bent to retrieve them but started. There it was again. He looked at the window of the tavern but what he saw, or thought he saw, was gone. Only the red neon flash of the tavern's sign. He plucked the keys from the white stones of the driveway and secreted them in his pocket. He thought then of Abby and imagined it was her he'd been seeing, and he began to shake.

"I can't." He tried to say more but couldn't. "I can't."

"Can't what?" Tell said.

Bent shook his head. "No, I mean … you can't. You can't drive. Give me your keys, too."

"I can drive fine." Tell took his keys from his pocket as though that settled things.

"No, you can't. Give them to me."

"I ain't givin you my keys."

Bent reached but Tell snatched them away. Bent wanted to lunge but hung his hands on his hips to stop himself. He shook his head.

"It's just like you," he said quietly.

"What is?"

"You'd really do it, wouldn't you? Get in the car and drive drunk and kill somebody. It'd be just like you."

"What are you –"

"All you think of is yourself. You … Insider training, Tell? Jesus. You're going to go to jail, and Machlon is going to go to jail, all because you couldn't –"

"Couldn't what?"

Bent shook his head.

"No. Couldn't what?"

Bent said nothing.

"I tried, okay?" Tell said. "I tried and Machlon tried."

"Tried what?"

"*Something.* Something to say *we're here* and the world can't just act like we don't matter and – Yeah, it was stupid, I screwed up and I screwed it up for Machlon."

"Nobody forced me," Machlon said.

"At least I tried," Tell said as though Machlon hadn't spoken.

"What about you, Bent? You owe a boatload of back taxes. You were gonna lose your house, Bent. You *are* gonna lose your house."

"I'll find a way to pay."

"With what? Your hours cut in half? And that crabbing you do on the side, like a boy trying to make enough for ice cream at the beach?"

Tell had moved in on him now and Bent squared up.

"If you hadn't run up so much credit card debt, you wouldn't have needed such a stupid scheme in the first place."

Machlon tried to edge between them. "Guys."

"Yeah? If you made a decent living you could pay your taxes. They'll take your house, and Jean and the kids'll be on the street."

Bent swung a clumsy blow but it went wide. Tell dodged easily then rose and struck with his left and Bent spun and fell and tasted grit. He rose to his hands and knees and hung his head and spat. A string of bloody saliva stretched and snapped. Machlon knelt beside him. Tell stalked a wide circle nearby, hands on hips, shaking his head.

"Why'd you do that?"

Bent didn't answer.

"Stupid fuckin argument. Why'd you do it?"

Bent hunkered on all fours, staring at the ground and spitting the last of the dust. Tell watched him, and dropped his arms, and walked up and took him by an elbow.

"Come on, get up, you're all right."

But Bent dropped his head and started to shake again.

"You're all right," Tell said, softer this time. "Get up."

Bent shook and shook, and Tell kept hold of his elbow and knelt down. Machlon leaned in and looked in Bent's face.

"He cryin or laughin?" Tell said.

"Both, I think."

Bent shook his head, and rocked back and sat, and rested his hands on his knees, and tears streamed down his face. "What's the point?"

Tell watched him a second, then sat full on the ground with him. Machlon lowered himself carefully. They sat there quiet while Bent cried, until after a while he thought how foolish he must look, a grown man sitting in the gravel crying. He laughed at the thought and his body started to shake. Machlon peered into his face and looked up.

"Now he's laughing."

"What the fuck," Tell said, and that made Bent laugh harder. That made Tell laugh then, and Machlon, and they sat there and laughed it out.

"I tried something," Bent said after a while. "It didn't work."

Machlon rose and staggered to the water's edge and hunched over. Tell went and waited with him. Bent wobbled over. They stood by, not knowing what to do but intent on solidarity. Bent tucked his hands into his pockets and stared at the ground. Tell gazed out at the lights on the bay. When Machlon had finished he wiped his mouth on his sleeve, and they trailed off out of the light of the parking lot toward home, the argument about keys forgotten.

The night was milky, the gibbous moon cast dizzy white light all around, and the stones of the lot crunched and shifted beneath their feet. At road's edge they stepped off into the ditch and winnowed single file alongside the high cord grass of the marsh. The far side of the road where boats were stored on blocks gave way to dirt shoulder, then marsh, and then the road closed in and cord grass rose on both sides.

Wind bowed the grass and it rustled gently. Otherwise the night was still. The summer creatures had gone south, or had lived their season and died, the autumn creatures slept, and winter ones keep silent always, conserving their energy for warmth or for the swift merciless attack of the predator. Drink had made Bent melancholy, and as they made their lonely progress along the marsh-swept way, he sang, like some birds do at twilight, like mourning doves, to comfort himself.

> Waded have I the miry march
> Where never a foot finds hold.
> Crossed have I also Gjallar Bridge,
> My mouth filled with grave-mould.
> The moon it shines, and the roads do stretch so wide.

He was in the rear and Tell tossed his chin back and snarled. "Give it a rest, all right, Bent?"

But Bent kept on.

> Then I came to those lonely lakes,
> Where the glittering ice burns blue;
> But God put warning in my heart,
> And thence my step I drew.
> The moon it shines, and the roads do stretch so wide.

"Knock it off!" This time Tell yelled.

But the night was strange, and the song an incantation, and Bent didn't want to stop nor to have Tell make him. He began to sing again and stretched out the words in ghostly tones like Bela Lugosi. "There *came* a *host* –"

"Shut the fuck up, okay?" Tell whirled. "Here's Machlon sick as he is, and you singin that hoodoo graveyard shit."

"I've got end-stage cancer. You think a song is going to upset me?"

"Sorry, Machlon, I didn't think."

"It's fine."

They walked on, and in the space created by the quiet each

had their thoughts. Their thoughts had weight, and each could feel the weight of the next man's as heavy as he could his own. Bent couldn't bear the quiet, and because he could not bear the quiet and because he felt all the anger go out of Tell and all the fight, he sang, weighting his words with the Lugosi voice because he thought it might cheer them a bit.

> There *came* a *host* from *out* the *north*,
> It *rode* so *fierce* and *fell*.

In the dark ahead of him he heard Machlon laugh. Good for you, Machlon, he thought, good for you, and he camped it up more for his sake, and because Machlon was laughing Tell couldn't object and even chuckled himself.

> And *first* rode *Grim* the *Greybeard*
> With *all* his *crowd* from *hell*.
> In the *trial-porch* shall *stand* the seat of *doooooom*.

A twig snapped or else a reed, and they stopped. They turned and looked about. The grey road stretched empty behind them then snaked away back of the marsh whence they had come. No one before them and no one behind, and no one in the reeds, either, for that way was only marsh. All was quiet. They were alone. They walked on and Bent resumed his song, but the mood had broken and he sang it as he had at first, as a dirge.

> Then every sinful soul did shake
> Like aspens in the wind,
> And every single soul there was
> Wept sore for every sin.
> In the trial-porch shall stand the seat of doom.

Bent's bladder pressed on him and he stepped to the edge of the road and unzipped and sent his stream down into a black pool at the edge of the marsh. He watched the water ripple and send circles out from the center, and watched his reflection swim and distort. He finished and zipped up, his reflection settled, and he saw beside it other reflections. Not Tell and Machlon but the things he had seen in the tavern window. He spun, expecting the visions to be gone and he and his friends to be alone on the road. But there they were still, those things. He threw himself back and stumbled and fell and the reedgrass caught him like a net. Tell and Machlon were frozen, and Machlon began to hyperventilate. Bent bounced back up and stared at them: three corpses, skin like reptiles and grey as ash. The ones he had seen in the mirror. What he thought he had seen that morning on the beach, and probably what Tell had seen behind him that day outside Little's.

"Who are you?" he said. "What the hell are those...costumes?"

The first corpse was the most freshly dead. His bones, where they showed, were still greasy, and he wore the tatters of the suit in which he had been buried. The second had lost his human features. Eyebrows, lips and nose were gone. The skin draped his cranium like crepe paper. Worms had bored into his belly, their tales waggled from the holes. The third was the most far gone, his stomach cavity hollowed out, the organs lost to the worms and the earth. He grinned a cavernous grin. The worst has already happened, the grin seemed to say. *Que sera sera.*

"Oh, they're not costumes," the first revenant said.

Bent looked around, toward the pub, looking for laughing faces in the windows.

"And this is no prank," the first revenant said.

Tell found his voice. "Look, buddy, I've had a shitty day like you can't believe and I'm not in the mood for games, so shove the fuck off."

He shoved the first revenant in the chest, and his hand came back wet with pinkish fluid. The revenant fell backwards and sat on the ground laughing.

Tell spoke but it came out barely more than a whisper. "Run." And he broke and turned.

Bent and Machlon followed. They got maybe ten feet, and the revenants shot into their path. Bent, Tell and Machlon pulled back and piled up on each other. The first revenant laughed some more, enjoying their fear.

"It's some kind of hallucination," Machlon said. "We've got alcohol poisoning or something."

"I assure you," the first revenant said, "we are no hallucination, and this is no game."

Tell remembered what Sandy had said. "Are you … I can't believe I'm sayin this. Are you ghosts?"

"Not ghosts. We were not that lucky. Ghosts are at least freed of their bodies. We're revenants. We are stuck in these rotting carcasses, as you see."

"Why?" Bent said.

The first revenant liked this topic.

"The pagans believed that every person had a set allotted life span, and if you died before it ran out, you had a reserve of unexpended energy and you would walk. Not dead, but not alive, either."

Tell snorted. "Horseshit."

The revenant drew very close to him. "They believed that unexpended energy gave you power. Sometimes dark power. The Romans prayed to their dead to take revenge on their enemies. Sometimes to tear them limb from limb. To remove their hearts and their livers."

Tell went quiet.

"Perhaps that is why we sense things. We sensed you three, your unhappiness, your desperation. Don't ask me how, I don't know, but that is why we are here. We heard you calling and we came. The pagans believed you would continue to walk until all your energy was used up and every last morsel of flesh had rotted from your bones." He held up his hands for inspection. "I am tired of waiting. And you can imagine how my companions feel. That is why we have come to you. You three despair. You see no way out. We've come to tell you: you are right. There is no way out of your present troubles. No way but one. We have no such earthly concerns as yours. We didn't wait for natural death for our troubles to be over. We ended them ourselves. That made us."

Bent looked from Tell to Machlon. None spoke.

"You understand?"

"What are these things?" Tell said, looking from Bent to Machlon as though they might know. "We're not killing ourselves."

"Why not?" The revenant rounded on him, speaking both with contempt and at the same time as though he couldn't care less. "What good are you? You can't pay your bills, Bent, and Tell, you've turned your boys into clutching covetous monsters and you and Machlon are about to go to jail."

Tell grew quiet.

"And then," the revenant said to Machlon. "All that awaits you is unendurable pain and, finally, an ugly, stinking death. Why suffer all that?"

Machlon imagined the pain to come on top of the pain he felt now.

Bent cursed the revenant and it moved in on him.

"And you." It moved very close and looked into Bent's eyes and spoke quietly so Tell and Machlon couldn't hear. "You can't care for your children, you know that. They will take your house. They will auction it on the courthouse steps. But you're a good father, you have made a contingency plan. The life insurance will pay."

Bent didn't understand how this thing knew all this.

"I've no clue how we know," the revenant said, as if he had read Bent's mind. "It has been this way since we became what we are."

"I don't understand, you read minds?" Bent said.

"Not exactly," the revenant said. "More like intuition. Impressions."

"Okay, you freaky fucker," Tell said, "what am I thinking right now?"

"I told you, it doesn't work like that," the revenant said, annoyed. "We simply sense unhappiness. In our current state, without the quotidian worries of life, we are simply more... present."

"This is a load of horseshit," Tell said.

"Think what you like," the revenant said. "But we are real, and we are offering you a way out. You boys have gotten yourselves into quite a pickle. So we'll take over. When the shit hits the fan, as the saying goes, we will be in your bodies to take the hits. If you change your minds, we will return your bodies and your lives in the terrible state in which we found them."

"Why would you do this?" Tell said. "If our lives are such shit, why do you want them?"

The revenant ignored him and drew close to Bent again, sensing the weak link.

"You will have left your family well provided for. Your children will be better off without you." He leaned in and whispered in Bent's ear. "Now that Abby is gone, what is left to live for?"

The first drew back then and looked in Bent's face, smiled as though he understood, and backed away.

"Think on it," the revenant said, then all three turned and

walked into the fog beyond the marshy verge.

Bent and Tell and Machlon stood silent, dead sober now.

"What the fuck *were* those things?" Tell said.

Machlon was pacing and hugging himself. "Holy shit, holy shit…"

Bent shivered. "Were they really…dead?" He thought of that morning at Little's. "Marshall …"

"What about him?"

"He said they were coming."

"Marshall ain't right in the head, Bent."

"He was right about this."

"So, what? You think Marshall talks to the dead?"

Bent turned on Tell, yelling. "Have you got any other suggestions?"

Tell didn't, and they all fell silent. They stood that way a long time, no one knowing what to say or do or think.

"Well," Bent said, "I guess we should…go home."

"Go home," Tell said. "The dead walk and you want to go home."

Bent sighed. "Where else can we go?"

Tell stared a second longer, then shrugged. Bent turned to Machlon.

"You going to be okay?"

Machlon nodded. "I think so." He shook his head. "Holy hell."

They stumbled forward and started off again along the marsh road, three abreast, walking silently, as the reedgrass fell away and the trees rose and hid the moon. None spoke, conscious that the world had changed forever, or that maybe it was they who'd changed, maybe the world had always been this way, only now the veil had been lifted from their eyes, and like mystics, finally they saw. And so they went silently, as holy fools, and when they reached the first house, Tell's, they stood about, none wanting to part, wanting to linger in their shared secret knowledge, their new shared questions about what lurked at the edges of their reality and what it could do to them, till finally Tell walked up the path to his door. Bent and Machlon moved on, and at the corner they stopped again, hovering in each other's gravitational pull, until the weight of what they knew but couldn't express became a pain that propelled them from each other, and they turned and walked their ways, Machlon up the hill and Bent east along the low road.

When Jean was four years old, in 1969, she went out into the back yard to dig a hole. She knew that if you dug through the earth, you would come out in China. Close enough, she reasoned, so every evening she knelt in the back yard digging because she knew the soldiers wanted to come home and they could come through the hole she dug.

Now, as she sat on the porch waiting for Bent, she thought about that. No more digging. Bent would have to find his own way home.

When Bent climbed the front steps a few moments later he found her waiting. He started into the house, but she stopped him.

"Not like you, coming home drunk, this time of night."

"Today wasn't great." Wasn't great. That's a fact, he thought. "I won't wake the kids."

He started for the door but she stopped him again.

"Can we talk, please?"

"I swear to God, Jean, now really isn't a good time."

"It's never a good time, is it, Bent, so now'll do."

He sighed and shuffled over and leaned against the porch railing opposite Jean. She looked at him.

"Can you sit?"

"I don't want to sit, I want to go inside, so can we please just get this over with?"

She'd felt bad until then, worried whether she was doing the right thing. She knew he was mourning Abby, and that made her angry, but she couldn't help but feel sorry for him, too. Him snapping at her gave her the push she needed.

"Nobody teaches you how to say these things, do they?" She said it almost to herself.

Bent was worried now. "What things? Did something happen? Are the kids okay?"

"The kids are fine. I want a divorce."

Bent was still in a daze, and he wasn't sure he'd heard her right. "What?"

"I've looked into it. We can do it ourselves, no-fault. Few hundred dollars."

"Wait, wait, wait. What are you talking about? We agreed we'd stay together for the kids."

"We never even talked about it, just like we never talk about anything."

Bent moved to the other chair and sat. "Okay, we'll talk about it. Just give me some time. Today hasn't been … Just give me some time."

Jean shook her head. "I can't. I just can't. You're always a million miles away, Bent." She laughed and cried a little. "Away with the fairies, my grandmother used to say. The silence, the … chasm between us? I'm tired of shouting across it trying to reach you. I just can't do it anymore."

"What about the kids?"

"Don't you think they sense the tension, Bent? Don't you think they feel it? Things'll be better this way. When they see you, they'll have one hundred percent of you."

"I can't be one of those fathers who only sees their kids on the weekends, I won't make it."

"We'll work it out. Joint custody, maybe."

He wanted to say more, but she sounded so certain. She had already decided. She was thinking about the details now.

"The house has been in your family, but the kids need continuity," she continued, "so I'll stay here with them and we'll keep the house in your name."

"What if I want full custody?"

"Please let's not make this adversarial, Bent. The mother always gets the kids in this state, you know that. It's better for them to be with me, anyway, you know that, too. Your distraction. Your dark moods."

Bent knew she was right, and he nodded. "Okay."

"Then, when they're out on their own, I'll move out and you can have the house back. Or you can have the house now and I'll take the kids and move into an apartment somewhere. But you'll have to help pay for it."

"How am I to do that with my hours cut in half?"

"That's why I suggested this arrangement."

Bent paused, looked around the porch, then out at the bay. "Where am I supposed to go in the meantime?"

Jean looked at him. "I don't know, Bent, but wherever you go, you'd better *be* there. You have to be where you are, Bent."

The wind picked up and far offshore the channel buoy rocked. Jean pulled her sweater tight around herself. Her chest tightened and she let the tears come and looked off into the distance, listened to the water lapping against the dock.

"Why wasn't I enough for you?" she said.

Bent thought of a million things to say. None of them were the real reason, but he couldn't tell her about Abby, or his father, so he said nothing.

Jean breathed out slowly through pursed lips and shook her head. She wanted a good cry, a better cry than she could have there with

Bent, so she took a deep breath and wiped her eyes.

"So." She stood and went to the door. "Don't wake the kids."

And she was gone inside the house. Bent sat and listened as the channel buoy rang out across the water. He sat there for a very long time, then he went inside and made up the couch.

~

Bent woke in the inky blue before dawn. He didn't know where he was at first, or really *when* he was, or maybe *if.* He lay as if floating and couldn't see for the dark, and he felt nothing and nothing felt real. Then slowly the frame of a window materialized, like grey pixels, then bits of a room, corners of things, a coffee table, the ratty tweed of the sofa. Then he heard Kip's happy panting, and he knew where he was. Bent lay absolutely still. He listened to the old brittle buoys grating against the wood of the shed, pictured bits of orange styrofoam crumbling like sawdust. He heard the water washing the pebbles of the little beach, white foamy edges like fingers up the sand. He strained more and swore he heard hermit crabs scuttling, their spindly claws articulating, and clams spitting tiny holes in the sand, and starlight falling blue to the earth.

It lasted only a moment, that brief space between sleep and waking, when he lay still and untroubled, savoring the simple fact of his own existence, the knowledge that he was alive and a day was dawning, a day that would bring sunlight and hot coffee and the faces of his children. But then the moment passed and he was awake, and the simple peace left him. A weight descended so that he could scarcely breathe, and he wanted to die.

At the foot of the sofa Kip nestled between his shins, chin on his knee. Bent palmed his snout, their ritual, and the dog's eyes closed. Bent ran his hand over the dog's eyelids, his peaked eyebrows and forehead, the fur soft as powder. The dog's tail thumped. On a normal Sunday Bent would dress and strike out with Kip, and together they'd walk the bluff till he reckoned Jean and the kids were up. So that's what they did now.

He dressed and zipped the fleece to his throat against the early December air, then drew on the army surplus jacket and knit cap. Kip jumped for the leash and Bent let the dog slip it from his hand with his teeth. He pushed the door and Kip trotted out before him bearing the leash in his mouth.

The wind had blown in the night and the last of the leaves lay in drifts. Kip bounced and leapt. The cold always brought him to life. Bent descended the hill, Kip ran ahead, dashing and whirling. Bent started down the beach as usual, treading the sand away from houses. Other mornings this felt good, to walk away, the distance, the aloneness of it, but now he felt small, as though he shrank with every step. The world had changed. Everything he thought he knew. Gone. He heard the revenant's words in his head. *No way out but one.* Was everyone who thought about ending it visited by one of these things? Is that why he had never seen them till now? His heart hammered. The landscape looked strange, like a movie shot in grainy video. He turned and called to Kip and made for the hill, keeping his eye on the houses.

He tried a different way. At the crest he made to turn left, but that way led to the marsh road. He thought of last night and shuddered. He dropped instead down the hill on the far side toward the north inlet, Kip a dervish on the road ahead. At the intersection he turned right and followed Kip onto the scrap of land that jutted like a tooth into the western bay. Kip circled every rock, sniffing crevices for rock crabs. Bent thought of last night, replayed it in his mind, sought evidence it hadn't happened. It *couldn't* have happened. Such things are not possible. But then he saw the revenant's horrible face in his mind, and he knew it had been real. Abby fluttered into his mind then, unexpectedly.

He looked up. The sea was black and stretched away into the grey sky, and the sky dropped to meet it. He looked at the new houses that had been built on what used to be a high grassy hill where locals picnicked. They were postmodern, all towering glass and odd angles. In the kitchen of the nearest house, a man and woman in white robes shuffled about, pouring coffee, sitting at the table with the papers, unaware of his gaze, his presence, his very existence, probably. He sank to a rock and folded himself against the air. A cold wind blew, but he wrapped his coat tight and let it come. Somewhere on the tiny peninsula Kip barked, found something to chase no doubt. Bent sat dead still on the rock and the wind beat, but he didn't budge. He closed his eyes and felt the wind come on, and felt his body balanced against it, in a kind of stasis, and he imagined they'd reached an understanding, the wind and him. Two works of nature, they had fought each other to a standstill, the wind swirling round, he letting it hug the contours of his body, vibrating to it. The nature of the wind was to tear down that which could be moved, the nature of man to build walls against it. Yet here he sat with no walls and yet was unmoved, and he imagined he sensed from the wind a grudging respect. He felt at that moment that he could just stay there, unmoving, forever, and in that stasis he would find peace.

But soon Kip grew bored with whatever he was chasing and came nosing for attention, and Bent drew the dog to him, and his coat blew open and he was cold. So he rose and turned, and the village loomed, and he and Kip started back.

From the porch he smelled bacon frying. The wind rattled the casement of the bedroom window, the one he still hadn't fixed, in what was no longer his bedroom. In the kitchen the children ate oatmeal. Bent ran his hand through Jack's hair and stole Ada's nose, though she was much too old for that. He took the coffee Jean offered and leaned against the counter. He looked at his family, at his children eating and at their mother, his wife, soon to be ex, frying bacon in a cast iron skillet given her by her grandmother. Nobody spoke. He thought of all the things he'd like to tell them, of how Kip was new-made by the winter air, and how once when Bent was a boy he'd gone walking after a hurricane and found a conch shell in a tree, and how he loved his children so much he sometimes cried. But Jack and Ada ate, and Jean cooked, and Bent drank his coffee and remained silent.

He thought of the revenants' offer again, and of how it would be if he did it. Where would he do it? What would Jean tell them? And in twenty years' time, when he'd been gone so long they had to look at photographs to remember what he looked like, would they remember this Sunday, when they ate breakfast in the kitchen with their father watching over them?

"What's wrong, Daddy?"

"Nothing, baby." He wiped his eyes and made as though the wind made them water. "Weather broke. Going to be a cold winter, looks like."

Ada swung her feet in her chair and rocked her head side to side and spooned her oatmeal, for children have no ear for small talk, or what it masks.

After breakfast the children bolted from the table. Bent shepherded their exodus with a swat, caught Ada on the behind but missed Jack, who swerved and evaded.

Jean was studying him, her brow creased over green eyes, and he saw his children in her face. Jack's serious brow. Ada's pout.

"Do you want to talk?"

He shook his head. "A little later. I want to get some things done around the house if I'm to be leaving soon."

He'd sworn to himself he would fix the window. Today without fail, he'd said. But when he'd fetched the tools from the shed and stood before it, he couldn't bring himself to do it. He couldn't say why, exactly. Something to do with memory, the thousand ways a family make their mark on a home. He looked at the window and thought of it rattling when he and Jean made love. Though it had been ages, he could feel her beneath him, smell her hair, and he thought, this window commemorates our shared existence, whatever that was worth to her. This window will remind her I was here. He stowed his tools and went to tend the traps.

It continued this way all day, Bent minding the quotidian tasks of a Sunday. All day he listened to the sounds of his family, Jean turning the pages of the Sunday paper, Jack and Ada out back with the Olsen kids, calling the cues of some game, the mysterious play of children, now laughter, now the skirmish that erupts and disappears like summer lightning, and Bent felt it all slipping away.

By five the light had gone and the sky was a smoldering fire. The world beyond the yard vanished. Most nights Bent cherished this time, when it seemed there was no world but this, this plot of land, this house, these two children. But tonight shadows lurked. He imagined he saw figures huddled just outside the ring of porch light. He strained his eyes till they stung but saw nothing, then looked away and felt it again.

By suppertime, he'd decided. If he'd made Jack go to bed early he'd have fought, so he let Ada stay up an hour late. He wanted to say his goodbyes all at once.

"Sing, Daddy."

Bent drew the covers round her chin and switched on the nightlight. "No songs. You've stayed up way past your bedtime and you've school tomorrow."

"I can't sleep." She stretched her words, taking sleep into two syllables.

"You can't sleep till you do."

"Just the first part."

"All right. First part only and then it's eyes shut."

Ada nodded to seal their agreement, and Bent sang:

> Reuben Reuben I been thinkin,
> What a grand world it would be
> If the men were…

Ada didn't know why he'd stopped, thought he'd forgot the words. "If the men were all transported," she helped.

Bent felt his throat constrict, and stole her nose to stall for time, and she batted his hand away and said it again, waving her hands impatiently. "If the men were all transported."

Bent nodded.

> If the men were all transported …

His voice cracked again, and he paused, and told himself she'd be better off, they all would. Another moment and he had his voice again, and he finished.

> Far beyond the Northern Sea.

Once Ada had nodded off, he went to the desk in his room, opened the bottom drawer and took out his life insurance policy. He read over the payout clause with care, pausing over each instance of accidental death covered by its terms. Satisfied, he returned the paperwork to its place and locked the drawer.

Downstairs, Jean nodded at his announcement he was off to check on Machlon. In the front hall he lay his wallet down on the table by the door and slipped into his army surplus jacket. In the living room, Jean sat on the sofa watching television. Bent stood in the doorway watching her.

"You know how I feel about you, don't you?" he said.

Jean looked up.

"Our marriage," he said. "You know where I keep it. Where in my heart I keep it, right?"

Jean nodded. "I know. I keep it in the same place." She frowned, studying him. "Bent?"

Bent shook his head. "I'm fine." He opened the door and left.

He crossed the yard and descended the hill to the beach and walked down the sand to the wave line. He knelt, dipped a few fingers. The water was icy. He stripped off his coat, then remembered that was what you did to keep from sinking, so he put it back on again. He waded in. The freezing water cut at his ankles, and he walked out to his neck, shuddering with cold, his legs stiffening. He stopped, closed his eyes, breathed in, and plunged. Cold. So co – can't breathe – fingers – can't – Hail Mary, full of – no, no – hold, hold – can't – air, air, air. He vaulted and broke the water line, took wheezing breaths, and kicked and sloshed for the shore. Back on the sand he gasped and choked in breaths. Have to get off the beach.

He reached the tree cover. Sank to the ground. Shivered, tried to get his breath.

Even this, he thought. Even this you can't get right.

They were right. Why can't I just be dead and have it over with?

He was shaking. The night was cold, and he saw his breath. Night noises whispered. In a house somewhere, someone washed dishes. Someone laughed, or cried maybe. Hard to tell. A cold wind is careless of feelings. Sat on slick matted leaves on the damp earth, beyond the soft light of windows, of streetlamps, he felt already gone from the world. He thought of his kids. Jack, Ada. And his heart surged. What was he doing? *You don't get to do this. You have kids. Go home.*

Then suddenly he was no longer cold. He felt sunken, gaunt. He looked down and saw his hands and they were not his hands. They were grey, wilted. Beneath the skin, delicate bones jutted. His clothes were not his, either. He ran to a car parked nearby, stared at his reflection in the glass. The face that looked back was not his own. It was the first revenant's.

~

The glass had fogged over and Tell rolled down the driver's side window. The streetlight in this corner of the lot was out and the dry stack blocked the moon. This was a good place. The dock master would find him in the morning. He didn't really know him. Poor bastard would be afflicted for a while and Tell was sorry for that, but better that than Louise should find him, or the boys. Already he mourned the life he was leaving behind, but he could see no other way. He couldn't go to jail. He just couldn't. He lifted the bottle. It was half empty, and he took a long pull and the whisky burned his throat. He reached for the pistol and held the grip, but he wasn't ready. He took another long drink.

Machlon lay on the couch, too nauseous to rise and go to his bed. The quilt had pulled away at the bottom and his feet were so cold. It was time for his pill an hour ago, but he just lay there and didn't move and hoped he froze to death in the night. Just never to wake up. How peaceful that would be. The release of it. It wouldn't be long now anyway. To just slip away in the night, an end to the pain. Right now that's the thing he wanted most in the world.

The first revenant was sitting on the far end of Bent's beach, though Bent never saw him. He felt the change was coming soon, so he wanted to be nearby, near the house. He knew where it was, of course. He and the other two revenants had stood outside many times now, watching, waiting, feeling for the right moment. And then suddenly it was here and he had rushed to the beach to make ready. He felt a rush, almost like he might pass out, and he knew it had happened. He looked down at his clothes, and he was no longer wearing the suit he'd been buried in. He was wearing an Army surplus jacket. Bent's. He rushed to the water's edge and stepped in past the white froth where the waves hit the shore and looked down at his reflection. It was Bent's face he saw. But he still felt like himself. He hadn't known if he would swap completely, become Bent, but no. Inside he was still him.

He sloshed ashore and trudged toward the road, sand clinging to his shoes and trouser legs. At the house he climbed the steps and tried the door. It was locked. Then he realized he would have Bent's keys. He reached in his pocket and located them and let himself in. In the hallway he stopped.

Jean looked up from her book in the living room, relieved he was home.

"You all right?"

He gave her an odd look, not the one he'd had earlier that worried her, but something else. Like he was surprised to see her.

"Yes," he said finally. "Fine."

Jean looked down. "Why are your shoes wet? And your pants? Bent, where did you go?"

Kip rose from his station beneath the kitchen table and slinked down the hall toward Bent. A few feet away he stopped, sniffed and began a low growl.

"Kip," Jean called. She looked at the other Bent. "What's wrong with him?"

The other Bent shrugged. Jean set her book down opened to the page she was on and rose.

"Kip." She stopped in the doorway. "Kip."

The dog began to bark. He padded from foot to foot, then growled, then barked again. The other Bent edged sideways to the stairs and ran up. Jean frowned behind him. Kip returned to a low growl, then a whine under Jean's soothing pat.

"What's wrong with you?" She knelt and hugged him around the neck. "Dumb dog."

Bent thought of what to do. He couldn't go home, of course. He remembered the park, how he'd felt something had been about to happen that morning that seemed so long ago. Now something had. Not knowing where else to go, he went there.

A heavy frost had settled and draped the grass like spider webs. Bent stepped and felt it shatter like burnt sugar. The park dropped off into a narrow strip of shingle beach on the western bay, and he stopped beneath a tall black gum at the edge. The tide was out and he smelt the froggy earth of the mud flats. Above him leaves rustled. He looked up. At first he saw nothing, only the tree's broad form, and the vague sense of light and dark, of shapes moving. Then he began to make out black hulks amid the branches. One of the hulks became clear, a turkey vulture, and at that the leaves erupted, and six of the giant raptors burst forth. They swooped and glided and lit on the pilings a few yards from shore. Still immature by the look of them, with grey heads and black beaks. They settled on the pilings and looked out over the bay, unconcerned with the interloper.

Bent deliberated his situation. He had no context in which to consider it. As far as he knew this had never happened to anyone before. He looked across the bay and imagined himself in a boat on the sea. Another species of his walking fantasy, but easier going. No force required, only to lie back on the wind-tossed waves. There are worse things. God knows there are.

After some time contemplating what to do Bent felt the same sensation he'd had on that other morning, that something was about to happen. He felt the urge to turn. At first the park was quiet. A fog had settled above the grass and walled off the village beyond, and he was alone with the bay at his back. Then he saw legs below the fog, and then a figure, and Tell emerged, in the body of the second revenant. There was nothing physical to indicate that it was Tell, but Bent recognized him anyway. By his walk, his bearing, something in the look of him. He didn't know, maybe it was the same as how people of long acquaintance could tell twins apart, but it was Tell all right. He approached Bent.

"You, too?"

"How did you even know it was me?" Bent said.

Tell thought about it. "I don't know, I just did."

"What happened?"

"One minute I was sitting in my truck, drinking a beer, the next minute, dead. Or undead, I'm not really sure. How did it happen to you?"

"Same, basically." Bent omitted his attempt to drown himself. "Why did you come here?"

Tell thought again. "Don't know. Why did you?"

Bent didn't know either, except for that feeling. They had been called to each other, it seemed, in that strange unaccountable way that happens sometimes, when one person needs another and the universe steers them to each other. Whether for their need or its own, who knows. Best not to ask.

Or maybe it wasn't the universe who did the steering, maybe it was the three from last night. Bent thought of that, too, and thought on what it meant, but decided he didn't want to know, or didn't care, at least not right now. Sometimes a person is just finished.

As Bent and Tell were trying to decide what to do, another

figure emerged from the fog. The face was the third revenant's, but they knew it was Machlon, the way you recognize somebody you haven't seen since grade school. You've both changed beyond recognition, but you know each other instantly. You see past the faces. You see each other's souls.

And then Bent knew how it had happened. "I tried to kill myself," he said. "I chickened out, but afterwards, I was … like this."

Bent and Machlon both looked at Tell.

"I was just sitting in my truck drinking a beer,' Tell said. Caving under their stare, he admitted the rest. "With a pistol in my lap. I wasn't going to do it."

"Apparently you were," Bent said. "Or maybe just thinking about it is enough. We wished for it and it happened?"

"Maybe," Machlon said. "I was lying in bed, and the pain was, you know, like it always is, and I just wished I would die. And then I was like this and the pain was gone."

"You feel no pain at all?" asked Tell, his hand on Machlon's shoulder as though he didn't credit it, even though he himself felt strangely new.

"I feel nothing," Machlon said. "Not a thing." And in a world such as he had been living in, this was as good as gold.

Tell looked at Machlon. "We gotta get you some clothes."

"I've no privacy left to hide," Machlon said.

"Still," Tell said. "Man ought to have pants."

Machlon thought about this. "Am I still a man?"

"I thought we were just meant to die," Bent said. "Wasn't that what they said? They didn't say we'd become them." He turned and crossed the boggy tide line to the water's edge and bent to his reflection on the steel water. He started at the horrid face that looked back, and dread rose in him. He turned back. "If we're them, are they us?"

Bent and Tell having both run to see if the revenants were in their houses, Bent arrived at his home.

At the sitting room window he looked in. Jean sat in the easy chair before the wood stove with a book, her feet curled beneath her, giving no sign that anything unusual had happened. The children would be asleep now. He watched awhile longer and was about to leave when *he* appeared in the doorway. Bent was briefly frozen in place at the sight of himself standing in his own house, him but not him. He looked like him, was dressed like him. Would his family notice any difference, the way he and Tell and Machlon had, or was that the kind of thing they just knew now they were revenants?

"Where is a towel?" the thing asked Jean.

Jean looked up. "Where they always are."

The other Bent nodded. He was as dazed as Bent was.

"We need to talk about when you're moving out," Jean said.

The thing ignored her, turned and started out. Kip appeared in the doorway and planted himself before the Other Bent and began growling and barking again. Jean jumped up and grabbed the dog's collar.

"What is wrong with you? Shhh! Quiet. You'll wake Jack and Ada."

Bent stared and ticked through a series of possible actions. He could break the window and climb through. He could brain the thing with a rock. He was roused from his stupor when Jack padded into the living room rubbing his eyes.

"What's going on?" he said, yawning.

Jack looked up then and saw Bent there at the window, this *thing*, pink and sinewy and gaping in at the glass, his face half-eaten, black round the edges where the flesh of his cheeks ended in a ragged half-moon and flapped against the exposed muscle above his jaw. Jean turned to see what the boy was looking at and screamed. Bent tried to call to her through the window, waved his arms and shouted, "It's me, Jean, it's me," but to her it just looked like a monster at the window – of course it did, for that's what he was now. Bent, and not Bent. He looked upon his family with the heart of Bent but with the eyes of a dead man, a stinking rotting thing. Jean hustled Jack upstairs and Bent knew he had to withdraw. As he went he heard her call for him to follow, the thing she thought was him, and turned and looked and saw it standing bewildered in the living room, a toy soldier, its battery running down.

Upstairs, Jean ushered Jack into Ada's room and barred the door and called the police. The thing she thought was Bent just sat in a chair in the corner. She couldn't understand why he seemed so unconcerned, out of it, almost. When the police got there, Bent, the thing at the window, had gone.

"What did he look like?" the lead police officer asked.

Jean looked at her children. They were quieter now, huddled together on Ada's bed, her daughter trembling like a paper flower, not knowing why but sensing her mother's fear, while Jack hugged his sister to him. The other officer was outside searching the yard. Jean knew that Jack had seen what she had seen, but she turned back to the officer and lied anyway.

"I didn't get a good look," Jean told her. For who would believe what they had seen?

Later, in his room, brown shadows flickered on luminous walls and Jean arranged the blankets around Jack for sleep. He told her the thing at the window had been his father.

"Don't be silly," Jean said. "Daddy's right in the next room."

Tell made his way to his house, keeping to the verges where tall shrubbery shielded him from the homes, turning away if a car happened by. It was risky, but he had to find out if that thing was in his house. When he reached home, he looked in the living room window, already devising strategies for what he would do if the thing were there, how he would make it swap back. It was there, sitting in the Barcalounger in front of the television, wrestling with a game console.

"Go, go, go!" his children yelled. "Look out for the red ones! They're poison!"

"Tell, it's past their bedtime, they've got school in the morning," Louise said, but there was no edge in her voice. She wiped her hands on a tea towel and smiled at the boys playing with Tell.

"Five more minutes," the thing said. "It won't kill them."

The kids cheered and angled their own avatars closer to his on the screen, jockeying for proximity to this new fun father. Tell sat watching until finally Louise sent the boys to brush their teeth and get ready for bed. He watched as the other Tell continued to play on his own awhile, then finally he left.

Bent returned to the park and told Tell and Machlon what had happened.

"There's one at my place, too," Tell said.

"What was he doing?"

Tell frowned. "He was playing Xbox with the boys."

Bent walked in circles. "What do we do? Shit. Shit."

Tell thought. "You think he'll go to your job?"

Bent thought. "He'll have to, or else it'll look strange."

"Then that's when you get him. Leave before first light, catch him going to the truck. Make him swap back."

"I'm going now," Bent said.

"After what happened? Wait till morning. Let things calm down a little bit. Maybe you can catch him before people wake up."

Bent didn't like it but saw the sense in it and settled.

Machlon didn't need to wonder whether his revenant was at his house. He knew the pain it would be feeling and knew it would seek shelter like a wounded animal seeks its den. It would climb into his bed and writhe as he'd done for months. He said none of this aloud, and Bent and Tell looked at his impassive face. He's no family to worry about, they'll be thinking. That for him it didn't matter. And they were right.

"I guess we should try to sleep," Tell said.

"How can I sleep?" Bent said.

"There's nothing we can do till morning, so you'll just have to damn well try," Tell said.

"*Can* we sleep?" said Machlon. Bent and Tell hadn't thought of that. They looked to each other. They didn't feel sleepy, just that urge that came at bedtime to lie oneself down and rest.

"Good question," Bent said.

On the road nearby, a dogwalker passed. Bent, Tell and Machlon ducked behind a tree. The dogwalker moved on and Bent held his hand to his heart.

"We can't stay here, obviously," he said.

Next to the park, over a colonial wall made of glacier rocks, was a tiny grove. They'd gone there as children, to hide when Machlon had been beaten or to work on various inventions, later to drink. Bent nodded toward it, and Tell and Machlon followed his gaze, and they crossed the grass and climbed over the wall into the grove. Ringed with trees that towered overhead, it gave good cover from all sides. The wall enclosing the trees provided additional protection. A good place to hide. They made themselves beds of pine needles and dead leaves and lay down, wondering what they could and couldn't do now. Bent had already noticed how quickly he had been able to move when he went to see if that thing was in his house, and he remembered how the revenants had shot ten feet on the marsh road in seconds. He thought of Jack and Ada and Jean and lay down waiting for dawn so he could go and get that thing away from his family, and they all closed their eyes and tried to learn if they could sleep.

~

They woke on a bed of brittle leaves just before dawn. The weather was blowy. Bent lay on his side, his arm for a pillow, and at first he didn't understand why he was sleeping rough. But then he looked around, saw Tell and Machlon asleep nearby, and remembered where he was. It hadn't been sleep, exactly, but they found if they let their minds drift they could go into a kind of trance, and it provided some relief. Though they were dazed and disoriented by their sudden change, they welcomed the grove's closeness, the shelter of the wall and the roof of leaves that shielded it from above. Bent lay back. The treetops rolled in the wind. The stars had descended. The sky was violet. Bent rose and knelt by Tell.

"I'm awake."

Bent had reached out to wake him but withdrew his hand.

"You sleep?" Tell asked.

"Not much," Bent said. "A little. I'm off to confront that thing. If it works, I'll come right back. If not, meet you here after sunset."

Tell nodded. "I'm going to my place as well."

Bent looked at Machlon.

"He sleep?"

Tell nodded. "Catchin up on what he missed the last month, I reckon."

Bent hid in the hedges by his truck. The thing appeared at six, walking out the front door, wearing Bent's clothes. It was risky. Neighbors would be up soon. But he had no choice. As the creature reached the car door Bent bolted from the bushes. The thing turned and Bent pinned him.

"What do you think you're doing?"

"This body wasn't being used so I took it." The thing laughed.

Bent slammed him against the truck, a new strength coursing through him. "What did you do? Undo it. Change us back."

The other Bent looked at Bent with pity and scorn. "It's what you wanted, isn't it? I saw you. In the sea. I saw you go under."

"I changed my mind," Bent said. "I came back out. I changed my mind."

"*Why can't I just be dead and have it over with*? Even once you were safe on shore. Isn't that what you thought? I'm sorry. This must come as quite a shock. But we both know it's what you wanted."

"It's not." Bent was crying now. "It's not."

"Then you should not have thought it. I'll take care of your family. I promise."

"I was only going to do it for the life insurance. My family won't get it if I'm not dead."

"No, you're not dead," the other Bent giggled. "Not exactly."

Bent wanted to attack again, but the truth of the words hit him. "What am I, then?"

"You're a stinking corpse."

"So, I'm not a ghost?"

The other Bent shook his head.

"And what happens when I rot away completely?"

The other Bent thought about it. "I don't know. I never got that far. Maybe then you really will be dead. Then you'll have what you wanted."

"No. No." Bent grabbed the thing by the collar. "Do it," he said.

"Whatever you did to swap, do it. Swap us back."

The thing merely smiled. Bent shook him, as if to force the change, but nothing happened. The thing laughed.

"It won't happen unless I wish it," he said. "And I do not wish it. Bit naughty of me, actually. We're not supposed to take bodies. It usually happens on its own. But I couldn't stand being dead anymore."

Bent slammed the other Bent against a tree. "Give my body back."

"I can't," the other Bent said. "I can't go back now. I won't."

"They're my family, not yours."

"Your family? That's a laugh. They *were* your family. You wanted out. You met hardship and couldn't hack it and wanted to be shut of it, with no thought to how your wife and children would get on without you."

"I didn't do it," Bent said. "I changed my mind."

"You didn't change your mind. You lost your nerve." He began mimicking Bent's thoughts when he was under the water. "*So cold. Air, air, air.*"

Bent let go and sank back. The other Bent was right. He had abandoned his family.

"You're dead," the other Bent continued, "and you might as well get used to it."

"But I didn't die," Bent said. "I'm in some halfway state. I'm stuck. If I can't be alive, I wish I would just die and have it done with."

"You can't. You left life too early. You left frustrated and angry and with unfinished business. Now you'll be restless and walk."

Bent slumped against a tree. "It's not what I'd expected."

The other Bent softened and nodded. "It wasn't for me, either."

Bent looked up at him. He didn't want to sympathize with the revenant who'd taken his life, but he heard with familiarity the note in the other's voice and was drawn to it. "What was your unfinished business?"

The revenant emerged from his reverie and drew himself up and waved in the air. "I've spent enough time on regrets," he said. "I don't want to think about it anymore." He turned away a few steps, then looked back. "My advice? Either find another body to take or make your peace with it."

The thing climbed into Bent's truck and backed out of the driveway to go to Bent's job. Bent sat in the driveway, breathing hard, until his gasps turned to sobs.

He thought about what the thing had said. Find another body. It seemed outrageous. Cruel. Just take somebody's body the way his had been taken? How could he do that to anyone? How could he put anybody through this? But then he remembered a body could only be taken if the person wanted it. That would be all right, wouldn't it? If somebody wanted to die anyway, he'd not really be hurting them. And if they had second thoughts as he did, he'd give the body back. That still left the problem of how to get that thing out of his house, but he would worry about that later. Jean had already kicked him out, so he didn't have to worry about getting himself back in, at least.

He didn't know how to go about it. The thing that took his body seemed to know what he'd been thinking and doing, to sense it from a distance. But he sensed nothing. So he sat in the bushes beside his house the whole day, and at full dark he set out and walked the quiet roads, listening, looking in at windows, hoping to overhear an argument, weeping, bitter reproaches of a spouse, some clue to point the way to a willing party. Then, out of nowhere, he felt drawn toward the river road, and he walked until he found himself at Norm's. The shop was shut and the windows dark, but a light glowed round the side, so he followed it. On the steps of the side entrance Pete sat, sobbing, and though Pete was the last person Bent in life would have expected to be suicidal, he found now that it made perfect sense, and suddenly he knew all the reasons. He knew everything about Pete the same way the revenant knew everything about him. Back taxes on the business, the business his father had started and Pete couldn't keep afloat now Norm was semi-retired. Wife leaving him. Taking the kids. "*Why don't I just kill myself…*" he heard Pete think.

Bent hesitated, then remembered he was no longer himself. Pete wouldn't recognize him. He recalled how terrified he'd been when he first saw the three revenants that night on the marshy road, so he spoke from the shadows at first, trying to make his voice as soft as possible.

"I can help," he said.

Pete leapt to his feet, and when Bent came into the light he fell back against the door jam, his terror and confusion familiar to Bent, and predictable.

"No need for that," Bent said, and spoke some more words to calm him down and assure him he was real. "I'll not hurt you. I can give you what you want."

"What I want?"

Bent felt sick to his stomach, but he tried to remember what the revenant had said to him, and he said those things to Pete.

"To kill yourself. I can do that for you, and you won't feel a thing. It's all true, what you're thinking," he said, hating himself for it. "You're running your father's business into the ground. Such a disappointment you must be to him. And your wife, she's no happier with you. You've lost her, your children can't stand being around you anymore. What's the point in carrying on?"

Pete wept to hear his own thoughts hissed back at him, and for the truth of them. He thought a moment, then the pain became too great and he wanted it over with.

"You're right," he said. "Do it." And he squeezed his eyes shut and waited for some fatal blow.

"Well … no," Bent said, rushing forward, "don't kill yourself."

He tried to lay a comforting hand on Pete's shoulder, but Pete shrank from him, so Bent took a few steps back and Pete calmed a bit.

"It's all true," Pete said, "everything you said. I'm a total failure. A complete loser. Do it. Kill me. I don't even care if it hurts, just do it."

He shut his eyes again and braced himself.

"It's not true," Bent said. "None of it. Your father loves you. Business is bad because of the economy, not you. And your father gives your suppliers such good prices, no wonder you're not making ends meet. And your wife, she's just angry because you work too much. Go to her right now and get on your knees and beg her to take you back. Tell her how much you love her and the kids, and that you'll do whatever it takes."

Pete had been listening hard, and nodding, and his eyes filled with tears.

"She's not having an affair," Bent said, "and neither are you, so you haven't that to fix."

"That's true."

"I've been cheating on my wife for more than a year," Bent said.

Pete leaned back and looked at Bent.

"Well, not now." Bent waved a hand over his deteriorated state.

"Oh, okay," Pete said. "I mean, no offense. You might be great with women. Maybe you're a really good dancer."

"I'm not."

"Women like to dance, don't they?"

Bent frowned. "I think so. Some do."

"Maybe I should take her dancing."

"Best to start slow, I think."

Pete buried his head in his hands.

"She wants me to help more with the kids. And she's right, I should. I want to, but by the time I get home I'm so tired all I can do is collapse on the couch. Sometimes I wake up there in the morning. Sometimes it's before dawn, and I go to the bedroom door, but it's closed. I listen and I hear her in there sleeping, breathing lightly, and I'm afraid, I don't know why, afraid of how much I fail her, I guess. So I go back to the couch." He began to cry and buried his head again. "I'm tired of living this way."

"Then don't," Bent said. "Change it. Don't give up without a fight. It's your wife, your *kids*. Do whatever you have to. Do anything."

"You're right," Pete said. "I'll sell the business if I have to. I'll get some 9 to 5 job. I'm going home right now."

He ran toward his truck. Halfway there he stopped and turned.

"Thank you. Whatever you are."

He got in the truck and pulled away.

Bent waved until the truck was out of sight. Then he was alone in the parking lot.

"What did you do that for?"

He sat on the steps, and knew he couldn't kill anyone, for that's what it would be. After a while he rose. Pete had left the door to the shop open, so Bent switched off the light and shut the door and left.

He started back to the grove, then stopped. He couldn't stand to be in company. He wanted to be alone, so he turned and headed back up Wright Hill Road. He stayed off the road when he could. Streetlamps were lit, and he dodged from tree to tree. The stone wall bordering the Appleys' yard provided cover the length of their land. He passed beneath a streetlamp and the light went out, and he shivered. He reached the corner where the basketball court stood, and beyond it, Little's. He still didn't want to go back, so he plunged down the embankment behind

Little's, crossed the railroad track and climbed up the other side into the graveyard.

The moon had risen, and its light cast blue shadows on the granite graves. Mist rose from the earth, and the boneyard looked a proper place of the dead. He thought about being spotted here, by an evening jogger, maybe. A corpse among the headstones.

On the far edge of the graveyard he passed through the slave section. Nubs of stone peeked from the leaves, initials their only epitaphs. J.H. G.W.C. On the leaves before a stone marked E.L., someone had left a teddy bear. Its fur, once white and spotted with polka dots, was dishwater grey. Bent wondered who had taken the time to remember a soul gone two hundred years, and he stopped and stood in silence out of respect.

He slipped amongst the headstones to the bottom, where the graveyard bordered woods. There had once been a church, Lutheran, built by the Norwegians who settled the town. But it was wood, and over the years the salt wind beat it ragged, and the Lutherans turned Catholic and did not rebuild and pulled the church down for firewood. Near the tree line stood ten or eleven headstones fenced round with iron, a private burial ground for the leading families of the old days. One bore the name of the man who had a statue in the small square beside the museum. There was the one the spine road was named for. In the center stood a monument larger than the rest.

> Here Lyeth Ye Body of
> S_____ A_____,
> Departed this Life on _____
> in the 50th year of his age.

An angel crowned the stone, but he looked more man than cherub. Featherless wings like arms, and eyes that looked surprised to be dead.

Almost nobody buried their dead here anymore. They committed them to the less lonely ground of the municipal cemetery in New Hope, where the richer tax base made for more manicured grounds. It was little visited, and he judged it a good place to spend the night. For a while, he tried to sleep, but he shifted from one side to another and couldn't settle, so he lay still and thought of his children, then Abby, and Jean. Poor Jean, stuck there with that thing. He began to feel grateful that she had asked him for a divorce. At least that thing would be moving out soon, away from Jack and Ada.

~

Mrs. Rutherford arrived at a quarter to nine as usual and turned her key in the lock, jiggling for the place where it unstuck. As she walked through the reading room she began to shiver. She checked the thermostat and found it off. Bent hadn't turned the heat up for her. His truck was in the lot, so he wasn't out sick.

She went to the circulation desk and tidied it in preparation for opening. At nine she glanced at the clock and waited for Bent to come say good morning, but he didn't appear. After a while she went looking for him.

"Feeling creaky this morning?" She stood in the doorway of his office.

He looked up from the computer. "Sorry?"

"You didn't come out to say hello so I thought I'd check on your old arthritic bones."

"Oh, oh. Yes, I'm fine. Fine."

He looked back down. He didn't look himself. He seemed dimly lit, was all she could think.

"Are you not feeling well, Bent?"

The other Bent didn't look up, just frowned over the documents before him as though confused.

"Give us a smile, at least. Maybe I'll tell you what I did in the war."

He looked up again, annoyed this time. "What?"

Mrs. Rutherford dropped her smile. "Nothing. Go back to work. I'm sorry to have disturbed you."

After dark Tell climbed the trellis outside his house where he knew Louise would be reading his youngest a bedtime story. But when he reached the window, it wasn't Louise reading to the boy. It was him. The other him. He couldn't remember the last time he'd read to either of the boys. Up so early and worn clean out time he got home, all he wanted was food, a beer and bed. Louise had stopped asking him to go dancing on a Saturday long ago. Were they sleeping together? Don't think about it. The thought made him want to climb through the window and beat its brains out, but this was his fault. He'd done it to them all. For the best, anyway. He'd made such a mess of everything. No other way out. Only a little while and the Feds would come and take him away. Then at least Louise could move on, find somebody else, somebody who could be the kind of husband she deserved, the kind of father the boys needed. He hadn't been either in a long, long time.

At nightfall Bent made his way back to the grove. Machlon lay amongst the ferns, snoring lightly. Tell stood and told of his trip to his own house.

"I was going to kill him," Tell said. "But when I looked in, he was reading a bedtime story to my youngest. They looked … happy."

"He's not their father," Bent said.

Tell shrugged. "I wasn't that great as fathers go. Always yelling, worried about money, racking up debts. Now the insider trading. Maybe they're better off."

"They're not better off. We'll figure something out."

Tell went quiet. Bent knew there were dark thoughts in his head, thoughts of worthlessness, wretchedness, and he didn't want to hear them for they mirrored his own, so he didn't sound him.

"Did you talk to yours?" Tell said finally.

Bent nodded. "He won't change back."

"What are we gonna do?"

Bent thought and shook his head. "I don't know."

"You know about death and the afterlife and all that. You were almost a priest. There has to be something."

"This wasn't in any of the books," Bent said. "You die and your soul goes to Purgatory, Heaven or Hell. That's it."

"Well, obviously not," Tell said. "You didn't read careful enough. Was there nothing in the fine print?"

"The fine print?"

"Well, you know. What they tell in mass can't be all of it. There's things they keep back, mysteries of the faith, for Chrissake."

"I thought you didn't believe in any of that."

"Well," Tell said. "That was before."

Bent sank to the ground. "I don't know. Let me think."

They sat quietly for a while, Tell trying to be patient while Bent thought. But he caught a whiff of something and followed it to Bent. He screwed up his face. "You stink."

Bent bunched up his shirt and sniffed and turned his face from the smell. He sniffed Tell. "You're no better."

Tell crossed his arms testily and shifted away slightly along the log.

They sat in silence awhile. Tell watched Machlon sleep, his chest rising and falling heavily, looking like he was out for the night.

"Machlon." He did not stir, so Tell called again. "*Machlon.*" But he slept on. Tell sighed.

Bent sank lower and leaned his head against the log. Ducked low as he was, Bent could not see beyond the wall and was grateful. Glaciers had carried these stones here millions of years ago and built this place for him to shelter in.

Bent thought of the traps. Nobody would tend them, nobody would remember, the coin they brought not being much. He pictured the blues trapped, no food, piled up in the wire cage probing for an exit, and decided he would go and turn them loose. He stood.

"Where are you going?"

"I've got to set the crabs loose."

Tell sat up. "One of a kind, you are."

Tell leapt to his feet then.

"Where are *you* going?" Bent said.

"Just realized. Something I've got to do."

"What?"

"Have a poke around the house, see if the Feds have been there yet, see if there's any paperwork or anything."

"It's too risky," Bent said.

"I'll be quiet."

Bent nodded. "What if Machlon wakes and finds us both gone?"

"He'll not rouse for a while yet. After you loose the traps, come back and stay with him. I'll be awhile. Long as I'm a bogeyman, I'm going to take advantage of the situation."

"What are you going to do?"

Tell smiled wickedly. "Tell ya later."

At his house Bent stopped and watched from behind the tree at the bottom of the yard. Behind the gauzy curtains the rooms were lit a boozy yellow. The children's windows were dark. He thought he could make out flickering movement in the living room.

He took the rocks of the jetty easily and found the ropes and hauled. He opened the cage doors and shook the blues into the water then filled the traps with rocks, shut the doors and sank them.

Back in the grove he watched the stars come out. One or two at first, then as if at once, the sky was full of flickering white lights. Once, Machlon woke and looked about as if surprised. He seemed to be waiting, lying frozen, his hands suspended as if braced for pain, then, feeling none, he turned on his side and fell back to sleep.

Bent's family would be done with supper by now, the children at their homework. Jean would have finished the washing up and curled on the sofa in front of the television. The other Bent would be ... what? Sitting with them? Bent felt jealous.

As he lay in the grove, Machlon sleeping soundly, his mind wandered. Now he was dead, would he learn if his father truly had died? Would he see him? Would he know him if he did? He had his seven-year-old's memory, and he'd looked at all the old photographs, over and over, but those wouldn't help now.

Bent looked at the sky and wondered about the time. He wished he could reckon the hour by the stars as sailors did. His body told him it was past one. He heard vague noises then, rustling, and he raised up to see above the glacial wall, and in the park he saw the most wondrous sight. Figures wandering in the park, figures like him, dead.

"Machlon.' He could not believe that Machlon might sleep through such a sight, so he whispered louder. "*Machlon*." But Machlon did not stir. "Still no pain," Bent said, and let him sleep.

He reckoned Machlon was safe where he lay, and if he woke he would surely see the miraculous event in the park and find him there, so Bent went over the wall. He was frightened at first, and moved cautiously, watched from behind a tree a long time, watched some figures sitting at the picnic table, some walking around, some just standing, doing nothing at all, then reflected that little could be done to hurt him now. He'd been watching one of the figures in particular, stood apart from the others, his back to them, looking out across the water.

Bent approached it, a rack of bones with bits of hide clinging here and there, no face at all, and patches of hair on a chalky skull. It took no notice of Bent, just stared at the black waters of the bay.

"Who are you?" Bent asked. "Who are all these dead people?"

The thing cocked its head like a dog would at a distant whistle. "Not dead," it said, "and not people either, exactly."

"What, then?"

"Revenants."

"What is a revenant?"

"Like you. Dead, but not gone."

"I'm not meant to be here," Bent said. "You see, I … well, somehow I've swapped."

"I know," the revenant said. "I saw."

"How did you see? You weren't here."

"I was. You just didn't see me because you hadn't changed yet. You didn't want to see."

"I want to undo it. Swap back."

The revenant shook his head.

"I can't?" Bent said.

"Not unless the other one agrees."

Bent felt sick. "Is there no other way?"

The revenant said nothing. Bent looked around at the wanderers in the grass. "Is this all those who have died in this village?"

"Not all. Some have gone."

"Where?"

The revenant did not answer.

"Will I go there, too?"

Again no answer.

"Why here? Why do you all gather in this park?"

The revenant shrugged. "Same reason as you. It's well hid. We hide in our various places during the day but come here at night. It's near home. As close as we'll ever get again."

"Why are you all still here? Are you waiting for something?"

But again it was as though he hadn't said a word.

"Are there only revenants in Easterly?" Bent asked.

"There are revenants wherever people die before they are ready," the revenant said. "Which is to say, everywhere."

"Is my father here?"

"I do not know your father."

The revenant wandered away as though he were sleepwalking and Bent let him go. He didn't look for Abby. He imagined what the accident must have done to her. He didn't want to see her that way. He hoped she wasn't there at all. He hoped she was one of those who had moved on.

When he returned to the grove, Machlon was stirring, and after he'd poked at his belly awhile and marveled at the absence of pain, he turned to Bent.

"Boy, was I out. What did you do while I was sleeping?"

Bent wanted to tell him what he'd seen, but worried first that he wouldn't believe him, then, when he considered how outrageous it would be not to believe Bent had seen dead men in the state they themselves were in, didn't know how to relate what he'd seen, the horror of it, and the loneliness, and the confusion.

"Watched over you, mostly," he said finally. "Tell did it for awhile, then he had an errand to run."

Machlon thought that was funny and laughed and drummed on

his belly.

"A dead man on an errand."

Bent reckoned it was funny too, then, and laughed with him. The laughter died off, and they were silent awhile.

Sometime after the moon had begun to sink, so about three or so, Bent reckoned, they heard crunching leaves, and as they turned, Tell leapt over the wall and collapsed in triumph against the stones, laughing like a truant.

"That was a thing of beauty, that was."

"About time. You've been gone half the night. I was worried Louise had called the police on you."

"And what do you think they'd do if they saw me? Shit out all the doughnuts they ate for a week."

"Anything seem unusual?" Bent asked. "Any warrants lying around on the coffee table?"

Tell shook his head. "Place was quiet as a church. There's a new big-screen TV. That'll be Louise spending my insider trading money. Hope she don't charge them cards back up."

Tell sucked his teeth, and Bent saw the sadness in his eyes.

"Anyway, then I had that thing to do I told you about. Man lives halfway down the river road. Takes time to get out there and back on foot."

"Who lives on the river road?"

"Benedetti who owns the oil company. I'm behind on my payments. He's been dunning me for weeks."

Tell threw a sack and it landed at Bent's feet.

"What's this?" Bent asked.

Machlon having slept through Tell's leaving was confused. "Why did you go to Benedetti's house?"

Tell filled them both in, told how he'd waited till they were all in bed, then jimmied the front door, opened it slow so it creaked and left it standing open and jumped the rail and hid under the porch.

"Hall light came on before long, and Benedetti comes downstairs in his robe. He looked outside but course he didn't see nothin, then he swung the door back and forth a bit to see was there a faulty latch. Finally he closed the door and went back upstairs. I gave it a minute, then went back up on the porch and did the same, opened the door real slow, workin that hinge to get a good creak out of it, then hid again. A moment later here comes Benedetti again, only this time he's worried. He's got a bat, and he looks all round the yard, looks left, looks right. Doesn't see anything, so he turns back, only this time he looks behind the door as well, like he's afraid something might jump out at him, then he closes it and goes back upstairs. I reckon he'll sit up rest of the night listening for that door." He burst out laughing again.

"Well I'm happy to hear you've had fun, scaring an old man witless."

"That's just for a start," Tell said. "Tomorrow there's to be thumping in the attic. Here." He reached for the sack and tossed it to Machlon. "Got you some clothes. Benedettis send their laundry out to be done. It was on the porch."

Machlon opened the sack and rooted around inside. He drew out a pair of trousers, stood up and held them against his waist to check the size, then climbed into them. He also found a T-shirt and a hooded sweatshirt.

"Benedetti's as skinny alive as you are dead," Tell said. "We just need to get you some shoes somewhere and you're all set."

Machlon pulled the hood up. "What do you think? Almost human?"

Tell eyed up him up and down. "You look like the Boston Strangler."

Machlon flipped the hood back and sat.

"When I was at my house, I went to see my kids," Tell said. "Sat by their bedroom window awhile, watched em sleep. I used to do that when they were real little, sometimes, go in and sit in a chair and just watch em. Couldn't believe I was so lucky."

Bent felt sorry for his friend, and for himself, and thought of his own children and longed to see them.

Machlon felt the sadness that had descended and spoke to break it. "Maybe I could haunt my old manager."

Bent stood. "I'm going to walk about a bit."

"You think of somebody to haunt?" Tell said.

"I've got someplace to be."

Tell nodded. "Back at dawn."

"I won't be able to get back until after dark."

"Don't you get seen," Tell said.

Bent nodded and was off.

When he reached the house, the windows were dark. All were no doubt sleeping within, his children in their beds, Jean in hers, with that Other Bent. He drew closer and mounted the porch. Just to look in a window, maybe, see that all was in order. As he reached the top, the wood creaked, and Kip's nails rattled as he approached the door.

"Kip, it's me." Bent knelt at the door and spoke to the gap. On the other side, Kip snuffled, sniffed the floor, his black snout poking into the gap near Bent's face.

"Kip." Bent reached and touched the wet nose. The dog strained beneath the door and tucked his snout into Bent's hand. Bent stroked the soft fine hairs above the black nose, and Kip whimpered. Somewhere in the back of the house he saw a light. Someone using the bathroom, probably, but he couldn't risk it.

"Bye, Kip." He scratched his snout in parting and padded down the stairs. Not knowing where else to go, he went to the shed.

Inside was as he'd left it. It smelled of rockweed and old wood and turpentine, and the filet table was pink from years of drenchings with dried fish guts. In the corner stood the stool on which his father set him to watch as he cleaned fish he'd brought home for supper, bluefish, usually, that swam into the shrimp net and got caught. He looked out the dirty window next to the door. The house was dark. The light was off. He could go.

But he didn't. He knelt and examined the space under the bottom shelf, which was stacked with traps. In his new body, he reckoned he could fit. He lay flat and slid under and tucked in like a herring in a salt chest.

He dozed off and on for the next few hours. When the black began to drain from the sky outside the window, he eased from beneath the shelf and slipped quietly from the shed. The wind was up. Fall's last moderating hand was loosening and winter was storming in. He had to hold the door tight to stop it slamming. When he heard the latch click, he left the yard and climbed the hill. At the crest he looked back at the house, and thought of Kip, sleeping fitfully against the door.

Since the change he'd lost track of the days, but not today. He knew what day it was.

He followed the train tracks till he judged he was abreast of the cemetery, not the graveyard in Easterly but the municipal cemetery in New Hope, then climbed the low hill and raised up to have a look. Through a stand of trees to his right he saw a black canopy erected over an open grave. He slid back down the hill and backtracked closer to the spot, then edged up, leaned against the hill, and waited.

The hearse turned in at the gate and swung round along the winding path between bare maple trees, trailing cars, headlights weak in daylight. The cortege stopped at the gravesite. The doors of the lead mourners' car opened and Abby's husband got out. He buttoned his black suit. Bent felt a stab of hate. The husband held out a hand to help Abby's mother from the car. She looked so small, crumpled. The other mourners kept their distance, fearful of the grief that overlay her face like a mark. The priest took her hands in his, then the husband led her to a chair. The wind had risen and a pelting rain was hammering at the canopy. The old woman shut her eyes against the weather and her grief. If they'd been able to bury Abby in good time, they would at least have had the last of the autumn weather. But the investigation had delayed it. They still had not found the driver, but they had done what they needed to do with Abby's body, and she could finally be laid to rest.

The pallbearers lifted the coffin from the hearse and carried it to the graveside. Abby had been Catholic. Why were they having an Episcopalian service? Must be the husband. And Bent hated again, and more deeply, and felt a tightness in his throat. His eyes stung. He pressed on them hard with the heels of his hands, but the tears came. Or at least what felt like tears.

The mourners were seated and the priest began the words of the burial service. "In the midst of life we are in death. From whom can we seek help?"

The priest's voice floated across as if Bent were underwater. He strained to hear but caught words only here and there. "Beloved." "Daughter." "Wife." He wiped his eyes so he could see. He watched the coffin and imagined Abby inside, and his breath caught in his throat. He held his arm against his mouth to muffle the sounds of his weeping. Flashes of Abby. In the sunlight at her window. Pruning apple trees in her garden. Smiling as Bent brushed a strand of hair from her lips.

The priest finished, and Abby's coffin was lowered into the grave. It descended and disappeared beneath the line of earth, and Bent sank back against the hillside. Whatever happened above at the grave he didn't know. His breath came in stabs, and his mouth hung open, spit trailing in strings, and his chest burned, and he begged to die. But he didn't die. He shook and convulsed and couldn't stop, and willed himself, die, die, just die. But still the ache and the tortured breath, and he lay there, curled into himself, buried his face in the grass and howled into the earth.

They had motored upriver. Tell wouldn't let anybody else pilot. It was an old aluminum v-hull, caked in rust, with a changeable engine that started when it felt like it. His father had no more use for it and gave it to him.

"What's she called?" Abby had asked the first time she climbed aboard.

"Piece of shit," Tell said.

But he guarded it jealously and shouted instructions and rebukes constantly. Sit over there, I'll lose plane. No, a cleat hitch, a cleat hitch.

"Argh, ya landlubbers," Bent chided. "Abaft the beam. Abandon ship!"

Tell scowled at first, but Louise and Abby laughed so he passed off as if he found it funny.

They could barely squeeze in. Bent let Louise sit up front with Tell, and he sat cross-legged on the deck and let Abby have the stern seat. A slow leak left a thin sheen of water settled always on deck, and his trunks felt wet. They headed northeast skirting the shore to the mouth of the river. The sun glazed the green water and gulls banked in to see if there was food to be had then turned and swept off again. The river narrowed as they passed the new condominiums on the western bank, storybook houses of distressed wood meant to replicate the weather-beaten saltboxes of the fishing villages, only no doubt cocooned in insulation, with central heating, not the pot belly stoves that heated the whole of Bent's and Tell's and Machlon's houses.

They chugged beneath the drawbridge. The light grew dim and the air cool, and Bent and Abby lay back and watched the steel grey underside of the bridge slide past. Bent stole a glance at Abby's browned belly, flat and smooth, then looked away.

As soon as the weather warmed this had been their routine, on weekends until the school year ended and nearly every day once summer started. Bent worked seven to noon at the grocery, delivering to all the old ladies. Most places that wouldn't keep a person busy their whole shift, but there were many old ladies in Easterly, women whose children had moved away and had children of their own who visited on birthdays and holidays, whose husbands had long since died, left them a meagre living put by weekly in the savings and loan, women whose only company in a week were the mailman and Bent. Tell hauled nets on his father's boat till one. Abby volunteered at the day camp till then, too. Bent didn't know what Louise did, nothing regular as far as he knew. Then they all met at the town dock. Machlon came for awhile but began to feel like a fifth wheel. One particular day, as they passed beneath the bridge, Tell suggested they climb onto the bridge supports. He idled the engine and steered the boat close.

"Go ahead, Machlon, climb up."

Machlon kicked off the gunwale and onto a support and Tell reached out and shoved off. Machlon turned to see that he'd been stranded. "Tell."

Tell just laughed.

"Knock it off, Tell," Bent said.

"Tell, come on, it's not funny," Abby said.

Tell laughed and Louise did, too. "You guys are such party poopers."

"It's not funny. Bring the boat back."

"He knows I'm only kidding around."

Machlon just stood there quietly, saying nothing, as if it was the most natural thing in the world to be sitting on a bridge support with no way off, but his face had fallen. Bent reached for an oar and held the paddle end toward Machlon.

"Grab it. I'll pull us over to you."

"All right, all right," Tell said, and he eased the boat alongside the support and Bent and Abby pulled Machlon back on board.

Bent turned on Tell wearily. "Why do you have to do things like that?"

Tell just laughed.

When next Bent went to collect him, Machlon begged off and didn't come again.

Bent watched Tell at the wheel. It seemed a natural part of him. His arms bloomed into it, and he held it loosely, in one hand, rubbing his belly with the other to draw Louise's attention to his toned abs. All year, since they'd left the junior high and moved into the consolidated school with the wealthy kids and met Abby and Louise, they had run together in a pack, but things were changing. Bent watched Louise steal glances as Tell ran his hand up to his chest and around his rib cage. Tell pretended he was scratching, but he was drawing with his fingers the outlines of his muscles – his pectoral, lat, deltoid, bicep – new muscles raised and hardened by the hauling of nets and lines, traps and anchors and barrels. Bent looked down at his own chest, his narrow rib cage, reedy arms, still the frame of a fifteen-year-old boy. They were the same age but Tell seemed much older. Louise had developed as well, her breasts nearly overflowing last year's bathing suit. Abby stayed lanky like Bent, but on her it was fetching. He longed to reach out and rest his hand on the lovely dip of her belly as she lay flat in the stern. Did she know? And if she did, was it a source of amusement? Was he just a boy to her? Tell followed the markers, the secret language in which they told him of sandbars and depth, a language Bent felt he should know in his bones but couldn't understand.

"Are you guys doing the summer reading list?" he said, searching for a language he could speak.

Tell rolled his lips. "Yeah, right."

"I'm on A Separate Peace," Bent said. "It's good."

"So am I," Abby said. "I love it."

The radio had gone to a news break and Louise flipped stations. A patchwork of static and bits of songs hissed until Louise hit on "Jack and Diane."

"I love this song." She jumped up and sang along, swaying and bobbing her head in time.

"Easy," Tell said. "You'll capsize us."

"My hips aren't that big." She ignored him and kept on.

From the north, a cabin cruiser appeared round the bed. It came on fast, and as it drew closer they saw that it was towing a shirtless teen on a wakeboard. Summer people. Most locals were still water skiing. Wakeboarding hadn't come to the staid boating community. Another boy on board opened a cooler in the stern and grabbed a beer. They'd set the cooler in the stern for ballast. Bigger wake, better wakeboarding. It would also annoy other boaters, most in the area favoring nice and easy sailboats over powerboats.

"Louise, sit down."

Tell waved the cruiser off with his left hand and tried to hold the boat steady as the wake approached. But the boys in the other boat shouted, egging Louise on. She sang louder, pointing at them and shimmying. The wakeboarder waved his free back hand then grabbed the board between his feet. Louise whooped appreciatively and danced *harder.*

"Go girl," one of the boys yelled. "Come on!"

"Louise, will you sit down!"

The cabin cruiser drew even and the boys whooped as they passed. The wake rushed and slammed into the side and the aluminum boat rolled and Bent heard the girls screaming as they hit the water. Bent plunged downward, felt his feet touch the sandy bottom and kicked up. He surfaced and shook his hair to see. Abby was bobbing nearby, coughing, and he swam to her. She leaned on his shoulder nodding and wiping water from her eyes.

"Assholes!" Tell yelled. The boys on board the cruiser held up their beers and the wakeboarder saluted, and all laughed as they disappeared round the next bend.

Tell looked at Louise treading water and smoothing down her soaking hair. "Why couldn't you just sit down?"

"What kind of a boat capsizes in six feet of water?" she said.

"I told you it was a piece of shit." Tell took hold of the port side and tried to right the boat.

"Well," Bent said, "it's a nice day for a swim anyway." And he began swimming in a circle around the boat.

"Come on, help me right this damn thing."

"You swamped it. Anyway, I'm in the middle of my afternoon swim."

Abby liked this small piece of revenge theatre and began swimming a corresponding circle counter-clockwise to Bent's.

"Come on," Tell said.

"Afternoon," Abby said to Bent as they passed each other.

"Lovely day, isn't it?" he said.

"Louise," Tell said.

"I don't know how to do it."

"You just grab the goddamn thing and lift."

"I can't," she said. "I'm not strong enough."

Tell pulled, and Louise floated nearby, and Bent and Abby swam circles around them and conducted polite conversation.

"Do you think the rain will hurt the rhubarb?"

"Oh I do hope not. I'm planning pies for the Labor Day picnic."

"Bent, come help me with this fucking thing before it sinks and we have to swim home."

"All right, all right."

Bent came to himself in the grass by the cemetery. After a while he felt well enough to rise and follow the railroad tracks back to Easterly.

At the railroad trestle he crossed the tracks and climbed the embankment on the far side and stood at the tree line by the playground. He skirted the edge of the yard and crouched by the propane tank on the side of Little's. He watched the road, waiting for a soul to pass, any living soul. A dog walker, anyone. But no one came.

Down the road he saw St Andrew's, its stained glass windows warm with light. He crossed the road quickly. A car turned the corner and Bent ducked behind a hedge. Its headlights rolled past and receded, and Bent rose and skirted the edge of the hedge to the church, dashed up the stairs and ducked inside.

He walked down the north aisle. Candles flickered with the displacement of air as he passed. It spooked him a little. He was a ghoul in church. He smelled resin. The wood of the pews had just been oiled. The confessional door was carved through with Maltese crosses in rows. He stepped in, sat and waited. Through the door, the church was a pattern of lights and darks. The only light entered through the crosses in the door. The screen door slid back. Bent smiled. It always amused him that a screen separated the priest from his penitents in such a small town. Surely Father Fintan knew the voice of everybody in his parish. But church is ritual. Much of life is pretense. Most people wouldn't be able to face each other without it.

"Go ahead, my child," the priest said.

Oh right, Bent was meant to start. He hadn't really come here for that. But he began. "Bless me, Father, for I have sinned …" He finished the prescribed remarks and went blank.

"What are your sins?" the priest asked.

"Well … I was idle, and … I haven't been spending much time with my family lately."

"It is difficult," the priest said. "People work so hard nowadays just to get by. Have you tried setting aside some time each week, a day where you do family things?"

"I could try, I guess, but I'm … not sure they want me around anymore."

"Of course they want you around, Bent. It is you, isn't it, Bent?"

Bent delayed. Should he admit it? What was the point of denying if the old man already knew? And his face was obscured by the screen. It wasn't as if he saw.

"It's me."

"I thought it was, but your voice sounds a bit raspy. Have you got a cold?"

Bent coughed. "Little one, yeah."

"I assure you, your family love you and they want to spend time with you. Take your children to the aquarium. Have a date night with Jean."

Bent nodded, and he imagined doing the things the priest suggested and his throat tightened and the tears rolled. The priest paused then, and Bent heard him sniffing, and for a moment he thought he was crying, too, but couldn't understand why.

"Do you smell something, Bent?"

Bent sat very still, as if that would stop his stench seeping through the grate. "No."

"Huh. Thought I smelled something. Anyway. Are these your only sins? It doesn't seem so very much."

Bent could think of nothing else, but he didn't want to let him go. He was desperate to keep him talking, but he could think of nothing and went quiet.

"It's been years since you've confessed, Bent. Years since you've been in church. Now both in one month. What's going on?"

Bent looked down at his grey hands, the hole that had exposed the knuckle of his left middle finger, the sinews shifting. "It's hard to explain."

The priest sniffed again. "Are you sure you don't smell anything?"

Bent froze again. "No, nothing."

"Huh. I hope I haven't got a brain tumor." The priest laughed gently.

Bent heard spraying this time. Through the grate he saw the priest spritzing air freshener.

In the grove he found Machlon was sleeping again.

"Thank Christ," Tell said when he saw him. "I was goin stir crazy."

Bent sat. Tell sniffed. "You stink."

"You've said."

"I mean on top of that." He breathed in and out, nose to Bent's arm like a dog. "You smell like fish."

"Oh that. I slept in the shed for a bit."

They leaned against the stones and were quiet, and watched pink light seep between the ashy branches and spruce needles. Bent said nothing of Abby's funeral, or his visit to the priest. Why did he never speak?

"I wish I had some coffee," Tell said.

"If you tried to drink coffee it would just spill out the hole in your stomach," Bent said.

"I'm saying just for the habit of it, the taste."

"We really are gruesome, aren't we?" said Machlon, who had awoken and sat stretching.

"Maybe we were before, and we're just now noticing," Bent said.

"Speak for yourself," Tell said. "What did I do that was so bad? I worked hard, kept a roof over my kids' head. Paid my taxes. Mostly. Am I to blame that things cost more than I made?" He was quiet for a while, then, "Some bacon would be nice as well."

"Well, Little's will be open soon," Bent said. "Why don't we just stroll down there, step up to the counter and order the breakfast special. I'm sure Sandy will be pleased as punch to see us."

Bent brooded quietly.

Tell looked at him. "You know what the problem is."

Bent waited, and Tell obliged him by going on.

"We're bored."

Bent held up his grey mummified hands. "Really? Is that the problem?"

"All right, yes, we're also dead. I get that. But we're going crazy with nothing to do. We'll need distraction if we're to tolerate this until you can find a way to undo it."

"*If* I can find a way," Bent said.

"Nights, nights are fine. We can roam about, stretch our legs a bit, see what we can see. But days. Cooped up in this grove, day after day, the three of us? We'll kill each other." He looked at Bent. "See what I did there?"

"I see, yes."

"So what I propose is, we wait until night, and then we break into the library. They've got those portable DVD players they lend out and loads of movies."

Then it struck Bent. If he was to find a way out of this, he'd need books, but it wasn't the Easterly Library that kept them. They needed to go to the seminary.

"The only books I know that might have the answers we need are in there,' Bent said.

"Welp, Machlon and I already did insider trading," Tell said. "What's breaking and entering next to that?"

It continued gusting all day, the sky solid steel, the sea battering the rocks at the little beach. Winter had come in the night, and Bent wondered if there would be snow. Winters in Easterly were cold, but on the Sound as it was, it was often spared the snow that blanketed the inland regions and instead a pale silver fell across the land and everything on it. Grass, trees, even sky and water were an endless expanse of grey. Most years Bent hoped for snow, for at least white was a color of sorts, but now he held his hands before him, his skin the color of stone, and he hoped it would continue grey all winter so he could hide.

At dusk, a mist settled and the wind dropped, and they listened to buoys clang as they bobbed in the waves. They heard the bell at St Andrew's strike ten, and Machlon shivered.

"I hate that bell. This town, this fog, it's as if there's a demon ringing it."

"Take heart, Machlon," Tell said. "You've no need to fear. We're the demons now."

In his mind, Bent called up a scrap of an old poem. It suited the occasion, and the mood, and he couldn't help reciting it.

All is not well, by dint of spell,

somewhere between the heaven and hell.

There is this night a wild deray.

The spirits have wandered from their way.

"Would you quit with the creepy songs?" Tell said.

Bent quietened. "It's a poem," he said after a while.

The walk to the island where the seminary lay would take all night, but it was a short boat ride across the bay. When the bells of St Andrew's struck eleven, they made their way to the marina. All the boats had been hauled and stored for the winter, but it wasn't a big boat they were after. They slipped among them, wrapped like carcasses and listing in their blocks, and peered out behind the one nearest the yard shack. Its windows were dark. Beyond the shack, a few cars peppered the lot of the tavern, and the low strums of guitar licks seeped from speakers within. Bent remembered the three of them that night stumbling unsteadily from the bar and wished he could take it all back. He turned away and tried not to think about it.

They walked the rocky border at water's edge looking for a skiff or motorboat. Usually the boatyard kept something in the water for small chores, attending the anchor buoys that bobbed offshore, clearing fouled lines. But there was nothing. They walked the length of the boatyard, then eyed the shore that ran behind the span of houses along that part of the inlet.

They thought of one more place to look. At the beach they stopped and pulled up into a dune to wait for the lights in the nearby houses to go out. The marram grass hewed in a thicket, and they nestled in amongst the yellow stalks. A few feet away the sand was dark up to the tide line, and tidal veins were etched in the sand by receding waves, and Bent thought how it takes small waves to leave such marks. The big ones crash ashore and pound the sand, leaving it hard-packed and taut. The small waves lap and caress and leave tiny strokes like wrinkles, the way life does, for the lucky ones.

Soon all the houses were dark. The living slept. They crawled from the dunes and crossed the last stretch of beach to the dock and found what they'd been looking for. Bill Hinckley's skiff. Most boats were in dry dock for the winter, but Hinckley kept his in the water year-round and fished for eels and bonito, striped bass and cod, and ate what he caught and not much else. People warned he'd die out there one day in that little boat, capsize in the chop and get hypothermia before a soul knew he was in the water, but he kept on. A man had to if he was hungry and wouldn't take a government check.

Bent and Machlon climbed aboard. Tell untied the skiff and leapt to the deck, let the momentum of his landing propel the boat away from its slip, and with a giddy rush, Bent felt with joy the rocking of the boat and the forward surge as they pushed off from the dock. After a while he looked back to see how far they'd got. They were at least two hundred yards from shore. The houses were grey hulks, no lights were lit. Bent turned front and saw Mouse Island.

The water was black and the boat bobbed on the winter sea. Bent remembered old ones told of the year the Sound froze, how people walked all the way to Fishers Island on the ice. But he watched the barren winter landscape as they rode and imagined the water beneath him a solid block of ice.

At the island they idled a moment just offshore. They studied its one house, stick-built, nineteenth century probably, what Bent's mother would have called carpenter gothic, and Bent wondered what kind of person sought such solitude. It was a summer house now, the island deserted in winter. Bent regarded the shuttered house and the reedy overgrown earth, the thistle and sea-buckthorn brittle and ragged and poking up between rocks. He shuddered and they motored on.

They crossed the bay, hitting and bouncing over the waves. Tell laughed aloud for it was good to be in a boat again. They approached the island from the west. Bypassing the dock, Tell cut the engine and they coasted into the shallows northwards, and he pulled up short amongst the cord grass and drove the anchor deep in the mud. They climbed ashore and felt their feet sinking in muck with every step. They got stuck a few times and took turns hauling each other free, their feet coming loose with great sucking sounds, and Bent worried their legs would get pulled clean off in the mud.

At the edge of the marsh they hit pavement and ran low across the parking lot. He led, of course, since he knew the place, and soon he realized his body still remembered the way. He turned and weaved left and right. They passed the dormitory, where they'd sat on their cots reading and playing cards until lights out at ten, and then you heard springs bouncing and quiet moaning. Past the chapel where he'd rung the bell a thousand times and cursed God as many. They rounded a corner and pulled up before the library steps and went round to the back door and huddled behind the trash cans. Tell signaled Machlon up. Machlon crawled onto one of the cans and raised himself up, looked in at the window, then dropped.

"Seems quiet."

Tell stepped out and Bent and Machlon fell in behind. They tiptoed up the back steps and slipped inside. The back door gave on to the storage room, where lesser-used volumes sat on raw wooden shelves. They pushed through the door that gave out to the main room. Bent remembered the smell. The wooden floors had been recently polished and shone in the moonlight pouring in through the tall old windows with bubbles here and there where the glassmaker had taken a breath.

They walked lightly, but their footsteps echoed against the plank floors and rounded cathedral ceiling.

"Let's make this quick,' Tell said. Bent ducked into the stacks and searched for the volumes he thought would be most likely to provide the very peculiar information they sought. He took Augustine and Gregory the Great, Peter of Blois and others. When he had filled all their arms with books, they turned to go and left the stacks. They stopped at the librarian's table to take some candles and matches, and when they turned to go came face to face with an old man with white hair in a priest's cassock. Bent reared back and the old priest screamed and priest and books clattered to the floor.

The priest lay motionless. Bent knelt and felt for a pulse and Tell and Machlon came running.

"Is he dead?" Machlon said.

Bent shook his head. "Unconscious." He ran for the phone.

"Forget that, we gotta go," Tell said.

"What if he's had a heart attack?"

"We'll call from a pay phone."

"There are no pay phones anymore."

"Goddamn drug dealers ruin things for everybody."

They ran for the door. On the way out, Bent pulled the fire alarm.

"Shit," Tell said.

They ran for the cover of the marsh and, gaining it, fell flat and pressed themselves into the grass. Soon they heard voices, then sirens, and red lights lit the charcoal sky beyond the marsh. A big engine idled, and voices shouted. Bent bellied up and peeked through the leaves. Two first responders led the old man, shaky but walking, out into the air.

"I'm telling you, he was dead. He was a dead man walking about…"

"Okay," one of the responders said. "Just sit and get some air …"

Bent stayed in the grove the rest of the night reading instead of going abroad, searching for any evidence that this had happened before, something that might tell them how to get back. Tell, emboldened by their successful raid on the seminary, went to the local public library before dawn and took some books for Machlon and a portable DVD player and some DVDs and spent the next day watching movies. They bickered occasionally, then mostly ignored each other.

Sometime the next afternoon they heard crunching leaves and peered over the edge of the rocks and saw the younger Bentson boys kicking through the leaves looking for arrowheads or some such. They dropped and lay flat against the ground, and after a minute the boys broke into a run, out of plain exuberance the way boys do, and were gone.

Bent hadn't found anything so far in the books, and as soon as it was dark, each man struck out for his own amusements, Tell no doubt to hover round the Benedetti place to wait for bedtime so he could spook the old man, and Machlon to Bent couldn't guess where.

Machlon slipped along the railroad track bed and climbed the hill at his house. He approached the window as he did every night and watched the revenant lying in his bed in agony. As he watched, he knelt on the rocks below his bedroom window as a kind of penance.

Bent just roamed. He stalked the neighborhood like a prey animal, slinking low between trees, behind rock walls. The wasting of his flesh left him a taut compact slab, able to slip in and out of spaces wide enough for a cat. As he passed the grocery, he caught sight of himself in the glass and stood watching, moving limbs, performing some basic human action like waving an arm, and marveled at the way his sinews rippled like the sleek pelt of a mongoose.

He felt he could leap to high places like a cat or from tree to tree. He wondered what would happen if he fell, would he fall like a cat, too, light and silent, or like a man? Or would his brittle frame shatter like crystal? He went to the wood and climbed the tallest tree, and clinging to the uppermost branch, swayed as the wind bent the branch back and forth, then with the next gust he let go and felt the momentum launch him skyward then drop him toward the earth. He hit, the sound like a bundle of twigs cracking, but felt no pain, and when he examined himself, his arms and legs, his outstretched fingers, he was all there, all except a nub of pinkie finger snapped off at the joint. As he brushed himself off, a red fox burst from the tree line and snatched the fingertip in its teeth and ran.

'Hey you!' Bent yelled. 'Come back here with that finger!'

He leapt up and took after the fox. The animal led him a merry chase and, when it had gained enough lead, deposited the finger in the grass to consider his catch. He pawed it and sniffed. As Bent drew close, it hesitated and seemed to consider whether to take it up again, and finally it turned and ran, leaving the finger on the ground. Bent reached it and knelt in the grass, taking the finger up, slightly insulted. Then he sniffed it.

'Don't blame you,' he said.

He clawed a hole with his bony fingers and laid the finger in, and swept dirt over it. 'Food for worms, at least.'

~

Bent emerged from the wood at the rise. It was nearly dawn, time he returned to the grove, be in before daybreak, don't be seen. But he looked down the hill and couldn't fight the urge. If he could only see them, just for a moment. He descended, and at the edge of his yard, their yard, he climbed high into a spruce tree and hid among its branches. The sky grew pink in the east. The door to the house opened, and he, that is the other he, stepped out onto the porch. Bent stared at himself below and his spine went cold. His brown hair, his long stride, the chambray shirt Jack and Ada had given him last Father's Day. Was that his sad look on the other Bent's face or was it the other Bent's? It was in some ways like the face Jack had inherited, but different, too. The difference of personality? Bent didn't know.

Below him, this other Bent climbed in his truck, *his truck*, cranked the engine, and without waiting for it to heat up properly, backed out and climbed the hill. Bent sat in a fog.

He was broken from his daze by the bursting of his children into the daylight.

"Hold your sister's hand," Jean called from the porch.

Jack reached for Ada's hand. She squirmed out of his grip and he contented himself with holding to the hood of her coat as they climbed the hill toward the bus stop.

Ada marched like a drill sergeant, swinging her arms stiffly. "Yankee Doodle went to town, riding on a pony, stuck a feather in his hat and called it macaroni ..."

Jack kept time pulling on her hood. Bent watched them till they turned the corner and fell from sight, and the tears ran.

He was stuck in the tree all day, but he didn't care. He sat thinking of Jack and Ada, replaying their time together in his head. At nightfall, he slid down the trunk and headed back for the grove, barely remembering to hide himself. The road was dotted with patches of ice, and he picked his way along, growing more and more cocky of his footing and less careful. His feet slipped from under him on black ice and he went down hard on his left shoulder. He lay there a moment, clutching at it, the wind knocked out of him. He felt something loose and clicking beneath his fingers. He probed it and the piece came away. He held it up and examined it in the moonlight. It was a length of muscle, about two inches long, dried and hardened like beef jerky. He didn't know why but he put it in his pocket. It seemed important, it seemed like a muscle was something you should keep. Then he began the business of trying to rise. He sat up and tried to push up with his hands, but his feet slipped and he went down again. He tried again, leaning to the other side this time, and fell on his hip, feeling a crunch in his pocket as he hit. He reached in. The muscle was pulverized.

'Great'.

He turned out his pocket and shook out the bits. He turned over on his hands and knees and crawled over to the grassy verge and sat, marveling how a person could get used to anything. He wondered whether that meant nothing was as bad as you'd thought it would be or it was all just as bad so no point in dreading one thing more than another.

He thought then for no particular reason of a time they were out for a walk, the whole family. They were walking down the street, Bent and Jean chatting and Jack old enough to understand the drift of grownup talk and even take part. Ada held to Bent's hand and was silent amid talk she couldn't share, and all of a sudden she stopped and let go of his hand.

"Everybody hold on!"

And she began the most outrageous dance, jerking her arms and swiveling her hips. They laughed and asked her why she'd done it, and she said they'd been ignoring her so she did the boogie. He didn't know why he should remember that all of a sudden, but it made him laugh and cry to think of it.

He returned to the grove and sat with his back against the stones all night looking in the books for a way to undo what they had done and finding none, and when Tell and Machlon returned at dawn he was surly and silent.

"Anything?" Tell said.

Bent just shook his head.

They spent the day dozing, and when he was wakeful Bent read through Augustine. He wrote at length in several volumes about the human desire to rise from the dead, and he wrote about how resurrection would happen. He wrote that even if you were eaten by a shark, God would know where to find the chewed-up, digested bits of you and on Judgement Day he would gather up the pieces and resurrect you whole. But he wrote nothing about Bent, Tell and Machlon's condition. He had been reading for hours, and sleep took him suddenly like nightshade, and he dropped off but would snap awake again and find only a few moments had passed. Even when he slept he didn't rest. He dreamt of phantoms and dark figures stalking his children as they played, of being shot, of sharks vaulting into the shallows and writhing with his children in their jaws. The living don't know what a gift it is to sleep.

At twilight Bent was still in a dark mood. The sun had dropped but the sky was silver. All day it had smelled like snow, and now it began to fall. Big powdery flakes like crab apple blossoms. It would stick. They all sat up and looked skyward.

"Early," Tell said.

They stood and walked to the stone wall. Machlon held out a hand and caught flakes that didn't melt against his skin, which had no warmth. They looked into his palm and watched the crystals land, their lacy edges glistening against Machlon's waxy skin. They leaned on the stone wall and watched the park turn white and listened to the quiet.

The brown grass of the park disappeared beneath the snow. The tips poked through like drowning men struggling to keep heads above water, but the snow kept falling and after a while even they sank and vanished beneath it. No living thing moved. Snow made mountains on every tree branch. Flakes slipped through the gaps in the tree canopy and dusted the floor of their grove, and Machlon walked into the wood and returned with a fallen branch of brown leaves and swept the snow away. In the distance they heard whoops and shouts, children bursting from houses to be first to put footprints in the snow, to make snow angels and snowmen.

Bent knew his children would be out in it, and he had to be there.

He had passed only a few houses before he saw people, children in their front yard building a fat snowman. He dove behind a hedge and ran along low to the ground. At the edge of the hedge, he saw another group taking turns hauling each other in a sled. He looked round, then looked up. He was hard by a maple tree, its last autumn leaves blanketed in white. He took a last look around, then reached for a low branch, braced a foot against the trunk, and hoisted, easy as when he was a boy. Easier. As a child, with Tell calling coward below, Bent climbed as though he was unafraid, reached for the farthest branches and shouted back good-natured insults. But he climbed slowly, feeling for the strong handhold, testing branches for weight before hoisting himself. But now he climbed arm over arm like an ape, not stopping to feel for the stable holds. What difference if he fell? It wouldn't hurt. At worst he'd snap off another finger.

He was safe for the moment amongst the branches, but he couldn't sit here all night and he wanted to see Jack and Ada. He looked up to where the branches of the maple he was in met the tree next to it. He climbed, leaned and jumped, and landed on a middle branch. He spidered down the trunk and round it then leapt to the next tree, and the next.

He reached the tree above his driveway and was quickly at the top. He sat camouflaged in the branches and snow. The sky was ash grey and the snow fell in fat flakes that together looked like sheets of falling lace. No one would notice him as long as he held still, but if he knocked any snow loose they might look up and then where would he be? There is no good explanation for a corpse up a tree.

The front of the house was dark, but pale golden light shone from the back and Bent knew they were in the kitchen. Finishing supper. The windows were sweating, the wood stove was burning, grey smoke puffed from the chimney. Snow had frosted the window panes and hung from the eaves, and the place looked like one of the Christmas houses his mother used to buy at the five-and-dime.

How had he become a man on the outside of his own life? He thought then how little had changed, that he was such a man even when he was in his own skin, tucked up warm with his family but worrying on all that was wrong, all that he wanted, not holding close to what he had. But you can't tell a person that, can you. Can't make them appreciate what they've got. His father always told him a man couldn't learn from someone else's mistakes, he had to make his own. Bent looked at his sinewy cadaver's hands. They never mentioned this in catechism. He'd asked the priest how bread and wine could be changed into the body and blood of Christ, and was told it was a mystery, and Bent couldn't understand why the priest thought that was an answer and not the sire of a thousand new questions. He didn't imagine they would change his beliefs, didn't want them to, really. The old man had the cure of souls for the parish, he really believed that, and it gave his life purpose. He believed a benign overseer watched over them all. Why would Bent want to take that from a man? He wished he had it himself. Still he wondered what effect his current state would have on the old man's beliefs and thought how he'd hunt him down and show himself if the old man weren't dead.

Jack and Ada emerged in their puffy winter coats. Ada looked like a marshmallow. Jack took giant steps around the yard and made Godzilla noises. Ada stepped deliberately, listening for the crunch. Soon she tired of this and began trying to follow in Jack's tracks, leaping from one footprint to the next.

Bent watched as they made a snowman. They dug beneath the snow of the hedges and collected pebbles for the eyes and nose, mouth and shirt buttons, and for a hat they gave it Bent's knit cap, and Bent watched from his tree and laughed. Ada jumped into the sled in the yard. Jack took the rope and pulled. Kip bounded after them, leaping like a porpoise through the snow and fluffing all their tracks into a froth. The sled nosed to the edge of the yard and dived down the crest, and at the bottom became briefly airborne. Ada yelped with delight, then the sled landed on the hard-packed snow of the road. The road was iced over and slick, and she made the sled shimmy by pulling on the sides. Jack threw the sled rope over his head and round his middle and like a husky hauled the sleigh up the hill while Ada cracked an imaginary whip and shouted, "Mush! Mush!"

Why was Bent here? That other soul was in his body, so why was it Bent still felt the ache, watching his daughter squeal with glee and his son proud to be a big brother, hauling his sister around the yard in a sled? And how is it he still felt that familiar pain, housed as it was in that rotting place inside him where a heart used to beat.

Jean came to the door and called them in. Jack and Ada were happily exhausted and made no fuss. Bent let them go, sat in his tree and felt profoundly alone. A man could choose to belong or not. He had chosen not to belong, and now he didn't.

His mood drew him to the graveyard. He travelled the tree line all the way there. At the railroad trestle he lacked tree cover, so he plunged down the embankment and ran across the old unused tracks and up the other side. He scaled the trees there and in that way crossed the road. He went three trees further, then dropped into the graveyard.

He walked to the back far off the road and sat, his back against the stone wall, and felt sorry for himself, his brooding so deep he barely noticed the day pass. By late afternoon, Bent had resolved to visit his family no more, not until he could find a way back. *It only hurts. Leave it.*

At dusk, the starlings began their murmuration. They burst from the tree line like a gust of wind and climbed, then whipsawed, beating a circle in the sky in one body. They plunged, then pulled up like a plane pulling out of a dive, then plunged again. They banked right toward the tree line again, then just before collision they climbed and started the pattern again.

Bent watched as the birds wheeled and spun, blackening the sky, the beating of their wings like a single pulse, and he laughed with the beauty of it. Whether the birds flew for joy or some other reason Bent didn't care, it was joy to him. He wondered that he hadn't stopped to watch them more often.

Abby had always been aware of birds, of animals, of the names of flowers and trees. She even knew of plant remedies, which had been thought good for fever, which for headache and upset stomach. She'd learned them from her grandmother.

Bent lay beneath the tree canopy thinking of Abby. He conjured her face in his mind and closed his eyes and tried to imagine her scent and remember her touch. He imagined how she would point to the starlings' murmuration, "look, look," she would shout, the delight she would take, the joy that would spread across her face.

"Oh, for God's sake."

Bent started and turned toward the sound of the voice. Coming toward him from amongst the headstones was Abby. He leapt to his feet. His throat was tight with a rising cry and he shook. He took a step toward her but she backed away, so he stopped. The damage done by the car was brutal, but it was still Abby.

"Abby. You look …"

"Like meat."

"I was going to say nice."

She snorted.

Bent shifted his weight. "You're not happy to see me?"

"I'm dead. I wasn't expecting to see anybody."

"I know the feeling," he said. "Let me hug you, at least."

He reached for her, but she pushed him away. "I don't want to hug you. You're dead. And so am I."

"I don't understand. They buried you. I saw the funeral."

Abby waved an arm. "I climbed out of the coffin at the mortuary. Walked right by Mister Neilan. He slept through the whole thing. They buried an empty coffin."

"I'm sorry this happened to you," he said. "I hoped you were resting in peace."

"I would be if not for you," she said.

"Me?"

"Yes, you. I'm dead. I'm not happy about it, but I've accepted it and I'm ready to move on. I can't, though, because of your constant wailing and moaning over me. Stop thinking about me all the time, for Christ's sake. You're keeping me here when it's time for me to go. You have to let the dead rest, Bent."

"I'm sorry. I just miss you."

Abby softened. "I miss you, too. But that was another life. That *was* life. It's over now." She looked around the graveyard and marveled at her circumstances. "I would have given anything for you to want me this much when we were alive."

"I *did*."

"Not enough to be with me. It's ironic. You kept me at arm's length my whole life. Now I'm dead and you won't let me go." She bent to a headstone and brushed it clean, then looked about. "It all seems so unimportant now, you and me."

"Unimportant? You were everything to me."

"No, I wasn't. I was the girl you wanted because you thought you couldn't have me in high school."

"That's not true. I've loved you from the very first moment I ever saw you."

"I've always loved you, too. But you were never mine. I should have accepted that." She looked off into the trees. "I want to see my grandmother."

Bent shrugged, trying to contain his hurt. "Go, then."

"You don't mean it."

"No, I don't."

"Fine. I guess I'll see you around, then."

She turned and stalked away among the headstones. Bent stood, stunned, trying to understand what had just happened. His life, or whatever this was, just got even more complicated.

Tell moved along the low road, from tree to tree as they'd learned to do, and landed in the great oak outside his living room window. He peered up into the boys' rooms. Lights out. They were asleep. He looked back into the living room window, and for a moment saw nothing, then Louise and the thing in his body swept into view. Dancing. They were dancing in the living room. Louise had accepted he was too tired to go out dancing on Saturday nights and had held out a hand to him how many times to dance at home. Just to sway and hold each other. He'd always refused.

Machlon had grown restless. After night fell, he left the graveyard and made his usual stop, which he still wouldn't disclose to Bent and Machlon. He passed Little's and dropped with the road to his house. His mother's rose bushes hadn't been put to bed for the winter. They'd be dead now. Won't come back next spring. He stepped gingerly in the last of the leaves around the back of the house, making no more noise than a foraging animal. He looked in at his bedroom window. The other him lay in bed. Pain seized him and he winced. It passed and his arms fell at his sides, spent. Machlon remembered that pain. He would be waiting for the next onslaught to take hold. That was his life now.

Then Machlon became aware that the other knew he was there. He froze and tried to make no sound, but it was no use. It's not because he made a noise that the other knew he was there. He just knew. So Machlon raised the window. The other hadn't the strength to move. He stared at Machlon, and Machlon knew what he wanted.

"You knew, didn't you?" Machlon said. "You knew about the pain. How could you not know?"

"I knew. I wanted it so badly, I didn't care. But this is so much worse than I'd imagined. Please…"

"No. I'm sorry, but I can't."

Machlon couldn't watch anymore, and he moved away.

He climbed the hill and found himself crossing the railroad bridge out of Easterly. He turned left, then right onto the long hill road. He climbed the long rise. It seemed to go on forever. He felt the sensation of peddling, the old days when he and Bent and Tell ground away at the gears of their bicycles, pushing themselves up this long hill, just so that when they reached the top they could turn and coast back down again. As their confidence grew they free-handed it, arms thrust wide, steering with their hips, the wind brushing their faces, the exhilaration of freefall. Machlon looked up and realized he had arrived at the county nursing home. He turned in the driveway and moved along the length of the building between the hedges and the wall. He looked at the sky. It was past midnight. The night shift would be on, just a few nursing assistants, maybe an orderly.

At the end of the long low-slung brick building he paused at windows, looking to see who lived behind them. In one room, two old women lay sleeping, their mouths hanging open as though they were freshly dead. It wouldn't be long for either of them. Even now their toes might be curling inward, one of the first signs, or so his mother had always said. In another room two old men sat each on the edge of his bed throwing down cards on a wheeled table between them. Hearts, looked like. At the end of the building nearest the woods Machlon looked in the last window. An ancient man lay in his bed, alone in the room. A television anchored to the wall flickered but he seemed not to watch it. After a while a nursing assistant entered. She leaned over and spoke to the man. He turned his head a little toward her and said something back but didn't look at her. He looked past her into the middle distance. The woman left and the man resumed looking off at nothing.

Machlon went around the back of the building and found a door. He turned the knob. It gave. He pulled up his hood and slipped inside. At the door of the room he paused and checked the name typed on a cardboard tab and slid into a plastic frame on the door. Janeway. Machlon entered the room, stopped just inside. The man spoke.

"Honestly, dear, I'm fine." Thought Machlon was the nurse, apparently.

"It's not the nurse, Mister Janeway. I'm just a volunteer. I saw the TV. Thought you might want company."

"Sounds like you need this bed more than me," the old man said. "You croak like a frog."

Machlon was aware of the rattle his rotting vocal cords made. He smiled at the man's bluntness. "Do you talk to all your visitors this way?"

"Never get any. Probably because I'm so rude." He laughed. "No, everyone who would visit me is dead. Except you, apparently. Sit down."

Machlon hesitated, doubting now whether he had judged correctly. He moved closer. No, he hadn't misjudged. The man's eyes were a milky white. He could barely credit his luck and passed a hand before the man's face.

"Don't bother. I can't see."

Machlon jumped back.

"Felt the air move where you waved your hand. Jumpy bastard, ain't you? Sit, sit."

Machlon moved a chair beside the bed and sat. The old man's cheeks were sucked in where his teeth should have been and his face looked like a rotting peach.

"Yep, I outlived em all," the man continued. "My wife passed a few years ago. And the others just dropped regular like flies after that. Gets so you read the obituaries to find out who's coming to poker night." The man paused, obviously thinking of something. And then he spoke it aloud. "My son died in Vietnam."

"I'm sorry."

The man nodded, accepting Machlon's condolences but not wanting to speak further of it. "So what made you want to volunteer your time visiting old bastards like me?"

"I don't know," Machlon said. "Everybody needs somebody to talk to. Seemed like a good thing to do."

"It's good to have a purpose. What's your day job?"

"Pharmaceutical technician."

"Good job. Good pay, benefits. I went in the Navy. Joined in '45. Fifteen years old. I lied about my age to get in. Everybody was doing it. Soon as you could go, you went. By the time I got through basic we'd dropped the bomb on Hiroshima and Nagasaki, so I spent the war as a cook's assistant on a submarine tender in the Philippines."

"Did you like it?"

"Hell no, I didn't like it. I thought I was going to be Audie Murphy, instead I spent four years spooning out chipped beef and scrubbing pots. It was all right, though. Better than getting shot at, I realize now. Every day we had to feed a thousand men. Breakfast, lunch and dinner. One night before the end of my duty shift I made a huge vat of oatmeal for next day's breakfast. Put it in the fridge, went to bed. Next morning I took it out and it was full of cockroaches. I went to throw it out, and the cook said, what the hell you doin? I said, it's full of cockroaches. Come here, he said. I heaved the vat over to him and he opened a bag of raisins and dumped the whole thing in, said stir that up, they'll never know the difference. And they didn't."

Machlon laughed.

"Ship sailed for its home port in Groton. Looked pretty nice around here so this is where I stayed. Went to college on the G.I. Bill, which means we were drinking in the afternoon, skipping a lot of classes and playing a lot of bridge."

"What did you do when you graduated?"

"Who said I graduated? Nah, too much drinking and bridge. After I dropped out of college, I took a job at Electric Boat. Welded the hull of the Nautilus. I did all right. But of course the pension wasn't much to speak of time I retired. That's why I'm in here instead of one of the private nursing homes. But it's fine, not like some of those hell holes you hear about on the news where they leave people sitting in shit-filled diapers for days. They're nice to you, the food's not bad. And look, you came to see me. Why did you come to see me? I'm glad you're here, but what's the real reason? Besides it being a nice thing to do."

"I did something not very nice to somebody."

"And you're looking to make amends. Now that's a nice thought. Well-intentioned. But have you made amends to the person you hurt?"

"He's dead."

The man turned his face toward Machlon. "You didn't kill him, did you?"

Machlon laughed. "No."

"Well, I'm glad to hear that."

Machlon leaned forward in his chair. "How much is enough? To make up for what I did. I thought I would come visit somebody who needed company, but I think you're doing me more good than I'm doing you."

"How bad did you do him?"

"*Bad.*"

"Well then, I suppose you've got to keep doing until you feel you've done enough."

Machlon thought about this. "Okay."

"Keep coming to see me, okay?"

"I will.'

Bent sat stewing in the graveyard for hours. After a while, he rose reluctantly and returned to the grove. When he got there, Tell and Machlon had already gone. He had been abroad enough, and the encounter with Abby had left him sad and disheartened. He stayed in the grove and slept fitfully. At dawn, he awoke. Tell was kicking his foot.

"Where you been?" Tell said.

"Got caught out. Had a good roam?"

"A-yut," Tell said.

"Haunt Benedetti again?"

Tell shook his head. "I'm bored of that. Anyway he got pretty shook up. Don't want to kill the man. It was movie night at the Baptist church on the river road, so I snuck into the deacon's office and watched through the register."

Machlon laughed.

"What's funny?"

"Tell in church," Machlon said and laughed, and Bent laughed, too.

Tell smiled a little. "And then I snuck into the library and got some new DVDs. Machlon?"

Machlon shrugged. "Just wandered."

He thought of the revenant in his body, writhing under his pain, begging him with his eyes to swap back every night as Machlon sat at the window looking in. He felt awash with shame, and his stomach felt like iron.

"As the souls of the dead should," Bent said. He waited for Tell and Machlon to settle. "That was too close the other day, the Bentson boys. We're too exposed here. This grove is too much in the middle of everything."

"What do you suggest?" Tell said.

Bent told of the graveyard, how quiet it was in back, and reminded them how nobody ever went there anymore. Late that night they went, each carrying the stolen books and DVDs. Bent led the way to the rear, and they settled on the edge of the wood near the slave section.

"We can even light a fire if we want, I think," Bent said.

"I don't feel the cold anymore," Machlon said. "Do you?"

"Just for the pleasantness," Bent said. "We can tell ghost stories."

Tell lowered himself and leaned back against the stone wall, folded his arms and looked about.

"Corpses living in a graveyard. So cliché. Could you think of nothing better?"

~

"Can you stop kicking your legs, please?"

Ada halted her absent-minded kicking mid-swing and looked at her father.

"What's the matter with you?" Jean said to the thing she thought was Bent.

The other Bent shivered almost visibly. So odd to be back in a live body. He was having trouble getting used to the stiff movements, the feel of blood coursing through his veins. Sounds were louder, sharper. Ada's kicks were like gunshots, and he'd jumped at each one until he'd cried out for her to stop.

"Nothing. Tired," he said.

All these new people. This noisy dinner. Was this the way it always was? Would always be? The wife wasn't bothered by the barking and banging of the children, was even amused by it. Was this what was expected of him?

Jean petted Ada's head. Thus reassured, she began kicking again.

"I have my book group tonight, don't forget you've got to watch the kids."

Watch the kids?

The other Bent tossed his napkin on his plate and pushed back from the table.

"Why is Daddy so grouchy?" Ada said when he'd gone.

Jean stopped with her drink at her lips.

"Daddy's just tired, Ada," she said after a while. "He's been working a lot."

"He didn't even go yesterday," Ada said.

Jean was quiet. Jack wasn't satisfied with his mother's answer and pressed her.

"He's so different. It's like it's not even him anymore."

She hadn't told them yet about the divorce. She was working out how to break it to them. Soon she would have to, though. Bent was worse than ever. It was hard to credit it. It was like he was another person altogether. He would have to go, soon.

~

They kept mostly to their routine, venturing out after dark, seeking their own diversions, and returning to the graveyard by dawn. They told where they'd been and what they'd done. Or Bent and Tell did. Machlon never would. They hunkered down and talked until they ran out of things to talk about, which happened more and more, a thing that bothered Bent. They read and burnt fires. Not for the warmth. As Machlon said, they didn't need that anymore. For the golden flicker and pop of wood and salty smoke. It felt like living, to do a thing purely for the pleasure of it.

Bent hunted his father everywhere, found himself searching yards and fields as he went his ways, even looking up into trees, for if he was in them, might not his father be as well? But he saw no one, no one dead, anyway. Only the living, and from them of course he had to hide. All this looking and he hadn't found him. His mother was right. He hadn't died. He had left them. Left him.

Soon after their decant to the graveyard they were sitting around, Bent reading the last of the books they had taken from the seminary, Tell and Machlon in reveries. Bent had tried to talk to them of his frustration, of finding nothing in the books that could help them. Machlon sympathized but he had no desire to return so he couldn't share Bent's keenness. Tell, for his part, took no interest at all.

"I'm finding nothing," Bent said. "What are we going to do?"

But Tell only nodded and hummed to himself.

Machlon broke the silence.

"I'm sorry," he said. "It doesn't matter for me, but I know how much you want to go back."

Tell stoked the fire with a stick. "I'm sorry for you, Bent, but as far as my situation goes, I've been thinking. Maybe my family is better off with the other me. I was a miserable bastard, yelling and moody as fuck. Remember how Louise used to love to have fun, go out, dance? Okay, maybe that's not your idea of fun but she loved it. I can't remember the last time I took her out dancing. To dinner, even. Always too tired. Last night, I went to check on things, you know. He and Louise were dancing. When's the last time I danced with her? Played with my kids? Maybe they'll be better off."

"Better off?' Bent said. "With that thing?'

Tell shrugged. "It won't be for long, anyway. The feds'll be coming for him soon.'

"And how will Louise and the kids get by? How will they pay the bills?'

"The bills weren't getting paid before.' Tell laughed but Bent and even Machlon didn't find it funny, and he stopped. "What do you want me to do? I can't go to prison. I can't do it. I'm staying right where I am.'

Bent thought of talking Tell out of it, but what difference would it make? There was no way for them to get back. He let him be. They sat and stewed and waited for dark.

They heard crunching snow then and looked up. Mrs. Rutherford was walking through the graveyard. They scrambled for the wood line and hid themselves behind the rock wall.

"You said nobody came to the graveyard. We're here one day and here's somebody already," Tell whispered.

Mrs. Rutherford stopped at a grave, her husband's, one of the last dug in this graveyard. She laid a wreath against the headstone and crossed herself in silent prayer, then stood quietly.

Bent watched over the lip of the wall. Her husband had been dead nearly twenty years and still Mrs. Rutherford visited him once a week. For her it seemed as though she just lost him. When she told funny stories of him, she still laughed as though they'd happened only yesterday. That's love, Bent used to think. As Bent watched her now, Mrs. Rutherford went very still, a different kind of still than when she'd been looking at her husband's grave, the way an animal goes still when it senses a predator. She lifted her head, turned, and, as though she were using echolocation, looked straight at him. Her eyes met his and Bent knew she saw him. He told himself he should hide but it was too late, and a longing came over him, too, to speak to his old friend.

Mrs. Rutherford strode directly toward them, and as she neared, Bent, Tell and Machlon rose as if summoned and stood sheepishly, as though caught doing something they shouldn't. Mrs. Rutherford stopped directly before Bent and studied his face.

"Oh, there you are, Bent."

Bent didn't know what to say.

"And who are these with you?"

Bent remembered his manners and suddenly he was making casual introductions. "This is Machlon."

Mrs. Rutherford offered her hand and Machlon took it. "Very nice to meet you, Machlon."

"Nice to meet you, ma'am."

"And this is Tell."

"Lovely to meet you, Tell."

"You, too. I've heard a lot about you."

"I've heard a great deal about both of you as well…though not recently," she said, looking up and down at their altered states.

"How did you know I was behind you?" Bent said. "And how did you recognize me? I'm a rotting corpse, for God's sake, we spend all our time hiding."

"I don't know. I just did. They say people who are close to death can sense things. Maybe it's nearing my time."

"Don't say that."

"I don't mean *today*, but for goodness's sake, I *am* however old I am."

Bent in this state and she still wouldn't reveal her age. It made him smile.

They invited her to their fire and added wood and kindling and got up a good flame to keep her warm, and she sat before it and warmed her hands.

"But how did you know that's not me?" Bent said. "The other Bent."

Mrs. Rutherford angled her head and waggled her eyebrows and Bent laughed.

"But Bent," she said, growing serious, "how did this happen to you?"

Bent cast his eyes down at the fire and couldn't answer. Machlon spoke up.

"We think…it's because we wished for it."

"Wished for it? For this?"

"Not exactly. We all wished we were dead, and the next thing we knew, we were. Sort of."

"Oh." Mrs. Rutherford threw her hands up and collected them in her lap. "I am sorry. For all of you. Bent...I never knew. Why did you not tell me? You could have talked to me."

She was Catholic and suicide was a sin. It was true they hadn't killed themselves, but wishing it seemed bad enough. Yet all she felt was sympathy, and Bent thought, what a good, good woman. His eyes stung and he blinked hard but couldn't stop the tears. He wiped his eyes.

"I don't know why I didn't."

Why could he never tell people what was in his mind? He thought a million things but when he imagined saying them aloud they sounded full of self-pity, so he stayed silent.

Mrs. Rutherford let him cry a moment. "Well, what's done is done. How to undo it, that's the question now."

"Bent's reading up on that," Tell said. He told where they'd got the books, and how, and Mrs. Rutherford laughed.

"That's very good," she said. "But there must be something else we can do. Are there others like you?"

Bent nodded. "Loads, apparently."

"What's happened to them?"

"As far as I can tell, they just stay like this," Bent said. "There's a whole herd of them in the park."

"What are they waiting for?"

"I don't know," Bent said. "I don't think they know. One of them talks to me a little. He said some have moved on, but when I ask him how he says nothing." He thought then of the revenant who seemed hardly to hear him, and of the others wandering in the park with no fixed aim in mind. "Maybe you can't get out of it. Maybe the idea is don't get into it in the first place. Live your life. Don't live a half-life."

He thought of his own life then, and Tell and Machlon of theirs, and they all fell silent, nursing their regrets.

"Well, you can't just live like this for all eternity," Mrs. Rutherford broke in.

"Surely we'll rot and crumble to dust eventually," Tell said.

Bent and Machlon looked at Tell. They did not find this comforting.

"Look here, Bent, I know you don't attend mass and you're no longer a believer, and I'm not arguing about any of that. But surely if anybody in this town would have heard of something like this or know where to look for a way to fix it, it's Father Fintan."

"That's a good point," Tell said. "I don't believe any of it, either, but whenever I see one of those shows about a haunting or somebody possessed and the people are running around trying to figure out what to do that's the first thing I say. *You need a priest.*"

"And how is it you're going to elicit this information from him?" Bent said. "*Asking for a friend?*"

"I'll simply bring him here and show you to him."

"He'll drop dead."

"I didn't."

"You've got some sort of shine or something. I don't know what that's about; maybe you were born with a caul. I'm a little afraid of you, actually."

"He's a Roman Catholic priest. They perform exorcisms. They expel demons from people's bodies and send them hurtling back into Hell.' She flung her hands out dramatically. "What's one risen corpse next to that?"

"Three." Tell raised a hand.

"You two will have to hide," she said. "We don't want to give the man a heart attack."

"You said he wouldn't die," Bent said.

"I'm only joking. But we don't want to overwhelm him, do we?

One resurrected body, well he's heard of that before. But three looks like overkill." She laughed at her own joke.

~

So they waited for Mrs. Rutherford to find a way to approach the priest. In the meantime they tried to occupy themselves. Bent had read every book they'd taken from the seminary and given them to Mrs. Rutherford to return. She drove to the security gate at the entrance to the island and when the guard approached her she popped her trunk.

"I believe I have something that belongs to your priests."

When the guard went round to look, Bent and Machlon, who had been hiding under blankets in the back seat, threw off the covers and dropped the books out the windows in two giant stacks.

"Well, bye bye." Mrs. Rutherford gunned the engine, executed a U-turn around the guard's station and accelerated back the way they'd come, laughing at the guard in the rearview scurrying to decide between collecting the fallen books and writing down the license plate, which they'd covered before approaching.

~

Bent tried to remember what he used to do when he lived and had a rare afternoon to himself, but nothing occurred to him. That was something else he'd noticed. He was forgetting things. Not events, not parts of his life, but feelings.

"That's awful, have you seen a doctor about that?" he said, and then answered himself: "Oh I think I'm past a doctor's help now."

He was talking to himself now, too. That was another thing.

He imagined presenting himself at the doctor's office as he was and trying to convince the doctor that the reason he had come was memory loss.

Some days he grew restless, couldn't abide idling in the graveyard till dark and hoisted into the trees and roamed. Once he returned to the grove. He dangled his legs and dropped. The park was empty, children at school and parents at work or home in the warmth by their stoves, and he had the place to himself. He sat down in the quiet.

And he thought, how is it that you can feel closer to somebody when they are far away than when they are nearby? When they're right beside you they can seem so distant, your goodwill distorted by some small quarrel that has passed between you, the rankling of some remark one of you has made, some action one of you has misunderstood or ascribed to impure motive. When they're near, they are discolored by every imperfection in each of you. When they're absent they are their perfect selves, and you are yours. If only we could love each other when we are present with the same clear eyes.

Why was he thinking all of this now? What was the point in considering his mistakes if there was no chance to amend them? Maybe he was depressed. He laughed out loud at the thought of it, imagined presenting himself at the psychiatrist's office just as at the doctor's and saying the problem was that he was depressed. Feeling a little down. A little blue.

Have you noticed that you're decomposing?

Never mind that, doc, let me tell you about the dream I had.

A county utility truck pulled up, and a man got out and set off running round the park. Just like that, in his high-vis yellow vest that said County on the back and his blue workers' coveralls and his black woolen cap. Not jogging, but running, like a boy running for the pure joy of it. He circled the entire park, and when he completed his circle, he vaulted a boulder, climbed into his truck and drove away.

Bent wondered if something extraordinary had happened to the man. Maybe a girlfriend had accepted a marriage proposal, or maybe he'd been named employee of the year. Maybe he'd won the lottery. Maybe he'd just then scratched off his ticket or heard his number on the radio as he drove and he'd pulled in here and done a victory lap. Maybe he was even now abandoning the truck at the county depot and telling his boss to go to hell.

It struck Bent then, all the strange or even ordinary things he'd seen people do for reasons he'd never know. Once while driving home by way of the river road, he saw a very old man shuffling along the sidewalk as though he were being prodded in the small of the back with a broomstick. He slowed down so he could watch him. Every few feet the man stopped and rested a moment, as though his unseen provocateur had relented, then he lurched forward again and continued on his way. He saw the man again the next day, only this time it looked as though the broom was poking him in the neck, and he hunched forward beneath its torments. He saw him yet again a few days later. This time the broom seemed to be up his ass. What could this malady *be*, Bent thought. But he never stopped to ask. You wouldn't, would you? A person can't do such a thing. Bent stopped seeing the man after that. From time to time he thought of him, even looked for him, took the river road on days when he couldn't spare the extra time just hoping to see him. But he never did, and he regretted it, and resolved that if he ever saw him, at Huntley's Dairy, maybe, or in line at the grocery store, he would strike up a conversation and maybe the man would drop some hint about what the matter was or even talk about it openly the way old people talk without shame about their ailments, just for someone to talk to. Or past the age of modesty, maybe, or maybe even out of some sense of responsibility. Pay attention, boy, this will be you, if you're lucky enough to live so long, or unlucky enough, maybe.

The day camp where Abby volunteered was over, so she'd taken to helping Bent with his deliveries. She rode behind him on the banana seat of his bicycle, and he shivered at the feel of her hands round his waist. At the stops she'd jump off the bike and help him carry the bags to the door, make conversation with the old lady who answered, then they'd hop back on the bikes and pedal to the next stop.

Many evenings they spent together, too. Silences became awkward, spaces in which Bent thought of reaching out and touching her, felt it was at once the most natural thing in the world and utter folly, and he blushed at his own foolishness.

Tell and Louise were out somewhere. They had been going off alone together, on walks, to collect driftwood for a fire, and when Tell had mentioned a planned hike to the end of Bluff Point and hemmed and hawed when Bent had begun talking about it as a group trip with Abby and him along, it was understood that Tell and Louise were a couple. Now Bent and Abby were two, not a couple but spending as much time together as they always had. Without Tell and Louise to give their outings a chummy feel, they sought for ways to keep things casual. Or Bent did. He felt his love but felt shame for feeling it and grew hot at the thought she might ever discover it for fear she would laugh. Not laugh, as Abby wasn't like that. Something worse. Tell him how nice he was, and how sweet, and how she only thought of him as a friend. He couldn't bear that.

Lacking Tell's boat and too young to drive, they walked to the town dock. They walked close, talking intimately about the smallest things the way teenagers do, and sometimes their hands brushed and Bent flushed and opened distance between them, hoping she didn't think he was trying anything and wanting so badly to try. At the beach they walked the shoreline west to the rocks, then east to the dunes and back again, the sand brushed white beneath a fat moon. Bent eyed its height to judge the time.

"What time do you have to be home?"

Abby rolled her lips. "It doesn't matter. He's there on the couch with his scotch and soda, watching movies on his brand-new VCR and he's fine fine fine. How'd you get out?"

"Out my bedroom window and down the trellis. My mother sleeps like the dead."

He didn't mention the Nembutal, taken two or three nightly these days. He lay awake in the early days, hearing her crying through the walls, sometimes softly, sometimes in sobs, until the pills took hold, and he hoped for the relief they brought her, and was happy when he heard the crying ease and finally stop.

They stopped at a dinghy tied to the lifeguard's station, which hadn't been manned as long as Bent could remember. They sat one each on the port and starboard gunwales and rocked the boat gently like a see-saw.

"See your mother lately?"

Abby shrugged. "She took me to lunch at the Green Onion a couple weeks ago."

"That's nice," Bent said.

"We walked around the mall and looked in the shops. We went into on, and all the clothes were really ugly, but she just kept going around handling dresses and tops, like she was stalling for time while she tried to think of something to say. I didn't know what to say, either, so I touched this twinset and said, This is nice, and she bought it for me. Like, she wouldn't take no for an answer."

"That's nice, I guess. That she wanted to buy something for you."

"That's what they always do. Buy stuff."

Abby told Bent about the day camp. Poor kids went there whose families couldn't afford sleep-away. She thought of the kids, black and Latino kids mostly but also poor whites, playing tag and softball and making pot holders by stretching rough cloth dyed red and yellow and blue on frames. They got breakfast and lunch every day and they ate fast, like somebody would take the food away before they could get it all down.

There was one boy, the smallest of the group, who was very shy and hardly spoke. He would do the solitary activities, the crafts, but wouldn't play with the others or mix at all, just stayed on his own. Abby always went to help him with his craft project and would talk to him as they taped little pieces of masking tape on an old wine bottle that later would take paint, or glued popsicle sticks together in shapes. She'd tell him stories, stories her grandmother had told her, old fairy tales she remembered from books. He never talked but he was listening, you could tell. One day Abby was playing softball and got hit by a wild pitch and they sat her on a bench and iced her leg. She was trying to be brave for the kids but it hurt a lot so she cried a little. And here came the boy, and he lifted his arm and produced a single Michaelmas daisy. Abby took it, the tiny sticky hairs on its stem tickling her thumb and forefinger, and it smelled of spice almost, minty and aromatic, and she laughed for the beauty of the flower and the boy, and thought that was the nicest thing anybody had ever done for her.

"How is it fair that I was born rich and he was born poor?"

"I don't see that fair comes into it."

"Well, it should."

"Doesn't, though."

He was still trying to think of something to say to make her feel better about her mother, and hadn't found that exactly, but maybe a way to explain it.

"I think maybe they don't know what to do with us sometimes. Like what we are."

"I wonder if you forget," Abby said. "When you grow up. I wonder if you forget what it was like to be a kid, and then maybe you don't understand your own kids."

They sat with their thoughts for a while.

"Do you ever miss the seminary?"

That was what his mother had done when she didn't know what to do. Instead of buying him clothes, she sent him away.

"God, no."

Abby smiled. "Cute.'

"No, I didn't mean –"

"Kidding.'

Bent, surprised by his own boldness, reached across and yanked Abby's hood up over her head. She nodded her head decisively, happy with what she imagined was her new look.

"I'm in the hood."

She winced then and lifted her bottom to relieve the pressure on her tailbone. She slid down the transom and sculpted herself against the hull. Bent mirrored her movement on his side. Now they could look at each other and see the stars.

"We'd sit at lessons all day, and go to mass, and hear about how to live a chaste life in service to God, then you'd lie in bed at night and hear bedsprings squeaking."

Abby's jaw dropped. "Were they…?" She pantomimed masturbation.

"Not all of them."

"Ha!"

They grew quiet, and Bent wondered what it would be like to kiss her. She sat silent on her side of the boat, thinking, Bent assumed, of other things. Her mother's long absences. Her father's interminable presence. Had he known what she was thinking about, he would have leaned across, knelt gently before her, and kissed her. But he didn't, and he never knew that she wondered why not.

Abby was young yet and not fully aware of her power, but she knew he liked her. Or thought she knew. So then why didn't he kiss her?

She knew boys thought her pretty, she saw them looking. Bent looked, too. Maybe that wasn't enough for him, though. Other boys liked her because she was pretty. Bent was so smart, maybe pretty wasn't enough for him. She thought of all the books he'd read, theology and history, and how he could talk about all the battles of the Revolutionary War and John Locke and the Founding Fathers. Abby was smart, too, she was in Group 1, and she read history books for school, but for fun she read novels. Maybe she wasn't serious enough for Bent.

Their thinking left another awkward silence and Bent struggled to fill it.

"You're not bored?" he said finally.

Abby half sat up, poised to go. "You're bored?"

"No, no. I'm not. I just worried you were."

"Why would I be bored?"

"I don't know. I mean, what do you do with Chas and Becca and those guys? It must be more exciting than sitting around in a smelly old dinghy all night."

"Oh, so that's it. Please." She shook her head. "All they want to do is drink and smoke pot."

"I just…I mean you're probably used to…I don't know."

"We don't have that much money."

"More than us. Did you ever have to go rock crabbing to get fifty cents for candy?"

"No," Abby conceded. "But you've got that great old house. I'd love to live in an old house like that."

Bent tried to imagine their lives, hold them up and see the sameness of them as Abby did. But all he could see was her, golden child in a house on the hill on the river road, and him, skinny creature, looking underfed, sitting in a tumbledown saltbox beaten bare by the sea. Ignorant boy. Couldn't spot the difference between rich and happy. But he had sense enough to see he'd embarrassed her by all his talk of money so he took up her compliment on his house.

"It is pretty cool. You can see all the way out to the sound from the top. Did I tell you we have a ghost?"

Abby sat up. "You do?"

"Well, maybe. I don't know."

"Did you ever see anything?"

"No, just, weird stuff happens sometimes. You find doors open where you left them closed, that kind of thing. There was this one day when people kept getting locked in random rooms. My cousin called and I said, Can I call you back? My mother's locked in the attic. Then she called again, and I had to say, Can I call you back? My grandmother's locked in the basement."

"What was your grandmother doing in the basement?'

"That's what interests you about this story?"

Abby laughed. "I know. I just mean you could never get me to go down in the basement. Especially in an old house like that. So what was it?"

"We never figured it out. That's what I'm saying. Sometimes I wonder, I don't know, maybe he is dead and it's him."

Abby sat up, looking serious. "Your father didn't leave you, Bent. He drowned. He's dead."

Bent shrugged. "Maybe."

Abby lay back. "Anyway why would he lock your grandmother in the basement?"

Bent laughed, which had been Abby's aim, and she laughed, too.

"Not in a mean way. I don't know. Just to let us know he's around."

"He's around."

"You really believe that? All that Catholic stuff? Our souls live forever and all that?"

"Not all of it. Like when the priest holds up the wafer and says it's the body of Christ? Not that. But I believe people live on after they die. That they watch over us."

"You've never told anybody what I told you, right? About my mother saying my father left us?"

"Of course not."

Bent nodded, satisfied. "If it is my father locking doors on people and whatnot to let them know he's around, I sure wish he would do it to me."

Silence descended again, and Bent knew he was brooding and knew Abby was looking for a way to help him out and tried to shake it off. Abby rose suddenly.

"Okay, you want oogie boogie stuff, let's go."

"Where?"

"Willettes.'"

The Willettes' house was dark. They'd called it the Willettes' house for years, though the Willettes themselves had moved away ages ago. The latest owners had left a year ago without explanation, fueling stories of something lurking within.

"What do we have to do, touch the porch, right?"

"That's it."

Abby paused.

"What are you, scared?"

"You go, if you're so brave."

Bent eyed the porch, moved along the hedge to inspect it from another angle.

"You're scared," Abby said.

"So are you."

"I'm a girl."

"The seventies happened. Gloria Steinem. You're liberated. Touch the porch."

Abby looked up at it. "This is stupid."

"Yes, it is. Touch the porch. Come on, there's nothing to be afraid of. Just the bottom step."

Over Abby's shoulder a figure loomed out of the dark. Abby screamed and leapt at Bent. As his eyes focused, he saw that it was just Marshall.

"Oh, hi, Marshall," Bent said.

"You know him?" Abby was clutching Bent's arms and he involuntarily flexed his biceps.

"Yeah. It's okay. You're not meant to wander, Marshall, remember?"

Marshall looked from Bent to Abby. As ever, it was unclear if he understood.

"He can't talk," Bent said. "Or doesn't. I don't know. Come on, Marshall."

Bent took a few steps, looking back at Marshall to coax him on. Marshall looked off down the road in the direction he'd been heading and waved.

"Come on, Marshall, there's nobody there."

Marshall yielded to Bent's gentle tug on his sleeve and let himself be led away. They walked in silence to Marshall's house. Marshall's grandmother answered the door with a bow of relief, an exasperated thrust of arms out to her sides and a lunge to haul Marshall in all at once.

"Oh, Marshall. Thank you, Bent."

"You're welcome."

"What's wrong with him?" Abby said quietly as they reached the front gate.

Bent shrugged. "He's always been like that. His parents died in a car accident when he was a baby. He's just never talked."

"God, poor Marshall."

They stood on the dark road. The moon had gone behind clouds and Bent could just make out Abby's features. He could feel her closeness. She shifted her weight onto one hip, trying to be casual, like she wasn't waiting for something to happen but readying for it in case it did. Bent shifted from foot to foot and wondered why this luminous girl would venture out at night to spend time with him.

"It's late. I'll walk you home."

By nightfall the air was thin, the sky silver and black. More snow. Bent missed Abby. He knew she probably didn't want to see him but still he walked the spine road to the park and found her there, sat round the picnic table with a group of women he recognized as some of the revenants that wandered the park at night. They were smoking cigars and playing Crazy Eights.

"Hello, Bent."

She didn't look up from her cards. Bent edged closer.

"You don't smoke."

"I'm dead. I'm a new woman."

"Is that him?"

Abby nodded. "That's him."

All the women looked at Bent and shook their heads.

"You're the one who's trapped her here," one of them said.

"I'm not doing it on purpose," he said.

A woman in hip huggers and a macrame fringe vest puffed on her cigar. "All you have to do is let her go."

"I'm trying," he said. "But I can't seem to manage it."

The woman snorted.

"You've been here a long time, I guess," he said, judging by her outfit.

"We all have," the woman said. "Some longer than others. My husband survived the crash that killed me. You'd think he would have been grateful at a second chance, but he's pined for me his whole life. Never remarried. No kids. Nearly fifty years later and he still won't let me go. Wasted his whole life. All of us stuck here because of somebody. Just like you. They won't let us go, so here we sit."

"I'm really sorry," Bent said. "Look, should you really be out in the open like this? Someone might see you."

The woman snorted again. "You never did."

"When?"

"Ever. We've seen you walk your dog here for years. You walked right by us. Just stood at the water's edge, letting out heaving sighs and thinking about everything you didn't have. It's very whiny. You can't change the past, kiddo. All you can do is let it go and try to find something else to love."

Abby left the group and went to Bent. "They're a little bitter. But Bent, you spent your whole life wanting what you didn't have and not appreciating what was right in front of you. Your kids, your wife. Even me. You just weren't very good at being happy."

"Well, I wasn't happy."

"Jesus, you could have been."

Bent sighed.

"I was going to leave you," she said.

Bent's skin bristled. "What?"

She nodded. "The day I died. I was going to tell you that I couldn't see you anymore. I loved you – love you – but I couldn't do it anymore. Waiting for scraps of attention, betraying my husband, your wife. I wasted my life on men who didn't love me enough. I was part of my husband's long-range plan – the perfect job, the perfect house, the perfect wife – and you were chasing some impossible dream from when we were teenagers. I guess I was, too, because I kept waiting for you. I can't understand why I settled for so little."

"It breaks my heart to hear you say this," Bent said.

"I should have said it long ago," she said. "You needed to hear it. So did I. Now, please, Bent, if you won't let me go, then leave me in peace."

She returned to the picnic table and her friends. Bent watched them for a moment, hoping she would change her mind, but she didn't look up, so he turned and left the park.

~

On a cold, clear Thursday morning Mrs. Rutherford coaxed the priest to the graveyard. They'd been told she might come, so Bent, Tell and Machlon were keeping watch and when they saw Mrs. Rutherford and the priest crossing the brown grass through snowy patches, they jumped the rock wall and hid in the wood. Mrs. Rutherford led the priest to their fire and stopped. The priest looked at the fire pit, confused.

"Is this your fire?"

"No, no. Now look here. What I'm about to show you may seem impossible. I'm not even going to tell you first or you'll think I've gone mad and you'll lock me up in a dementia ward. I'm just going to show you." She withdrew a whisky flask from her purse. "Here, you'd better drink this."

"It's nine o'clock in the morning," the priest said.

"Trust me."

The priest looked at the flask, then at Mrs. Rutherford. "What is this all about?"

"Last chance," she said, but still he refused the drink so she replaced the flask and turned toward the wood. "You can come out now."

Behind his tree, Bent hesitated. This was a terrible idea. The priest was almost as ancient as Mrs. Rutherford, he would have a heart attack. Bent stayed concealed.

The priest threw his arms out and let them fall at his sides. "What are we looking at?"

Mrs. Rutherford cleared her throat but Bent didn't stir. She cleared her throat again, more theatrically.

"Dem-en-tia ward…"

Bent stayed put.

The priest laughed nervously. Mrs. Rutherford picked up a stone and hurled it at the tree. "Bent!"

"Missus Rutherford," the priest said, "are you sure you're all right?"

Bent took a deep breath, reminded himself of the need to get back to his children, and stepped out, but the priest was fixed on Mrs. Rutherford and didn't see him.

"Would you like to sit down a moment?" the priest said to her. "Or we could go back to the rectory and…"

He stopped then. Someone was there. He turned, struggled to focus for a moment because Bent's body was like a kind of camouflage against the trees, but then he saw him. Bent. For a moment the priest said nothing. He only stared. Then his eyes went dull, his skin grey, and he fell face down in the grass.

"You see?" Bent said, rushing forward. "We've killed him. We've killed Father Fintan."

He rolled the priest over and removed his tattered suit coat for a pillow and eased it beneath Father Fintan's head. Mrs. Rutherford produced the flask, unscrewed the cap and dribbled whisky into the priest's mouth. He swallowed and came around. Tell and Machlon, hearing the commotion, had emerged from the wood to help and appeared now behind the priest as he lifted his head. Mrs. Rutherford waved them away and they dropped behind a boulder. Father Fintan looked at Mrs. Rutherford then turned and looked at Bent, who hung back. Mrs. Rutherford offered the flask, and the priest accepted it and took a long drink.

"We have an interesting theological problem," Mrs. Rutherford said.

After some persuading and more whisky they convinced the priest to sit at the fire and they told how Bent had come to be in this state. Once all was told he of course agreed to help if he could and vowed to begin his research straight after noon confessional.

"Though I scarcely know where to begin," he said. "What's happened to you is... I don't know what it is. The Resurrection, Lazarus, a few other accounts of raisings from the dead, if one believes them, those were true resurrections. They were miracles, done through the power of God. I'm not aware of anything like this in the canon or theological writings."

"What about accounts of people who rose from their graves? I've found some of that in the ecclesiastical and historical chronicles."

"Those people rose in their own bodies. They attacked the living, they rioted among the animals. Wandered through villages calling out names and those called later died of plague. That kind of thing. They were stories people told to explain tragedies, deal with grief. Also, *they weren't true.* The dead *do not rise.*"

Bent held his arms aloft, living rejoinder to the priest's otherwise reasonable assertion. "And yet."

The priest sighed and drank.

~

Jean found a space a few storefronts up from the shop and parked. She took a cloth shopping bag out from under the seat and locked the car. Just in front of her, a cherry picker marked New Hope Public Works stood on the side of the road at the intersection, and two city workers in the bucket were fastening one half of a Christmas banner to the light pole. A man walked by and Jean detected the scent of cloves. She couldn't tell if it was coming from the man or from somewhere else, a nearby kitchen, perhaps. She wondered what a man who desired to smell of cloves would be like. Was it just a Christmas thing? Would he be a romantic, flowers and music at night? Or was he simply self-centered? Maybe his wife just bought him the cologne and he wore it like a dutiful husband, she decided.

She walked along the sidewalk. The shops had Christmas decorations up already. She stopped at the window of the toy shop. A giant carousel had been erected as the centerpiece of the window display, and it was nestled amongst piles of fake cottony snow dotted with plastic fir trees and little plastic children pulling little plastic sleds and skating on a little plastic ice pond. The carousel spun merrily, and Jean watched the horses rise and fall. It was the kind she had always wanted as a child, the kind she had always hoped to get for Ada. She walked on.

At the butcher shop she turned in, the bell above the door tinkling. Her father looked up from the register, smiled, and came out from behind the counter wiping his hands on a towel. He held out his arms and she walked gratefully into them.

"How's my little girl?"

Jean smiled, tried to put on a good face, but her father saw through it. He held her by both shoulders at arm's length, tilted his head skeptically, then drew her back into his arms and patted her head gently.

"It'll be all right, baby." He clapped her back decisively, then let her go and went back behind the counter. "What'll it be? I just did some nice porterhouse. Or maybe ribeye?"

Jean winced. "That's too expensive, Dad. Just give me some chuck. I'll make a stew."

Her father ignored her and drew a porterhouse out of the meat case. "It's Christmas."

"Dad…"

"Just a few small cuts. And I'll put some stew meat in there, too, Ebenezer."

Jean pressed her lips together. There was no point arguing, and if she was honest, she knew when she came that he would do this. Her father went to cut the porterhouse. She watched as he trimmed the fat, then began to slice into the tenderloin, his hand rising and falling in a smooth steady rhythm like he was playing the piano. Her father had been cutting their food by hand her entire life, and most of his own. As a child she used to run to meet his boat on the dock and watch him clean the day's catch. His hands moved deftly, deliberately, with a kind of automaticity that lent his movements an almost somatic quality, one that both made her feel safe and made her worry that he would cut himself through lack of attention. But no. Not her father. Even now he was steady as a rock.

"Jesus, Dad, that's too much."

"Freeze it." He sliced thick slabs. "You always need meat in the freezer."

Jean rocked gently on her heels. She hated doing this, but she didn't know what she would do without it. Especially once Bent moved out.

Her father called from the back counter. "You guys coming for Christmas, right?"

Jean nodded. "Mmm hmmm."

"Bent, too?"

Jean paused. It probably wasn't a good idea, but the kids would be heartbroken.

"I don't know yet."

Her father nodded. His slicing grew slower, and she could tell he wanted to say something. "You can always come to us. You know that, right?"

Jean tried very hard not to cry. "I know, Dad. Thanks."

Her father nodded, still slicing slowly as though he wanted to say more, but he went quiet and returned to his old rhythm.

~

The priest worked long hours and in secret. He started with the word Bent had given him, the word the thing in the park had told him. The thing Bent now was. Revenant. After a lesson in online research from the librarian in the central library in New Hope, the priest searched for the word. He expected to find perhaps a few stories and only after much reading. He was surprised instead to discover reams of information. Scholarship and historical and ecclesiastical chronicles. He found accounts from England, Scotland, France, the Netherlands, Iceland and other places. Stories told as true. Some he could read online and did, some existed in published volumes, which he drove to university libraries to read. William of Newburgh wrote of an impious man who died after falling from the rafters of his bedchamber where he'd been spying on his cheating wife. After he was buried he began to walk abroad at night, pursued by a pack of barking dogs and poisoning the air with the putrefaction of his body. As the foul stench spread people began to die. When the plague had carried away most of the town, two young men dug up the corpse, cut out its heart and burnt the body to ash. That was no solution here. An anonymous monk at Byland Abbey told of a man who rose from the dead to gouge out the eyes of his mistress. Thietmar of Merseburg told of a priest murdered on the altar by the risen dead.

There were dozens and dozens of violent revenants, there were a few who returned briefly to right a wrong, but nowhere could the priest find mention of anyone whose body was forcibly stolen by a revenant. Even if one believed these stories, and how could he, none of them showed any way to help Bent. He kept looking.

~

Jean was updating the records of the students she'd treated that day, all minor things, thank God, and she was surprised to look up and see Mrs. Rutherford in the doorway of her office.

"Missus Rutherford."

The old woman hovered on the threshold. "I hope you don't mind. I remember Bent telling me you use this office on Wednesdays, so I thought I'd pop in."

Jean leaned back in her chair. "Please God let me have a mind like yours when I'm whatever age you are that you won't tell anybody."

Mrs. Rutherford waggled her eyebrows. "Fancy a coffee?"

They took Mrs. Rutherford's car to Little's and found a table, and Sandy brought them two mugs and filled them at the table. Mrs. Rutherford looked at Jean over the top of her cup. She looked tired.

"How are things?" Mrs. Rutherford asked.

They chatted for a while about this and that, work and the kids and the museum.

"I'm sorry about Bent's hours," Mrs. Rutherford ventured. "I know that's probably the last thing you needed."

Jean breathed out. "Oh, *Bent*."

Mrs. Rutherford put down her mug. "What's wrong?"

Jean thought about whether she should say anything. Bent's taciturnity had infected her. People talk to each other, don't they? She has a right to vent to a friend, hasn't she?

"Well, I don't know if he said anything to you, but we're getting a divorce."

"No, he didn't. I'm sorry to hear it."

"I always told myself, hang on for the kids, he's a good father. But I just can never seem to reach him. Anyway. I thought this would make a change. But he's worse every day. Now he barely even notices them, and the other day he yelled at Ada over nothing."

Mrs. Rutherford folded her hands and pressed them against her lips. "Is he...living elsewhere?"

"That's the other thing. He was supposed to move out, I thought maybe he'd stay with Machlon, but he just keeps coming home every night, a lot of the time *drunk*. I lock him out of my room, so he sleeps on the couch."

Mrs. Rutherford spoke almost to herself. "That's not good, is it?"

"I don't know what to do. This is so unlike him. I don't want the kids seeing this."

"I think he's...going through something."

"Has he said something to you?"

"Not as such."

Jean breathed out, and it came out as a cry. She hated crying in front of people, but for some reason it felt okay with Mrs. Rutherford.

"Oh dear." Mrs. Rutherford plucked a napkin from the holder and handed it to her.

Jean wiped her eyes and blew her nose. "I don't know what

to do."

Mrs. Rutherford considered a moment, then took a deep breath. "I think I need to show you something."

The car rumbled over the pebbled dirt track into the graveyard. Jean watched the headstones pass and thought they were going to visit Mr. Rutherford's grave, but Mrs. Rutherford drove past it and around the bend and stopped the car near the trees. The old woman opened the door and got out, so Jean followed her.

"What's this?" she asked.

Then she smelled smoke, the fragrant woody scent of burning logs. She noticed a low fire at the tree line, and three figures huddled around it. She looked at Mrs. Rutherford, concerned.

"This is not going to be easy to understand," Mrs. Rutherford said.

Jean looked at her, perplexed, and then back at the fire. One of the figures rose and stood, motionless, watching her. Then it began to approach. As he drew closer, she saw what he was, if it could be called "he." And she didn't know how, but she knew it was Bent.

She stared at him, and then shook her head as if to wake herself from a dream. She looked at Mrs. Rutherford for an explanation. Mrs. Rutherford's eyebrows were furrowed sadly. Jean looked back at Bent, and he reached for her, but she shook her head and backed away, hugging herself. Then she turned and ran. Mrs. Rutherford brought her hands to her lips in a steeple.

"Jean!"

But Jean kept running.

Mrs. Rutherford turned to Bent. He threw his arms in the air and looked at her wide-eyed.

"Don't be angry with me, Bent. She had to know." She rushed toward her car. "Jean!"

Bent followed. "I'm coming with you."

"No, you stay here. She needs time."

"She's my wife. I'm coming."

And before she could say anything more, he jumped into the passenger seat.

"Oh, *Bent!*"

But there was no time to argue, so she climbed behind the wheel, shifted into gear and went after Jean.

Jean ran and ran. The crying made it hard to breathe but she couldn't stop. Couldn't stop crying and couldn't stop running. She ran down the marsh road and past the marina, to the edge of the village and out onto the main road. Her chest heaved and her lungs burned, and the rushing air dried her throat and her eyes stung. At the bridge to the new yacht club she couldn't run anymore, and she doubled over and threw up in the ditch.

Mrs. Rutherford's car pulled up behind her on the verge and stopped. Bent and Mrs. Rutherford got out. Jean turned, leaning on her knees and panting for breath, and looked sideways at Bent.

"Jack saw you," she said. "In the window that night. That was Daddy, he said. I told him he was being ridiculous."

Bent didn't know what to say. He took a step forward, but she backed away.

"I'm sorry," he said.

Jean was shaking. "What's going on? How are you alive right now? And what is that thing in our house with my children?"

"I'm working on that," Bent said.

Jean paced back and forth.

"I'm sorry to interrupt," Mrs. Rutherford said, "but Bent really can't be seen."

So Bent and Jean went beneath the bridge to talk, Jean looking back every few feet and Bent rearing back to give her space. It was colder under there, and films of ice sheathed the tidal pools between the rocks. Jean shivered and hugged herself. Bent thought of offering her his coat but it stank and he knew she wouldn't want a dead man's coat anywhere near her anyway and didn't blame her.

"I expect you want to know when this happened," he said.

"I know exactly when," Jean said. "The moment that thing came in the house, Kip started growling at it. The dog knew before I did." She looked at Bent, searching. "How is this possible?"

"I don't know. I've figured out how it works, but I don't know why."

Jean couldn't believe this was happening. "So tell me how it works."

"A dead person – a revenant – can swap bodies with a living person if the living person is willing."

"Who would be willing to do *this*?"

"You don't know beforehand. The revenant just senses somebody who's open to it, and then they swap. They want to live and they take advantage of the fact that you want to…"

Jean looked at him. "Want to die."

Now Bent was shivering, but not from the cold.

"So when you went out that night…"

Bent felt a pit in his stomach. "I didn't do it. But…"

"But you thought about it."

Bent looked down at the rocks. "Yes."

Jean looked at him, first with sadness and then with more disappointment than he'd ever seen in her face.

"How could you do this to us?" she said. "You left your kids with a stranger. You left me with a stranger. I might have slept with that thing."

Bent looked up. "You didn't—"

Jean shook her head. "I've been making him sleep on the couch. I thought he was you. I thought you were refusing to move out and sulking about the divorce. How could you do this, Bent?"

"I was depressed. I told you I couldn't not see my kids."

"Well, congratulations, now you never will."

"Don't do that." Bent sat on the rocks and watched the water passing under the bridge. "I miss them so much. It's killing me."

Jean threw him a bitter smirk. "Funny."

"That's not what I meant." He shook his head. "I never even wanted kids. You made me have kids. You forced my hand."

"Oh, ho, ho, ho, no way, buddy. You were the one. You had these huge hang-ups about losing your father and your mother sending you away. *You* wanted kids. You wanted to make this perfect family because you thought it would fix everything."

"Hey, don't psychoanalyze me, okay?"

"Well, it's true. I *never* wanted kids."

"Then why did you want me to move out? Why didn't you just leave them with me?"

"Because I want *my* kids."

"Well, so do I."

"You've got a funny way of showing it. And then we weren't enough for you. Abby came back to town, and you went all agog."

Bent looked at her, surprised.

"Oh yeah, I knew," she said. "I knew everything. Every time you saw her, I knew. You came home smelling like sex with that shit-eating grin on your face, and I had to sit at the dinner table with you and act like everything was fine in front of our kids. And then she died, and you were despondent. I even felt bad for you. That made me so angry. You put me in the position of feeling bad for the death of a woman you were cheating with. That's why you did this. You didn't miss your kids. You missed Abby."

"No, it wasn't Abby! I came home after Abby, didn't I? And I didn't do it. That thing just…You were right, I was depressed. And when I thought I wouldn't see the kids…I thought I wanted out. Of everything."

Jean looked at him. "That's the difference between a man and a woman. A woman would never leave her kids. We'll stay no matter what. Men can leave because they know that."

She drew back, shocked at herself. There's so much she would never say to him when he was alive. She never wanted to hurt him. But now she'd said it and she saw it land and it cut him badly. Well, good.

Bent picked up a stone and hurled it into the water. The splash echoed against the steel of the bridge.

"What do we do?" he asked.

"Oh no, there's no *we*," Jean said. "You got yourself into this, you get yourself out. As for that thing in the house, I'll deal with it. I have to go, the kids are going to be home from my parents' house soon."

Bent rose. Jean thrust out her hand to stop him.

"You stay right there. I don't want to be in the same car with you. You make your own way back."

She left him there under the bridge and climbed the bank to Mrs. Rutherford's car. Bent listened as the motor started and the sound of the car receded into the distance.

Jean raced home, hoping she'd catch that thing where it was most days, and sure enough, when she got there she found it snoring on the couch. She stood in the doorway with the front door still open so she could run if she had to.

"Hey."

She waited, but it didn't stir.

"*Hey!*"

Still no signs of life. She laughed bitterly. Signs of life. She edged into the room, plucked the remote from the coffee table and launched it. It connected with its forehead with a satisfying crack. The thing jolted awake. It looked around, massaging its forehead, then noticed Jean.

"Shit." It sat up, touched its head and checked its hand for blood. "What was that for?"

"Get out of my house."

The thing feigned hurt. "Babe, what did I do?"

"Give it up. I know you're not Bent. I know what you are. Leave."

The thing kept up the pretense. "I know I'm not myself lately, babe, but –"

"Leave or I'll call the police."

Its shoulders dropped, its face became impassive and its voice flat.

"You do that and poor Bent will lose his meagre part-time job. Not a good time to be trying to make it on one income. Especially on a school nurse's salary."

Jean tried not to show anything, but she was nearly hyperventilating with rage.

"And oh, the *scandal*," it said. "People talking round the dinner table, kids taking that to school, Jack and Ada, the teasing…" He clicked his tongue.

Jean ran through her options. She couldn't think. She pointed at it.

"I'll see you dead."

She picked up Jack and Ada from school, a bag packed for each of them in the back seat.

"What's this for?" Jack said.

"We're going to stay with Amma and Poppa."

"Is Daddy coming?" Ada asked.

Jean looked in the rearview mirror, then back at the road. "Daddy has to work."

Jack spoke quietly. "Good."

~

After she dropped the children off, she drove straight to the graveyard and jumped out of the car so fast Tell and Machlon didn't have a chance to hide.

Jean ran toward Bent, not even bothering to close the door. "I need to talk to –" She spotted Tell and Machlon then and reared back. "Holy hell."

Bent ran to Jean. Tell and Machlon stood, not knowing what to do.

"That's Tell and Machlon, I guess?" Jean asked.

Bent nodded. Jean turned and walked in little circles, breathing deeply through her nose to keep herself from hyperventilating.

"Are you okay?" Bent asked.

Jean nodded. She calmed herself and told Bent what had happened.

"We have to do something," she said, still out of breath. "They think he's you. They're going to remember you as a monster."

"The priest is working on it."

"You told Father Fintan?"

"Mrs. Rutherford thought he might be able to help."

"Well, tell him to hurry."

Bent nodded. "I'll go see him now. You'll be at your parents'?"

Jean nodded.

"That's good," Bent said. "At least I don't have to worry about you for the moment."

He walked her back to her car. She turned and held a hand up to Tell and Machlon. "Bye, guys, I guess."

She climbed in and Bent shut the car door. The moment she pulled away he went straight to St Andrew's. He didn't even wait for dark.

The priest did not have good news.

"I've read every revenant account I could find," he said. "Almost all of them medieval. There is nothing that fits your situation."

Bent nodded and dropped his head. He hadn't really expected the priest to find anything, but while he searched there was hope. Now there was none.

"I'm sorry," the priest continued.

"Thank you, Father."

"For what? I have failed you utterly."

"You can't fail someone if you try."

"What will you do?" the priest said.

Bent sighed and stood. "I don't know."

"If this were a medieval story, I suppose you might go on a quest."

"Save the maiden, find the key, capture the castle? That kind of thing? Complete three tasks and recover my body?"

It sounded awful said aloud, and the priest blushed, though he knew Bent meant no harm. "What does all this mean?"

"Mean?"

The priest struggled to put it into words. "Augustine wrote that visitations of the dead to the living happen only through the permission of God, and only in the mind of the person visited. But here you are, in the flesh. You're not a figment of my imagination. Both Mrs. Rutherford and I have seen you. And surely God would not allow this. My whole life there's been God, Heaven and Hell and Purgatory, and the Scriptures as allegory. Where does this fit?"

The priest looked sad, almost frightened. Bent felt sorry for him.

"You're looking to me for answers? We're both in trouble."

The priest stood. "I'd better go. I've got to say mass in half an hour." He paused. Everything had changed. How would he say mass when he'd only half an hour before been sitting in his office with a corpse? "Too bad we weren't trying to kill you, we could just chop off your head."

Bent had started toward the door, but he stopped at this. "What?"

"Yes," the priest said, adjusting his collar, which was bunching, "in a lot of the tales, that's how they killed the revenant. Chopped its head off with an axe."

"Why didn't you say so?"

The priest grew worried. "Well, no, that won't help you. You want your life back. This will just kill you."

"But if we swapped bodies, then killing me will kill him, won't it?"

"I don't know, the chronicles don't say anything about that."

"It's worth a try," Bent said.

"Bent, wait. You don't know if this will work."

But it was too late. Bent ran from the office and was gone.

The sky was glowing orange, and he hurried along the beach to Boatwright's shed. He found what he was looking for and returned to the graveyard. He ran to Tell and Machlon and produced the ax and held it toward Tell.

"Here, I need you to cut my head off."

Tell laughed nervously. "What?"

"Just do it. I won't feel it."

"I'm not doing that."

Bent turned to Machlon and held out the axe. "Machlon."

But Machlon shook his head frantically and sat before the fire hugging himself. Bent let the ax drop. Suddenly he screamed.

"Goddamnit!"

Tell bent to the ax, keeping one eye on Bent, retrieved it gingerly and handed it to Machlon, who tucked the handle beneath him and sat on it.

"What am I going to do?" Bent yelled. "I have to get that thing away from my family."

"How do you know it'd even work?" Tell said. "It might not even kill that thing. How do you know you wouldn't just be left alive and headless? You'd have to carry your head around like that saint in church statues."

They heard crunching snow. They turned. A man was walking toward them amongst the headstones. Bent and Machlon made to scatter but Tell leaned forward and squinted.

"That's me," he said.

They stood to meet the man as he approached. It was Tell's revenant, the one who'd taken his body. Tell stepped to him and they stood, face to face.

"Well, this is weird," Tell said. He turned to Bent and Machlon. "Have I put on weight?" He turned back to the other Tell. "I always did in the winter, but this…." He looked the other Tell up and down. "Been enjoying my life a little too much, eh?"

The other Tell ignored this. "I need to talk to you."

"How'd you know where I'd be?" Tell said.

The other Tell looked around at the headstones. "You didn't make it difficult."

Tell nodded. "How's my kids? My wife?"

"The FBI came to the house last night."

Tell turned and went to tend the coffee. His hand shook as he poured, Bent saw.

The other Tell continued. "Two agents. You bought some stock?"

Tell nodded. "So they know."

"They're saying I'll get eight to ten years and a hundred-thousand-dollar fine. I can't go to prison. I'll die in prison."

"Dying twice," Tell said. "That'd be some kind of record, wouldn't it?" He looked to Bent and Machlon, laughing nervously. "You must've known," Tell continued to the other him. "You sense these things, don't you? You got that I was thinking of killing myself. You didn't get why?"

"We get what we get," he said. "I don't know how it works. I wasn't dead that long. Look, I want to swap back."

Tell turned and fed the fire.

"Do you hear me? I want my body back." The other Tell drew forward. Bent and Machlon stepped up and he stopped.

Tell stood and turned. "I'm sorry for your troubles, pal, I really am. But see that's why I was sitting in my truck with that gun in the first place. Then the next thing I knew, here I was. You stole my body, as it turns out, at a very convenient time. So, sorry, but I can't do it."

The other Tell took another step, then stopped. Bent and Machlon stood beside Tell but made no move, and nor did Tell. They knew now how it was done, not the hoodoo of it but the idea. Both parties had to be willing. And Tell was not.

The other Tell saw he would not get what he wanted and he turned and stalked off toward the road, and soon he was gone.

"Well, that broke the monotony," Machlon said.

Tell watched the road in the direction the other Tell had gone. "Only a matter of time now."

"You're just going to let him go?" Bent said. "This is your chance. He wants to swap back."

"I can't."

"Are you nuts? He wants to swap back," Bent said.

"I can't."

"I would give anything to be back with my family. You're really going to do this?"

"You'd be going home," Tell said. "I'd be going to jail. Am I a bastard? Without a doubt. But I think about it and I start shaking. I can't do it. Let's hope he's right. Let's hope he dies in prison. Then my family will get the insurance."

Bent kicked the stones of the fire pit. "Fine. You want to stay like this, stay. But I need to think of my kids. I'm going to make that thing swap back."

His truck was not at the house, so he went to the museum. His pickup was in the parking lot. He couldn't do anything here. He rolled back the tonneau cover and crawled onto the truck bed then rolled the vinyl back into place. He scooted on his back to the wheel cover and leaned back. The truck was his, but he felt like a criminal, lying in wait for a driver to hijack. After a long time he heard the door of the museum open and footsteps crunching on the snow. The driver's side door opened, there was the squeak of cold leather, the door slammed and the engine cranked, sputtered, then turned over and growled low. The driver waited, then grew impatient and gunned the motor a few times, and Bent felt the truck back out of the space, turn and lurch forward.

Ten minutes later, the truck turned, rolled over gravel and stopped. The driver's side door opened and slammed and Bent heard the other Bent's footsteps trail away on the stones. For a moment there was tinny music, then it was gone. Bent snaked to the bottom of the truck bed and peeled back the tonneau. He saw water and to his right the faint traces of red neon flashing on and off. The Sea Witch.

Bent waited and felt the truck bed go cold beneath him. He heard tires on gravel, and other footsteps, and snatches of music as the tavern door opened and closed, and more and louder voices and laughter as the tavern filled, but the other Bent didn't return, so Bent climbed from the truck bed, found room amongst the reeds near the truck, and waited.

This other Bent wasn't the same as him. The children could tell. Not what he really was, but his indifference, his lack of care. He didn't love them, and they knew it. Oh *God*. He had *left* them. Or tried to and left the door open for that thing to take his place. How could he have done such a thing? He'd thought he was doing what was best, but no, he had only told himself that. He'd been a coward. He realized, too, that he'd surrendered control of how the children would view themselves, whether they felt they were loved.

The sky was black, starless. A skin of ice rimmed the reeds, turned translucent further out, then thin as paper before it dissolved into black water, lapped by a gentle tide. On the rocks nearby the black prehistoric shell of a horseshoe crab lay cavity up, like a discarded infantry helmet, molted probably, or perhaps eaten, hollowed out, its tiny legs and guts devoured by gulls. Behind the blue-black clouds he watched the ghost of the moon sink. Juke music flared then vanished as the pub door opened and closed. Distant footsteps ground stones, engines churned, headlights swept and tires crunched then hummed when they met asphalt, and cars rolled away.

Then Bent heard him, his feet crushing salt laid to keep the doorway free of ice. Bent peeked out. The lot was empty but for his truck. The other Bent had closed the place. The steps crossed the lot, came round the truck, bent to the lock, aimed with the key and missed. He swayed, steadied himself and tried again. Bent surged from the reeds and caught him by the shoulders, flipped him on his back. He straddled him, pinning with his knees, and punched hard three times. The other Bent let out his breath but otherwise did not react. Too drunk.

"Do it," Bent said, his fist raised for another strike. "Whatever you do to swap, do it."

The other Bent lay on the gravel and groaned. Bent punched again.

"Now!"

The other Bent turned his head to the side. "Drop dead," he said, and laughed, and coughed blood. Bright red flecks spattered the white gravel. It bubbled from his nose and down his chin. He lay there and laughed and Bent fumed. He drew back and punched again, and again, and heard the sound, like a tennis ball against a racket, and watched the other Bent's head jerk with the impact. Then he wrapped his hands around the thing's throat and squeezed.

The thing began to choke, and it grabbed at Bent's hands, trying to pry his fingers loose, but Bent bore down. He squeezed and squeezed, and the thing's face was red.

Then Bent felt himself grow faint. He felt dizzy, and he slackened his grip, and then the bartender was on him and hauling him up. He wrenched himself free and ran toward the road, and into the marsh, and heard the bartender's voice thin in the cold air ask the other Bent, was he all right.

He cursed himself for his weakness. He'd had him. What happened?

The next day was a Wednesday, so he waited in the bushes outside the school until Jean came out. He signaled to her, and she got in her car and reached over and opened the passenger door. Bent army-crawled from the bushes and climbed into the car and closed the door. He pulled a blanket from the back seat and threw it over his head while Jean pulled away and drove him to the graveyard. Along the way he told her what had happened.

"I don't suppose you'll cut my head off," he said.

"*No.*"

Bent sighed. "All right."

"You don't even know if it would work."

Bent dug at the dirt with his foot. "I have to go away for a bit. I need to think."

"Where?"

"I don't know. There has to be a solution. I'm going to walk awhile. Think."

Jean nodded. "Okay."

Bent nudged her. "You going to be all right?"

Jean sighed. "I'll keep them busy."

"I meant you."

She nodded. "I'll be okay. We're fine at my parents' for the time being."

Bent looked at the sky. Dusk was falling. The birds were going quiet.

"I'd better go."

Jean shivered in the cold. "Where?"

The priest had mentioned a quest. There were no tasks to

perform, nothing he could do to get his family back, but the idea of a pilgrimage appealed to him. This would not be a pilgrimage to something but away from it. Away from the life he could no longer bear to look on from the outside.

The shoreline stretched out to the east and the west. He closed his eyes, pictured the coast in his mind. How far could he get keeping to the shore and shunning roads? Much of it would need to be done at night. Lord's Point, where beach houses perched on wooden stilts feet above the tideline. Stonington Borough, where he would have to skirt the rocks around the tip of the point. But he reckoned he could reach the end of the long beachfront at Misquamicut at least before he would be diverted by the marshlands beyond, muddy, impassable on foot. He could figure things out from there. He had dreamt of walking, so he would walk.

"East," he said.

Jean nodded. "Be careful."

Bent laughed. "Careful of what?"

Jean shrugged and nodded, then got in her car and drove away.

Bent tried to think of what to say to Tell and Machlon, how to explain why he had to leave, and he thought of the questions they would have – where would he go, when would he be back – questions he didn't have answers for. So he left without telling, that night. Took nothing, needed nothing and was sorry for it. A corpse needs no food nor no blanket to keep him warm and that's sad, for they provide a comfort beyond mere physical relief. He just walked away. He was starting to think it was what he was best at.

He walked all night, this ground being familiar and uninteresting to him. He was three hours going the length of the river road, as there was no shoreline, only rocky embankment sweeping down behind houses to the cove, and he picked his way slowly, slipping on rockweed and green algae incandescent in the moonlight. By five he had reached the pub on the edge of New Hope. He could go on, but for the next few miles the houses closed ranks from the expansive lawns and spacious properties of the river road to the tightly packed Colonial homes of New Hope's historic district, postage-stamp lots and little or no setbacks, then the shop-lined main street, and even if he made it that far before people began stirring, there was the drawbridge. He couldn't risk crossing it except in the small hours.

Just beyond the pub lay the boatyard, boats hauled out for the winter. Bent ran to the nearest boat. He reached up and hooked a hand round one of the tarpaulin ropes and hauled himself up. From atop the tarp, he undid the knots on enough ties to open a gap, then hung off the edge and looped himself like a snake through the gap and onto the deck. He re-tied the ropes from the inside then turned and crawled on all fours to mid-ships. He pulled on a cabin window. It slid open and he climbed in. The tarp pressed against the windows and made of the lounge a tight cozy space like a cave, or a tomb. Bent lay back amongst the pillows of the nearest sofa, curled up on his side and closed his eyes.

When he awoke, daylight had lit the tarp up blue. He looked for a clock, but the helm instruments were frosted over. Trapped till dark, he ducked through the door beneath the helm and went below decks in search of diversion. He found a bookshelf in the captain's cabin stacked with true crime and Louis L'Amour novels, and, probably for its title, *Two Years Before the Mast*. He'd never read it so he lay atop the bedspread with his back against the headboard, switched on a battery-powered reading lamp affixed to the wall, and opened the book. Soon he grew restless, and he lay back and tried the trick of hypnotizing himself. He thought of one thing and then another but could get hold of nothing, and after a while he sat up and tried reading again. But he read the same sentence over and over and each time couldn't remember what he'd read. Finally he gave up and lay still waiting for dark.

~

For several weeks, there had been a series of cross-border raids between Bent's, Tell's and Machlon's, one of them sneaking in when a house was empty and stealing something, then sending a ransom note, sometimes accompanied by a photograph. Partly it was to alleviate the boredom of winter and the curtailing of their territory, but there was something else, too. They were growing up, they realized, and so they devised little games to postpone it a while longer. Sometimes the one who hadn't stolen the item was enlisted to help retrieve it, sometimes not. Bent entered his room one night to find Tell and thought he had caught him in the act of theft.

"Ah hah!"

He realized then that Tell had come not to steal but to hide ransomed goods. He clutched in his hands Machlon's two-foot-tall stuffed tiger, tattered and missing an eye, won at the fair when Machlon was eight. Tell opened the bedroom window, leaned out and sat the tiger on the roof propped against the side of the house.

Machlon soon appeared to claim his property. He narrowed his eyes at Tell, then at Bent, whose presence made him an accomplice, though it was his own room. "Okay, where is it?"

Bent and Tell stood shoulder to shoulder, looking innocent. Machlon searched the room, homed in on the bed and swept back Bent's quilt dramatically only to find the space beneath the bed empty. He flung the pillows aside and, finding nothing there, either, turned suspiciously on the closet. He yanked the door open and swept back the clothes in clumps.

"The note says it's in Bent's bedroom. Give it up."

"Does it actually say in Bent's bedroom?" Tell said.

Machlon looked around, then settled his gaze on the window. He started for it but Tell blocked him.

"Oh no no no,' Tell said. "That would be too easy."

"Fine." Machlon turned for the door.

"Machlon, you wake my mother and she'll kill us all."

Machlon stopped briefly and executed a dramatic turn in the doorway. "Call me The Shadow." He slunk off down the stairs.

Soon they heard him cursing quietly and they looked out the window to see him climbing from the trellis onto the roof. He stopped to remove a splinter from his hand, then crawled on all fours to the window, then reached out and retrieved the tiger from the outside wall where it leaned. He crawled toward the window with the tiger in one hand but Tell shot the bolt. Machlon rapped on the glass and whispered, his voice hollow through the glass. "Let me in."

Tell laughed.

"Okay, Tell, ha ha ha. Now let me in."

Still Tell just laughed.

Machlon knocked louder. "Open up."

Tell pretended not to understand. "What? I can't hear you."

"Come on, it's cold out here."

Machlon knocked, and Tell laughed, and it had that edge in it. Not just laughing, then, but sneering. It was funny till it became mean-spirited and Bent lost heart for the game. He unlocked the window and Machlon climbed in.

"Why do you do this stuff? It's twenty degrees out."

"I wasn't gonna leave him out there. Anyway, what's he still got that fucking thing for? What kind of guy keeps a stuffed animal?"

So Bent thought it was Tell climbing up the trellis this night to do more mischief, or Machlon, maybe, to hide some item of Tell's for revenge. But when Bent went to the window, it was Abby cresting the trellis and crawling onto the roof. He opened the window and helped her in.

"What are you doing? It's freezing out there."

"Oh good. It is you." Abby heeled out of her snow-caked boots. "I wasn't sure this was the right window. I spent the climb thinking how I *was going to explain if I tumbled into your mother's bedroom."*

Abby threw her coat on a chair and tucked her hands in her back jeans pockets, rocking a little on her heels. "So. What's up?"

"Uh, nothing. I was just reading." Bent threw his book down on the bed. Abby took it up, tried to take an interest in its contents, then laid it back down. She looked for something to occupy her and wandered around the tiny room.

"Everything...okay?"

Abby slumped in the chair her coat lay on and bumped her head on the sloped ceiling. "Sorry to burst in on you like this."

Bent sat on the edge of his bed. "Your father?"

Abby nodded. "I came downstairs to get some hot chocolate and there he was, drinking and watching some World War II documentary. He started mumbling about my mother and I just left."

Bent reflected on the difference in their positions, him wishing his father was here and her wishing hers wasn't.

"Sorry."

Abby rose and flipped through his record collection, idly at first, then finding a 45 she really wanted to play, she placed the album on the turntable and held the needle above it.

"Okay?" she said.

Bent nodded and she set the needle on the fat lip of the disc. A few repeating rasps and then a low crackle, and "Everybody Hurts" began to play. Abby turned to Bent, smiled and rolled her eyes at herself.

"So predictable."

She sat cross-legged on the floor near the collection and Bent sat opposite.

"What's this one?" she said periodically and Bent told her about the album and the band, pointing out things in the liner notes. Every time the song ended Abby returned the needle to the beginning. They sat

listening quietly for a while. When Michael Stipe told his listeners to hold on, Abby turned to Bent.

"Can I stay here tonight?"

She insisted she would sleep on the floor but of course Bent wouldn't allow it. He took his sleeping bag down from the top of the closet and lay it out on the floor next to the bed, the only space available that could accommodate his endlessly lengthening legs. He gave Abby some pyjamas and she tip-toed to the bathroom to change. When she returned, she climbed under the bedcovers and Bent eased his lanky frame into the sleeping bag.

"What happens to people?" Abby said above Bent in the darkened room. "All my parents' old photos show this smiling, happy couple. How did things go from that to this?"

"Maybe they're disappointed in their choices. What did they want to be? Like what did your father want to be?"

"Exactly what he is. A rich asshole. No, I don't know. He never talks about anything. He just went to college, then law school, and now here he is. My mother talked about a Christmas tree farm."

"A what?"

Abby laughed. "Yeah. She wanted to buy a plot of land and grow pumpkins for the fall and Christmas trees for the winter and serve cider and have hayrides. Then they got married and, I don't know, they both did what they did."

Bent thought for a while. "Maybe the people they used to be don't like the people they are now. Maybe they blame each other."

They lay quietly awhile. An icy snow began to fall, and they listened to the tiny pellets rap at the window. In the darkness, Bent felt Abby's hand slip into his. Eventually they fell asleep.

Bent came to himself and realized he was still in the boat, waiting to continue his flight. The restaurants would be busy till nine or ten. He stayed put till he heard the dinner crowd thin at the pub, and the rattle of recyclables being carried to the curb. When the last car door shut and its driver motored away, Bent emerged from the tarp, dropped to the gravel and headed out. By midnight he was across the drawbridge, grey and studded like an old battleship, and headed east.

~

Machlon crouched in the bushes. He had started out looking for Bent but had kept going and now here he was. Arnold had said keep doing until you feel like you've done enough. The superstore's loading dock stood open. There were no streetlights in the back of the store where no customers ever came and the only light came from two floodlights on either side of the bay door. The night was dark and the lights could barely penetrate it, their beams casting two pools of white directly beneath them and not much more. The only other light was a glow from inside the warehouse bay, where Machlon could see aluminum shelves stretching to the ceiling packed with crates of food. A white van was backed up to the door. Machlon checked the driver's side. The keys were in the ignition and a baseball cap sat on the dash. He pulled the door handle gently, eased the door open and took the cap. He brushed back his hood, put the cap on with the brim low over his eyes and pulled the hood back up.

The warehouse bay was deserted. He took a dolly and, moving quickly, began stacking it high with crates of non-perishables. Canned beans: kidney, baked and black beans. Bags of flour. Canned peaches and pineapple and carrots, peanut butter, dried spaghetti and linguini and ziti, soups and rice, baby formula and brightly colored boxes of cereal with cartoon characters on them. When the dolly was full he steered it to the van, digging in his heels to give his wispy frame traction as the dolly veered and swerved, loaded the items then wheeled back for more. When he had filled the van, he lay the dolly down.

"Hey!"

He turned, keeping his head down and trying to see through upturned eyes. A man was walking toward him from the bowels of the warehouse. Machlon turned and quick-stepped toward the van. He heard running and quickened pace. He ran for the van door but before he could reach it he was spinning and slammed against the side of the van.

"What the hell do you think you're doing?"

The man had him by the collar. Machlon kept his head down but felt the man's grip slacken. He looked up as much as he dared. The man's face had darkened, and he stared at Machlon, his brows knitted. He still held loosely to Machlon's collar and Machlon knew he wouldn't be able to break free by force. The man had seen him. What else was there to do? Machlon lifted his hand and pushed back his hood, then swept off the cap. The man was frozen, staring, couldn't believe what he was seeing.

"Boo," Machlon said.

The man stumbled backwards and fell to the pavement. Machlon climbed into the driver's seat and locked the door, replaced the cap and hood, turned the engine over and pulled away. In the rearview mirror he saw the man sitting on the ground staring at the place where Machlon had been standing a moment before.

"Sorry," he said.

Machlon drove across the river to New London and onto the access road. The back door of the food bank, where people left out-of-hours donations, faced the river so offloading was easy. When he had finished he drove the back roads toward Easterly. It was unlikely that the man on the loading dock had reported his van stolen by a corpse but you never know. Crossing the bridge he looked downriver. He saw the Revolutionary War fort, its stone obelisk rising high above the landscape, and beyond that, the lighthouse in the middle of the channel just beyond where the mouth of the river opened up into the Sound. At the first exit he turned off onto the surface roads and by a long and winding path that avoided any public areas he made his way home, reflecting that he would likely never pass this way again. It was almost light when he reached the river road. He pulled the van into the parking lot of the old, decommissioned railroad station, parked in back and walked the rest of the way. He made it back to the graveyard as the sun was cracking the horizon.

"Cutting it a little close, ain't you?" Tell said.

"I'm here, aren't I?"

He sat by the dying fire.

"Bent's disappeared. You aren't to run off, too, and leave me alone in a goddamn graveyard, understand?" Tell said. "What did you do that's got you back so late?"

Machlon shrugged. "Nothing."

~

Bent walked night after night, through the nature preserve, Lord's Point and Stonington, past Quiambaug Cove and Wequetequock, through Westerly all the way to Misquamicut. He walked the long beach, its restaurants and arcades boarded up for winter. At the eastern end of the beach he stopped. This was the end of familiar terrain. Up till now he knew how and where he could walk to avoid people, but from this point on he had travelled only by car, never on foot, and had no idea how far he could get. He looked back the way he had come, he looked ahead, and turned in slow circles on the beach. When that didn't help him decide, he sank to the sand and sat, legs crossed like a child, and watched the surf. He sat and thought till the thoughts stopped coming and he found a kind of peace. Then he rose and continued east.

He walked for several nights. Sometimes a thing caught his attention and he stopped. He climbed a wooden observation tower that gave a view of marsh to the south and houses to the north, and he leaned on the railing and watched people move about inside their homes. At a bumper car track, closed for winter, he sat in a garish yellow car. Sometimes he walked for hours without rest. He no longer got tired as he had when he lived.

At first he racked his brain for ways to get rid of the revenant. He had failed to strangle it, he wasn't sure why. He could ambush it at the house and try to chop its head off, but then where would that leave him? His kids fatherless and him stuck in this body forever and no chance of swapping back. That's where strangling the thing would have got him, too, come to think of it. He decided to put it out of his mind and let his subconscious work on it.

He found it easier to think when he walked. His mind felt his body wandering and so it wandered, too. It was democratic in its thoughts, spent as much time on the quotidian as on the epic events of his life. Were there a lot of these? Not so very many. Not as many as some. His father's death. Then there were Jean and the children, and of course Abby, who had provided some of the best days of his life and one of the worst. And there were the things he knew. It was a lot. He had gathered knowledge greedily, hoarded facts like canned peas. He knew that Agincourt was won by mud and that Falstaff was really Sir John Fastolf and no coward. He knew a pope once accidentally killed a boy by having him painted gold. What did it all matter? It changed nothing. The world cared nothing for such facts. It cared for the nightly news, for martyred leaders and tweets and hula hoops.

His thoughts tumbled down on him like meteors, none connected to the last. It worried him.

His mother told of getting oranges and stockings for Christmas and sharing a small bird with carrots and potatoes. It was like Dickens. He thought she was telling tales. Years later she had still made her mother's Depression meatballs, a bit of meat and mostly bread. His father ate them without complaint, though it must have seemed a comment on his ability to provide.

Her grandfather once got lost in the woods, his mother told them. It was back home, in the old country. He wandered for three days, slept in trees to escape wolves. He had no food, only water from stagnant pools. The dirt lodged in his teeth. On the fourth day he came to a farmhouse. The farmer shared his supper. All he had was cabbage, and grandfather hated cabbage, but he ate every bite and always ate cabbage after that. It didn't matter that the story had been stolen, the moral wasn't difficult to spot and Bent and his sisters and even his father fell short.

The stylites lived on the tops of pillars and the people gazed up at them.

Hermits left the towns to lie by themselves in caves and contemplate the creation, and the people moved their towns to be near them.

He would have liked to be a holy fool, but he was too attentive of hygiene.

Even if there is a prime mover, how could it be understood when interpreted through a human mediator? Any construct is a human one, and therefore inadequate for understanding the arbitrary power it seeks to explain. It is corrupted by human ego.

He'd asked those thousand questions prompted by the mystery

of the Eucharist and still had no answers. Maybe if his life had gone differently. But that was childish, self-centered. Had things really been so bad? Ordinary human problems, no more. Even the death of his father. Traumatic, yes, but nothing compared with the great sorrows of the ages. Boethius languished in prison and was tortured to death.

What was he? If myths are stories we tell ourselves to make sense of the world, what was he to make of himself? Was he even real? Had this happened? Or was it his imagination? Was he really dead? Had he ever been alive? Was this what happened when you die? You have nightmares of a monstrous *you* left behind? No, it must have happened, because Tell and Machlon were the same as him. Or maybe he had conjured them as well.

In times past people didn't understand wind and weather and the sea, so they invented gods. Strange gods and terrible gods, gods that turned to swans and raped young girls. They even invented people. Mothers who killed their children. Was he somebody's invention? A boogeyman to explain some incomprehensible grief? No, that was impossible. He had to pull himself together. So to speak. Ha ha.

We are pattern makers. Often the patterns we make strain credulity.

He wondered if he was going mad.

A few nights' walk brought him to a park he thought he knew. The gatehouse was dark. He ducked under the boom gate and followed the drive till it opened up into the place he remembered.

He recalled the Friday night Machlon rolled up to his house in his mother's '68 Rambler. He'd just gotten his driver's license and had told Bent to pack a bag. Bent slid in and pushed over the pizza Machlon had brought and tossed his rucksack in the back.

They drove north half the night, what Route 1 calls north even though from Easterly it's almost due east all the way to Cape Cod. They ate pizza from the box and wiped their hands on the floor mats. In Rhode Island they stopped for drinks at a chain ice cream shop and decided to buy a soda from every one they passed, who knows why. After a while their stomachs were queasy and they poured out the soda as soon as they'd paid for it and tossed the cups in the back. The floorboards filled with paper cups.

Sometime past three they pulled into a park. There was a gazebo in the middle of a pond and they crossed the narrow, slatted bridge to it and slept beneath its cupola.

The next year Machlon went off to college in Boston, and then the terrible thing happened to his mother. Go back to school, everyone said. There's no point sitting around this house, where it happened, thinking on it all day. This is your chance to get out. So Machlon had gone. But he hadn't stayed gone long. A month or so afterwards, a friend drove the Rambler home and parked it in front of the Machlon house and took a train back to Boston. Some friends had noticed it and called Bent and told him. He called the college, and after some convincing, got them to tell him that Machlon had been checked into a mental hospital. It was a breakdown, he guessed, though no one called it that. Machlon was out of it, was all anyone would say. Thought Jesus lived at the Trumbull Airport.

Now Bent picked his way through the thorny woods, and after a while broke into the clearing of the park. He crossed the bridge to the gazebo and sat back against the wall, knees drawn up. For a while he captured the mood of that weekend and laughed to himself. Then it drained away. He curled on his side and bundled his coat for a pillow and tried to sleep.

~

"How's your penance coming?" Arnold said. Machlon had since learned his full name: Arnold Janeway.

"I don't know," Machlon said. "I did something, a sort of mitzvah, but I think I caused more trouble in the process."

Machlon told him of the grocery raid, leaving out the part about frightening the van driver nearly out of his wits.

"Robin Hood, eh?"

"Does it still count? That I gave food to the poor, even though I robbed somebody to do it?"

"I don't know, what am I, the Dalai Lama?...Well, I guess if you ask me, a lot of poor people got food to eat and some big corporation just lost a little stock. I'd say you're in the credit column."

Machlon felt satisfied with that answer.

"Still, I think you'd better not do it again. You don't sound like a very good thief. You're liable to get yourself thrown in the hoosegow. If you want to do community service, so to speak, why don't you start a food drive at your office?"

"The thing is...I don't work there anymore," Machlon said. "They laid me off."

"That's rough," Arnold said. "How are you managing? Does your wife work?"

"I'm not married."

"Never?"

"Never."

"Why not? There I go being rude again. But hell, a person shouldn't be alone."

"When we were kids, we all did everything together, you know? Then everybody started pairing off and I was the odd man out. After a while I got used to being alone. Well, not used to it. More like I lost the knack of being around people. Everyone else, they make jokes, they go to parties. People would say witty things and I'd try to think of something funny to say back but I couldn't. So I just listened. After a while I worried they were waiting for me to say something funny back so I stopped going."

"You're a good listener. That's a virtue. Most people aren't. That's why they talk so much. They only know how to say what they want. Don't know how to listen to what other people have to say. You're an introvert, that's what you are."

Machlon thought about this. "Am I?"

"Don't you think?"

Machlon considered it. The aptness of the label surprised him. "I suppose I am. I wish I'd met you thirty years ago so you could have told me. I might have done things differently. You're a pretty smart old bastard."

"Like hell. I'm just old. You gotta work pretty hard to get to my age and not learn at least a little something. I've done all kinds of stupid things in my time. Careless, thoughtless things. My son could have gotten a college deferment. He was a straight A student. I think he went to the war because I supported it. For the life of me now, I can't think why."

He grew quiet, and Machlon saw how with effort he pulled himself out of it.

"*Ve grow too soon olt and too late schmart.* That's what my grandmother used to say. I don't know why she said it in a German accent. She was from New Jersey."

"My father killed my mother," Machlon blurted out. He didn't know why.

Janeway was quiet a moment.

"El maleh rachamim," he whispered. "It means God full of

compassion. It's part of the Mourner's Kaddish. I hope your mother is in a better place. And I think you ought to give yourself credit just for staying upright all these years, don't you?"

It was the first time Machlon had thought about it that way. They sat quietly for a while, just enjoying the peace Janeway had given Machlon. When Machlon finally spoke, it wasn't with sadness. It was because he felt Janeway had earned the right to know.

"I have cancer," he said.

"I know. I can smell it. Don't be offended, you can't help it. But I could smell it the first night you came to see me."

Machlon considered the stench of death on him that the old man was mistaking for cancer and wondered if he smelled as bad when he was alive.

"What are they doing for you?"

"It's end stage. There's not really anything they can do. I look… dead. I don't want people to see me. It will scare them."

The old man nodded. "It's not so bad," he said after a while. "Dying. I've lived my span of years and you're young yet and losing time, I know. But the actual process isn't so bad, if they can keep you comfortable. And if you can get shut of the fear. You just have to take what comes. How long?"

"I don't know. Not long now, I think. I just…if all of a sudden I don't come see you anymore I wanted you to know why. I wanted you to know I didn't just leave you."

"Thank you," the old man said.

~

Bent woke to a grey dawn. He unfolded his coat and slipped it on. He crossed the narrow bridge to the land and sat at a picnic table by the water. A sparrow landed soundlessly on the wood near him. It cocked its head, hopped closer, regarded him, hopped again, and looked up at him intensely, seeking food.

"I have nothing."

Bent opened his jacket and showed the lining, the empty pockets. The bird cocked its head again and hopped even closer. Bent snaked a finger in at his throat and felt around, hooked a maggot and drew it out, held it out to the sparrow. The bird leaned to it, one snapping motion like an animatronic president at Disney World. He turned his head – click – and aimed a black eye at the maggot, then with a peck took it up and launched, bobbing toward the tree line like a wind-up model airplane. Bent couldn't decide whether to be happy or depressed.

He looked around. The park was not the way he remembered it from that weekend, or didn't feel the same, anyway. Such things never do. An observation so tedious it hardly bore mentioning. Still, what else to do? Roll over and wait to rot? The sky was lightening. The park would open soon. Probably no one would come, but you never could tell. He rose and headed for the tree line the way he had come.

In every town he came to, a scrum of dead congregated, sometimes a great number of them, sometimes only a few. Sometimes on beach front, sometimes on grassy headlands. At such times he felt like he was dreaming, the movements of the dead around him slow, like a movie running at half speed. In one farmer's field, they wandered among the cows, who chewed hay and blinked impassively. Maybe they couldn't see them. But in the barn, horses nickered and whinnied, agitated, so maybe the cows were too simple to know the difference between the living and the dead. In every group Bent sought his father, walked among them studying face after face. He didn't know why. If he was anywhere he was likely to be in Easterly, and he hadn't seen him there, so his mother was probably telling the truth. He had left them.

He took to spying. Eavesdropping, really, just to hear people again. He lurked beneath kitchen windows and listened to dinner conversation. He came much closer than he should have, but he longed to hear human voices, see television light flickering on upturned faces. So he drew nearer. Once he was chased by dogs, but when they saw what he was they ran. Once in an upstairs window a boy waved at him. He jerked back and began to back away, but saw the boy wasn't afraid and stopped. Very young he was, five or six, hair like ripened wheat, skin white as candle wax. Bent waved back and flicked his hand to send the boy from the window. The boy shook his head and smiled sadly, and Bent realized he was dead, too. Newly dead, obviously, for his face was uncorrupted. Bent waved once more and backed away. He did not want to hear the keening he knew went on in the rooms below.

He thought then of the story of his life. He held a job, and raised two children, and kept a woman on the side. Aren't his children something to see, though? But that's as much Jean's accomplishment as his. More. And what was he? He wondered why we can't just be happy with what we have.

Abby, Abby.

Life had always been too much for him, too big a risk. Every good thing he had, every good thing that happened, he held a part of himself back, kept himself from enjoying it too much. Remembering that first, momentous loss, he became acquainted with life as a thing that took. The wheel spun and you were given a father. It spun again and he was taken away. Was it worth loving if you might lose the things you loved most?

Ahead of road trips, his stomach churned. He calculated crash rates, mapped routes along back roads away from the more heavily travelled interstates, chose driving times when drivers would be most alert and accidents least likely. He could have been an actuary. He was beset with visions, images of their car in flashes like photos taken by a forensic photographer, the twisted wreckage, his children in horrible attitudes of death, cracked open, bloody, and him the survivor who would always have to remember, the Banquo. *All my pretty ones? Did you say all?* When they reached their destination safely, his children would be up for hours past their bedtime, incapable of sleep, recounting all the wondrous things they'd seen on the journey, and he would look back on it and think, Yes, that was great fun. I wish I had been less afraid.

People will only wait so long. Smart ones, anyway. Abby's father bought her a car for her sixteenth birthday, so their outings were no longer limited to where Tell could take them in the boat. The new thing for those with cars was dinner at the Roundup next town over then to the movies across the street, where they played Rocky Horror Picture Show *every Saturday at midnight. Abby asked Bent at school that Friday if he wanted to go, and of course he said yes. But when the car pulled up outside his house on Saturday evening, Chas sat next to Abby in the front seat. Tell and Louise were already in back. They looked like two couples. Bent backed away from the window and turned out the light.*

He was in his forties when he met Jean. She had been roped into acting as a chaperone for a class that visited the museum. For awhile they were just friends, but slowly they fell into dating, and then one day Jean told Bent she was pregnant. Good Catholics, Jean's parents wanted them to get married, so that's what they did.

It was a small service in Jean's parents' back yard, with a white tent set up in case it rained. The night before the wedding they sat on the porch, rocking gently in the swing, both quiet, something there to be said, but no one saying it. Finally Jean spoke up.

"I don't want you to marry me because I'm pregnant. I want you

to marry me because you love me."

"I do love you," he said.

It's not that it wasn't true, but...

Abby came home that summer and asked to see Bent. She and Chas had separated, she said. Did Bent want to go to a movie or something? And then she looked at Bent's hand and saw the wedding ring. No one had told her.

"If only you'd come last summer," he said.

"Our timing," she said.

Bent turned and took her hands in his.

"It's not that I don't want to. I just can't. I won't be a man who leaves his child."

Abby nodded. "Of course," she said.

Bent said nothing.

Abby smiled sadly. "Send in the clowns."

Bent continued east. He found close places to hide days, in thickets, in sheds and barns if he was lucky. Nights he walked, and thought about where he was, *what* he was.

What doesn't kill me makes me stronger…What a crock.

He had read his Augustine. If you were completely without sin, a martyr or saint, you went straight to heaven, and if you were completely wicked, directly to hell. He was no saint, sure, and this no heaven, but he was no devil either. He thought then of the last two categories, and much the most crowded, the not altogether good and the not altogether wicked. These went to Purgatory to be cleansed by fire. *The fire shall try every man's work of what sort it is.* Was that where he was? Was he, as Gregory wrote, working off his sins in the place of their commission?

But why limit himself to Christian notions? He'd left those behind so very long ago. He thought then of the Roman pagans, who conceived the afterlife as a place of punishment and sought to comfort their dead with feasting at their graves. Comfort, and placate, too, for the dead were not only to be pitied but to be feared. He thought of the Viking Valhalla. Wait now, what happened to the warriors who didn't go there? He couldn't remember.

What had any of this to do with him? He was dead as they were, but had found no Heaven, no Hades, no Valhalla. He just wandered about, like the old men in the mall who nobody paid attention to.

I know, you love being alive, you do not want to die; and you would like to pass from this life to the other in such a way that you do not rise again dead, but are changed, alive, into something better. That is what you would like, that is what ordinary human feelings desire, that is what the soul itself has, in I do not know what kind of way, engraved in its deepest will and desire.

Augustine again.

He became aware of his surroundings. He was on a grassy cape looking out to sea. Up ahead in the east the sky was grey, the grey of nothing, the grey of impossibility. The walk had brought him no answers. He turned around and made for home.

~

Machlon sat in the hard-packed snow outside his bedroom window, back to the wall, knees gathered to his chest. Inside, the other him lay amid blankets he knew were soaked with sweat and stinking. He could almost smell it. He'd been shocked when he looked in at him. His face was white, as though he'd been drained of blood, and Machlon couldn't recognize himself. After looking a moment he could bear it no longer and sank to the ground. The revenant had known he was sick. He took his body anyway. But still, that kind of suffering can never be understood until it's felt, and nor can the suffering Machlon had embraced by his unwillingness to reveal himself to the other him now, to allow it to take his body back.

Machlon left his vigil at the window and walked to the nursing home. He looked in at Arnold's window to make sure he was awake before going in to visit, but the bed was empty. Not unmade, the covers thrown back as though Arnold was off for a test somewhere, but made up with hospital corners. And all of Arnold's things had been taken away. The walls were bare. Arnold was gone.

Machlon returned to the graveyard and sat in front of the fire. He had kindled it but it was dying, and he hadn't the will to add wood or even to move.

"What are you doing, sitting here in front of a dying fire?"

He hadn't even heard her approach. He looked at her a moment, then shrugged and looked back down.

"I was worried I'd come too late," Mrs. Rutherford said. "Bent's gone abroad?"

"Bent's disappeared."

"What do you mean disappeared?"

"Gone. A few days now."

"Well, I'm sure he's fine. He probably just needs to be alone." She studied Machlon. "What's the matter?"

It was hard for him to speak. "Somebody died."

"You mean somebody besides you and Bent and…"

Machlon nodded, and Mrs. Rutherford sat beside him. "Oh, I'm sorry. Was it someone you were close to?"

He couldn't explain why Arnold had meant so much to him. He barely knew him. Still, he nodded. Mrs. Rutherford sat with him quietly. After some time had passed, she stood up, even now crisply, not with the creaky hesitation of age.

"Let's go for a drive."

Machlon looked up at her miserably.

"No point in wallowing. It will do you good."

They drove along the river road, watching the lights twinkling on the bay, then turned left at the church, circled over to Groton and its little beach. In season you had to pay and there was a guard in a shack at the entrance, but now the shack was boarded up for winter, and Mrs. Rutherford breezed past and wheeled into the parking lot.

"Hold on," she said.

Machlon didn't understand, but then Mrs. Rutherford gunned the engine and steered straight for the edge of the long parking lot where the tarmac abruptly dropped off into the sea. Machlon clutched the grab handle and screamed.

"Oh, Jesus."

"That's right, just hold to the Jesus handle and enjoy the ride," she said. "Sorry, Lord."

She raced headlong toward the edge but just as Machlon thought she was about to go over she slammed on the brakes and the car skidded and came to a stop at the edge of the drop-off. Mrs. Rutherford whooped.

"Harold and I used to do that every time we came here," she said.

Machlon clutched his chest and tried to catch his breath.

"You're not dead yet," Mrs. Rutherford said. "Not quite, anyway. Enjoy it."

They continued the circle home through town and up the long hill road, past the chicken farm with its rows of long sheds.

"There must be thousands of chickens in there," Machlon said. "That's no kind of life."

Mrs. Rutherford pulled into the church next door and studied the chicken houses for a long time, then turned to Machlon.

"You're right," she said.

She got out of the car.

"What are you doing?"

Mrs. Machlon began to cross the field that separated the chicken houses from the road. Machlon watched her a moment, then climbed out and followed.

"This lady's crazy," he said as he caught up with her.

"What are they going to do, arrest an old woman?" she said. "Tell them I've gone round the bend." Frost heaves had turned the grass and dirt to waves. "Good thing I wore my Buster Browns."

They stopped at the first chicken house and Machlon turned to Mrs. Rutherford.

"Go on," she said.

He took a deep breath, thrust the doors wide and jumped back, expecting a tidal wave of chickens, but it didn't come. He stepped inside. Hundreds of chickens stood under heat lamps, clucking, shifting aimlessly.

"Go on, chickens." He swept his hands in the air, but the chickens just stared. He stepped up to one of the rows of heat lamps and shooed at the chickens. "Go on, chickens. Go, go, go." They scattered at his approach but still made no break for the door. He put his hands on his hips and sighed and turned to Mrs. Rutherford.

"Why don't they go?"

"They're afraid of you," she said.

She blundered forward into their midst waving her arms and stamping her feet and the chickens scrambled in all directions. Machlon pushed his cap down on his head, leaned forward and broke into a run toward the chickens, shouting as though he had jumped out of an airplane. The chickens burst away from him.

"That's it," Mrs. Rutherford said. "You've got them going now."

Machlon rushed the length of the house, the chickens scattering in a wave before him like the wake of a boat, then turned and ran back, herding the chickens before him. Those at the head of the pack ran for the door, and he whooped as the others began streaming out after them.

He ran to the next house and did the same, then the next, and the next. As he emerged from the last house, he saw the chickens streaming across the field in all directions, some toward the tree line, some toward the side roads, some toward the high school at the top of the hill. Machlon whooped and waved his cap, chasing the few stragglers toward their friends.

"Go, chickens, go!" Mrs. Rutherford shouted.

"Go, chickens, go!" Machlon echoed.

They watched a moment longer.

"Now let's get out of here before we get arrested," Mrs. Rutherford said.

They scrambled back across the field to her car and pulled away.

Back at the graveyard, Machlon paused, his hand on the door handle. "What just happened?"

Mrs. Rutherford smiled. "Before Harold died, he made me promise that I would never stop having fun. And I never have."

Machlon studied her ancient face, full of tiny rivulets but with eyes that shined bright. He smiled, shook his head, and got out of the car.

When Machlon reached their fire, Bent sat before it with Tell. They scolded Bent and made out to be cross, but they were glad to see him, he could tell. They asked where he'd gone and what he'd done, and he told it mostly, though some parts were hard to explain so he left them out. It felt good to be back, and the fog that had begun to confuse him on his walk left him and they passed the night talking amiably.

~

Tell sat on the ground at the back of Little's the next morning, listening in on his old life beyond the window, the morning talk of his former companions, when they began to talk of a chicken break.

"Somebody let em out. They found all the doors open."

"Why'nt they keep em locked?"

"Why would they lock the doors of a chicken house? You think the chickens know how to use doorknobs?"

"I'm saying to keep people out."

"Who would wanna let a thousand chickens loose?"

"Somebody did, obviously. Some of those chickens are probably halfway to Rhode Island by now."

Tell ran low toward the railroad bridge, taking the risk of crossing the bridge so he could pluck the morning paper from the lawn of the house just shy.

"It's crazy," Tell said, back in the graveyard and reading the article. "Who would do such a nutty thing?"

"Kids, probably," Bent said. "Anything in there about the insider trading?"

Tell shook his head.

Seated by the dying fire, Machlon chuckled.

"What?" Tell said.

Machlon smiled. "Nothing." He laughed again. Tell watched him, and Machlon looked up and saw Tell looking, then looked down, then broke into open laughter.

"You did this?" Tell said.

Machlon just laughed.

Bent looked at him and couldn't help laughing himself. "Machlon, did you?"

"You should have seen it," Machlon said. "Chickens running everywhere, squawking, wings flapping, feathers flying. It was pandemonium."

Tell threw down the paper. "What are you, stupid? Why would you do that?"

"Do you know how those animals are treated? They barely have room to move, never get to go outside. They just lay eggs until they get too old, and then they get the chop."

"It's in the newspaper, Machlon," Tell said. "They're investigating. You want to attract attention to us?"

Machlon laughed. "How's this going to attract attention to us?"

"They're going to look for who did this."

"And you think they'll suspect the undead?"

Tell looked at Bent. "Don't you have anything to say about this?"

"They're waterfowl," Bent said. "Technically."

Tell turned back to Machlon. "Goddammit, Machlon, what the hell is the matter with you? We've spent months hiding in a graveyard, making sure nobody ever sees us, then you go and pull a stunt like this. That was really stupid."

"Shut up."

Tell and Bent both froze. Neither could believe it.

"What?" Tell said.

"You heard me. *Shut up.*"

"What's got into you?" Tell said.

Machlon stood. "I'm sick and tired of your crap, Tell. My whole life I've been putting up with your shit. I'm done." He squared off with Tell, reached out slowly, placed his fingers on Tell's shoulder, and shoved. "You want to go?"

Tell looked at Bent, who stood with his arms crossed, one hand over his mouth to cover a smile. Tell looked back at Machlon and laughed uncertainly.

"I mean it, Tell. I'm fed up. You want to go? Let's go."

He shoved Tell again. Tell didn't move, just stared in disbelief, and Machlon leapt back, threw off his hoodie and began stalking back and forth before Tell, his arms thrust wide.

"Jesus, Machlon," Tell said, "have you ever even been in a fight?"

"I'm serious, Tell. I'm grateful for what you did with my father, but all these years you've been running your mouth at my expense. I've had it. What are you going to do to me? I'm dead and I feel no pain. If you want to go, now's the time. Do you want to go?"

Tell laughed nervously. "No, I don't want to go, Machlon."

"All *right*, then." Machlon retrieved his hoodie and struggled back into it, punching his hands into the armholes.

"And don't call me stupid anymore, either."

"Okay, I won't."

Tell sat and leaned against the stone wall. He looked at Bent.

"You want to go?" Bent said.

"No, I don't, at all," Tell said.

"Good thing for you."

~

The next morning they heard footsteps and turned to see the priest picking his way through the fresh-packed snow that had fallen during the night and iced over. Tell and Machlon hid. The priest moved forward purposefully, his head down against the wind and a scarf wound over half his face. He looked like a traveler who'd come from a far-off land, and so he had.

"Mrs. Rutherford is ill," he said.

"Is it serious?"

The priest nodded. "If you're to see her, I think it had better be tonight."

Bent nodded. "As soon as it's dark."

"She was fine yesterday," Machlon said after the priest had gone. "She chased the chickens, too. I hope it wasn't too much for her."

He looked at the fire sadly. Bent put a hand on his shoulder.

"No, no," he said. "She's very old, Machlon."

"How old?" Machlon said.

Bent chuckled sadly. "Nobody knows."

Mrs. Rutherford was pale, and so small beneath the blankets it seemed they might crush her.

"I'm ready to go," she said. "I've done everything I wanted to do, mostly. I'm ready to see Harold."

She had no doubt that's where she was going, no thought that she might be stuck as Bent was, and Bent didn't, either.

"I'm sorry to leave you," she said. "I hope you find your way. When you do, look me up."

"If I make it," Bent said, "will you finally tell me what you did in the war?"

Mrs. Rutherford managed to angle her head on the pillow. She looked at him gravely, then raised her eyebrows. Once, twice. Bent laughed, then grew quiet, then began to cry.

"Don't be frightened." She took his hand and patted it. "Don't be frightened."

The next morning, early, as the fire still burned, the priest emerged from the morning fog. He pulled up a chair, faced it toward Bent, sat and leaned in. He hesitated a moment, and in that brief hush Bent sensed why he had come. Grief rose in his chest.

"When?"

"A few hours ago. She called me during the night and said it was time and asked me to come deliver the last rites. I did, then I sat with her. She dozed on and off, and we talked when she was wakeful. She told me to thank you for coming to see her. At about five, she took a deep breath, and exhaled, and then she passed."

Bent wiped his eyes.

"She was in no pain," the priest continued.

"Good. That's good."

The priest turned his hands over in themselves for warmth, and fretfully. "Do you think she'll be..."

"Like me?"

The priest nodded. Bent shook his head.

"She lived her life to its natural end and had no unfinished business," Bent said. "Wherever the restful dead go, she's there now."

The priest nodded, taking comfort in this pronouncement from Bent, who it seemed was in a position to know. Now the priest sought pastoral care from the flock. The priest pressed on.

"Do you...know any more now?" he said.

"Of this state I'm in? No. I've no more knowledge than I had before. No idea what I am, no idea what comes next. I only know that those who have completed their business in life move on, and those who haven't linger."

"Would you like to attend the funeral service?"

Bent said he would, and so, three days later, just before dawn, he ducked in through the rectory door, which the priest had left open for him, travelled the musty corridors through the residence to the church, and secreted himself in a confessional. The mass took place at ten, and though the mourners didn't know he was among them, Bent listened to the words spoken by the priest and cried for his lost friend.

"The wise shall shine brightly like the splendor of the firmament, and those who lead the many to justice shall be like the stars forever."

He had now attended two funerals as a corpse, neither of them his own.

He went to the park to seek the revenant. The park looked like an over-exposed photograph, flashes of white snow and black trees and the water of the bay like a pool of developer fluid spilled on the print. There were fewer revenants now, and they were less active than before. One sat leaning against a tree with his knees drawn to his chest. Another huddled under the picnic table as though hiding. The one he'd spoken with when he first found the group sat on the bench looking at the water. Or he looked in the direction of the water. What he saw Bent didn't know. Bent went to him and stood, waiting for an invitation to sit. The revenant didn't look up but Bent knew he was aware of him. It did not offer him a seat. Bent sat anyway.

"Why do you come here?" the creature said.

Bent glanced at the revenants wandering in the park. "Have the rest gone to…wherever they were meant to go?"

"There will be others."

"You didn't answer my question," Bent said.

"You didn't answer mine."

Bent shrugged. "Where should I go? Where can I go?"

The creature nodded. "I thought the same when I first came here."

"When was that?"

The revenant inclined his head, trying to remember, but after a moment he seemed to forget he was trying to remember something and went back to gazing at the bay.

"Will anybody come to tell us what to do?"

The revenant shook its head.

"A light. Isn't there meant to be a light?"

The revenant laughed.

"What about family to meet us?"

"Mine are still living. Most, anyway."

"Is there nothing you can tell me?"

The revenant smiled and looked unbearably sad.

"What did you think?" he said. "That you would die and suddenly everything would make sense? That you would exist outside time, like God? See all that's ever happened from above, beginning to end? You're human. There are no answers. Only questions."

Had Bent expected answers? Well, isn't that what was promised? He'd stopped believing in God and an afterlife long ago, but part of him still thought, when the time came, *maybe*. But no.

Bent wanted to sit, to be companionable, so he looked at the water along with the creature, but its sadness was like a cloud and he felt it spreading toward him and couldn't bear it. He rose and tried to think of something to say in parting, but the man had no interest in words, or in him, so he took his leave in silence.

~

They heard fluttering. It grew closer and louder, and they looked up. A blackness moved toward them in the sky. It drew near and rippled and pulsed and exploded into hundreds of crows banking over the graveyard. They flew overhead and Bent and Tell and Machlon threw their heads back to watch. The crows reached the tree line and landed. The branches were thick with black. One cawed, as if barking an order to the others, and they settled on the branches and brooded.

Tell looked at Bent and Machlon. "This seems like a bad sign."

They sat quiet, out of things to say. Tell crossed his arms.

"Christ, I'm sick of sittin around here."

Bent's gaze drifted to Machlon, who acted as though Tell hadn't spoken. He sat studying the ground, waiting, it seemed like.

"Where do you go, Machlon?"

Machlon was quiet awhile and watched the water in the slice of cove visible through trees beyond the tombstones.

"I go to my house," he said finally. "I look in at the window. He lies in bed and writhes and cries and prays to be dead. I think he's praying to me."

Bent tried to think of something comforting but Tell snorted.

"Better him than you," Tell said.

Bent turned on him. "That's a shitty thing to say."

"Stupid thing to think," Tell said.

"At least he thinks about somebody besides himself," Bent said. "You've abandoned your wife and children to the care of that *thing*, even now he wants to give your body back."

"Oh and you gave so much thought to your wife and kids before you tried to check out."

Bent threw himself at Tell and in an instant they were rolling in the grass. Tell got him pinned and struck three blows on his jaw but Bent flipped him and was up. He kicked at him but Tell seized his ankle and yanked him off his feet. He charged him but Bent rolled away and got up. They got in close then, wrestling and landing punches where they could. Bent got Tell in a headlock. Tell reached an arm around to try to break free but Bent took it and twisted it behind his back and pulled as hard as he could. He heard a sound like seams ripping, then felt it through his fingers, and Tell's arm came off in his hand. They froze, stunned, staring at each other. Tell looked at his gaping shoulder socket, then both looked down at the arm.

"That's going to leave a mark," Machlon said.

They all laughed then, soundless, joyless laughter, till tears came.

Tell slumped against the fallen tree. Bent came to him and held out the arm and sat beside him, and Machlon sat, too. Tell cradled the arm in his lap like a baby and wiped his eyes with his remaining arm.

"I'm slipping," he said. "Losing myself."

"So am I," Bent said.

Machlon nodded. "Me, too."

Bent stabbed the ground with a stick and let go and it stuck. A last patch of snow was spattered with flecks of dirt and pine needles. The stick looked like a dead soldier's rifle stuck upright at a grave and hung with a helmet for a marker.

"I've been forgetting who I am," Bent said, then shook his head and grimaced; that wasn't what he meant. "Not who I am, or was, but how it *felt*. Sometimes I can't get at it. Can't feel it. But then other times, I think, my god, my *kids*. My *wife*."

Tell and Machlon listened and knew what he meant. Bent felt like there was more to say, so much more he wanted to say, but then there was too much to say and thinking of it wore him out, so he fell silent. So did they, and the silence was kinetic, like they could feel each other thinking, like the frenzy of each man's thoughts was buzzing in the air around them like a bee swarm. They sat, Tell holding his arm, and let the night pass.

Tell spent most of the next day trying to sew the arm back on. Bent had felt so bad he broke into the grocery the night before and stole a sewing kit. Tell would hook a seam and pull the thread through and the rag of flesh would come off in his hand. He'd cut it away with the tiny scissors and try again. By late afternoon he'd managed to re-attach it with rough zig-zagging stitches, but he'd had to cut away so much tattered flesh that the pieces no longer matched with the shoulder and the arm didn't fit right and hung out at an odd angle. Tell looked down, raised and lowered the arm a few times, then tore it off and hurled it across the den.

"Sorry," Bent said.

They sat quietly for a while.

Tell laughed a bit. "Do you remember that night we walked to the creek by the airport and sat in the reeds watching the planes land?"

They remembered and laughed quietly.

"We got drunk on whisky Machlon stole off his father," Tell said.

They laughed harder then.

"He beat my ass next day," Machlon said.

"Yeah," Tell said. "Sorry."

Machlon waved his hand. "The runway lights were so blue," he said.

They sat quietly and saw it in their minds. They'd walked from the cinema, along the road where the Christmas tree farm was, and climbed the fence and sat amongst the cat o' nine tails opposite the National Guard landing strip. The flight path went right above their heads and the planes glided over like sharks and floated down and nosed right in between the two lines of blue lights.

"What made you think of that?" Bent asked.

"I don't know," Tell said. "It was a nice night."

Bent and Machlon nodded.

"It was," Bent said.

Above them a crow called.

"What do you think happens when we die?" Tell asked. "I mean *really* die."

Bent smiled and shook his head. "I have no idea."

Tell looked out at the cove and thought about this awhile.

"I have to go back," he said finally.

Bent and Machlon received what he'd said but didn't look at him.

"The FBI?" Bent said. "They'll come for you."

Tell shrugged. "You were right. What am I doing? That thing is ready to swap back. I need to see my kids."

At nightfall, Tell rose and looked around. "Let's see, do I need to bring anything? Oh yeah." He bent and retrieved his arm, eased it into the sack and cinched it and looked at Bent. "At least you have pockets."

He threw the sack onto the shoulder that still had its arm and turned to Bent.

"I'm crap at goodbyes, so…"

"Yeah," Bent said, and they clasped each other firmly, and then Tell turned to Machlon and they hugged and slapped each other on the back.

Tell turned and moved off through the headstones, then turned and, walking backward, called out, "You might see me again."

"Thinking of changing your mind?" Bent asked.

Tell shook his head and pointed at the ground. "My burial plot is here."

He turned and walked off.

Bent and Machlon puttered around a bit and didn't know what to do. It was full dark and they could each have gone their ways as usual, but they were bothered. Machlon was restless and twitchy. Finally he turned to Bent.

"It doesn't seem right," he said. "Somebody ought to be with him when he…goes."

Bent had been thinking the same. It wasn't as if he was going to die, at least not right off, but it seemed like they should be there to see him off. They moved quickly to catch up and hoped it hadn't happened already. When they reached the park, Tell was standing near the water, waiting. They reached the tree line to the west.

"Tell," Machlon said.

Tell turned and spotted them. They became aware then of a shape on the far edge of the park and turned. Tell's revenant stepped from the shadows and stopped. Tell turned to Bent and Machlon and smiled, then turned back to the revenant. They walked toward each other and met in the middle.

The revenant looked down. "Where's my arm?"

"Oh, right." Tell reached into the sack and drew it out and handed it to the other Tell. "I saved it for you."

The other Tell held the arm out and looked at it, then at Tell.

"Long story," Tell said. "I tried to sew it, but I don't know... maybe you can do something with it."

The revenant set the arm in the snow, then stood. He and Tell looked at each other, and in a moment it was done. Tell, back in his own body, looked back at Bent and Machlon and raised a hand. They waved back, and he turned from them and walked off toward home. The revenant bent and retrieved his arm and looked accusingly at Bent and Machlon.

Bent raised a hand. "My bad."

The revenant gave him a last dirty look, then tucked his arm under his arm and walked away.

Machlon walked abroad for a while, but Bent returned to the graveyard. He sat tending the embers when a rare visitor sent him scurrying for the tree line. A very old woman hobbled carefully through the grass and stopped at Mrs. Rutherford's headstone. She stooped creakily and set a potted chrysanthemum before the stone. Poor woman. Had she anybody left now Mrs. Rutherford was gone? The woman stood and regarded the headstone. Bent saw on her forehead a smudge of ash. Was it that late in the season? His nose tingled. There was a pungent sugary smell in the air, like burnt syrup. The sap was running.

The warmer air had been softening his skin. Fissures had

opened here and there on his body, and the last of his fluids were oozing from the openings. At this rate he would be completely decomposed within weeks. He pictured himself, the last of his flesh, like brittle book binding, evaporated in the warm air, his brownish bones like a carcass in the desert, one dung beetle ranging over a rib searching out some morsel left behind by the worms. If he was going to do something, he had to do it soon.

When the woman left, he returned to the fire. Memories pained him. He wished they would stop, but on they came.

They sat at the kitchen table on a summer evening, windows open to the warm night, playing Uno. Ada hated to lose, and they let her win sometimes, as you do with small children, but they wanted her to learn sportsmanship so sometimes they played to win. Good luck, though, convincing Jack to let his sister win at anything if he could help it. Whenever Ada knew she was losing she grew sulky and slammed down cards or game pieces when it was her turn, and on this particular night she had slid into a three-hand losing streak.

"Uh oh," Jack said. "Ada's being a bad sport."

Their attempts at discipline were weakened by the fact that they found Ada unspeakably adorable when she was angry, and the angrier she got the more adorable she became and the more they struggled not to laugh. Even Jack found it funny.

"Bent," Jean said, trying to maintain composure. "Explain to Ada again about why it's important to be gracious when you lose."

Bent explained about how games were meant to be for the fun of it and how if you made it less fun people wouldn't want to play anymore, but Ada glared at the cards like they were somehow doing it on purpose. She tried very hard to look menacing and Bent and Jean tried very hard not to laugh. The crickets chirped outside the windows and June bugs pinged at the screens and the beauty of the night added to their mood.

"Uno!" Jack yelled when he was down to one card.

Ada's face darkened.

"Ada's gonna lo-o-oose, Ada's gonna lo-o-oose..."

"Jack."

They went around again and Jack threw down his final card and thrust his fists in the air and Ada flung her cards on the table.

"You cheated! You wanted me to lose!"

"Ada, what did we say about being a good sport?" Jean said, but Ada sulked, and Bent and Jean worked hard not to laugh, and then they couldn't help it and laughed anyway.

"Stop laughing at me!" Ada said, but Jack shoved her shoulder and then she laughed a little in spite of herself, and then her good humor returned. They played till long past the children's bedtimes.

Even now Bent laughed to think of it, and he looked back on his life and thought that if he told it as a story, he would tell a happy one.

Machlon returned to the graveyard and found Bent there.

"No desire to roam?" Machlon said.

"Nah."

"Me, neither."

They lit a fire without worrying it might be seen. They lay on their backs and felt last autumn's rotting leaves, wet and black from a winter covered by snow, and talked of old times.

Bent thought of the time in sixth grade when he and Machlon and Tell and other neighbor kids had lingered on the basketball court in the fading light and chugged round the blacktop like a train singing "Locomotion." It was April and the air was still thin and cold, but they were boys made vigorous by spring. They sang there in the graveyard and Bent could smell the spring air and the blacktop. They rose and chugged among the graves, steering between the headstones and singing and dancing the "Locomotion."

They fell back in the leaves, laughing and breathless from the effort.

"Who else was there?" Bent said. "Dave Styre…"

"Bonnie Mack."

Bent nodded. "Bonnie Mack, and Mike Buermeyer, and Tracey Keller."

"You had a crush on her, didn't you?"

Bent smiled. "I used to sit cross-legged on my bed with a Magic 8-Ball and ask it questions about her."

"Dear Magic 8 Ball, will Tracey Keller fall in love with me and marry me and run off to Hawaii with me?"

Bent nodded. "Exactly. And it was Decidedly So. But then she got really tall."

They laughed together, and then grew quiet.

"How come we had to die to talk like we used to?" Bent finally said.

Machlon's smile faded. "Yeah," he said. "I wonder why that is."

They grew quiet again, and Bent sensed if he wanted to know anything else of Machlon he ought to ask it now.

"Are you mad at me, for not being with you after your mother died?"

"What? No."

Bent shook his head. "I should have gone back to Boston with you. I could've taken a leave of absence."

"That would have been crazy. Nobody takes a leave of absence from Yale. I'm not mad at you at all, Bent. I was glad you got out."

Machlon was quiet for a while and Bent worried he'd upset

him. He shouldn't have mentioned it. But then Machlon spoke.

"When they came and got me and told me I was going to the hospital, at first I was relieved. It was a lot, you know? But then we got to that place, they had the RA take me, and he left me there. I watched him go through the security doors and walk off down the hall, and I looked around at all these strangers and I was so alone."

He put more wood on the fire, stacked it carefully, and the fire surged and hissed.

"I couldn't talk to any of them. Most of them barely knew where they were. They were stoned on anti-depressants and sedatives and they were wandering the halls doing the Thorazine shuffle."

Bent frowned, and Machlon rose to demonstrate.

"It's this walk you get when you take it. They walk and walk and walk, they never stop, and they shuffle, like this." He walked along in small quick steps and hardly lifted his feet. "In the mornings we had group therapy," he said, sitting down again. "Everybody in the group was supposed to say why we were there and how we felt about it. This one boy who'd tried to hang himself had been there for a week and hadn't said a word. Finally somebody asked him why he wanted to kill himself. And he said, 'Well, my girlfriend left me, and my parents got divorced. My sister's a heroin addict. My dog died…' And I don't know what came over me, but when he got to the part about the dog I burst out laughing."

Machlon chuckled now thinking of it.

"I don't know why. I mean, I felt really sorry for the kid, but I couldn't stop laughing. They were all staring at me, and the kid was looking at me with this really hurt expression, but that just made me laugh harder."

Bent pictured the scene and though it wasn't funny he started laughing, too. They both laughed, and then their laughter died away.

"I don't know why I did that," Machlon said.

Bent didn't know what to say, but he wanted to say something to make Machlon feel that what he'd done hadn't been so bad.

"I was cheating on Jean," he said.

Machlon looked at him, surprised. He looked down, and his face contorted, and Bent thought he was going to cry. But he snorted, tried to control his face, then burst out laughing. He tried to stop but couldn't and held up a hand.

"See? I'm doing it again."

And Bent burst out laughing then, too. They gave in to it and laughed long and hard, rolling in the leaves and pounding the ground with their fists and screaming with laughter as the tears rolled.

"I can't breathe," Machlon said, gasping.

Bent laughed, and then his laughter died in his throat.

Can't breathe.

And he knew how to get the revenant out of his body.

Toward morning their talk died out, and they sat quietly as the orange dawn floated above the sea to the east, and then Machlon spoke the words they'd both known he would say before the night was out.

"Will you be angry if I go, too?"

Bent looked at him and smiled sadly, then looked back at the dawn. "Are you not afraid?"

Next to him, he felt Machlon shrug.

"I am." He stopped there, as if the fear didn't seem to matter. "The pain was so bad. God, Bent, I can't tell you how bad it was. I would have done anything to end it. But it isn't right. He wants to live, that's why he took my body. I understand that. But what he swapped for isn't living. Now he'll soon die. So I'll go back, and maybe he can swap with somebody else, somebody willing. I don't mind dying. It was the living I couldn't take anymore. It's nearly over now."

The next morning early they left the graveyard, the sky the color of mourning doves. They walked along the track bed, stepping on the crossties to avoid the unstable shifting rocks of the track bed. Bent's stride was too long for the gaps and Machlon's too short, so Bent took two ties at a time and Machlon took short halting steps from one tie to the next. It felt strange to be about in daylight. But it was still early and they could walk the tracks all the way to Machlon's house hid beneath the high slopes.

Ahead the track banked hard left, and they stopped. From here it veered toward the river road. To the right, at the top of the slope, would be Machlon's house. They started to climb, dug their feet in and clutched tufts of grass and hauled themselves up. But sometimes lingering patches of snow clogged their path and they slipped back down and had to regain the ground they had lost. Eventually they gained the top.

Machlon's bedroom was in back, and they peered in at the window. The other Machlon lay small and still beneath the covers, pale and shockingly thin, the quilts barely rising with his breath. Bent looked away. He couldn't stand to see his friend so wasted, even if it wasn't really him.

Machlon turned to Bent. "I hate to leave."

"I'll be all right."

They embraced, and Machlon turned back to the window and drew up the sash. Inside, the other Machlon's head turned at the sound. Machlon climbed in and shut the window behind him. For a moment he watched Bent through the glass. Bent nodded. Machlon took a deep breath and turned around. He walked toward the bed as the other Machlon watched, and Bent turned away. He didn't want to see.

~

Bent went into the empty church and used the phone in the priest's office to call Jean. She drove to the graveyard to meet him and he told her his idea.

"Are you sure this will work?"

He nodded. "I think so. It will kill him at least. If I'm stuck like this, then I am. At least he'll be gone and you and the kids can go home."

"So you're going to just abandon us and kill yourself? Again?"

"Do you have any other ideas? Because I don't."

"I don't, either."

Bent looked toward the woods. The trees were swaying in the wind. He smiled. "Do you remember that trip to Maine?"

They'd left the children with Jean's parents. They'd lain in the grass on a sweeping hill and watched fireworks over Penobscot Bay, then gone back to the one-room cabin on stilts and crowded together in the shower, its cheap plastic walls shaking as they moved together.

"We nearly broke that shower."

Jean laughed. "And I went out onto the deck to look at the lake and you stole my towel."

She'd shrieked and giggled and they wrestled their way to the bed and made love again.

"That little breakfast place," he said.

They'd found it the next morning and had coffee and crullers by the lake.

"That was a good time," Jean said.

"Yep," he said. "Lots of little memories."

Jean glanced at him and then back out toward the woods.

"We could have made a go of it, you know. If you'd tried."

"I know," he said. "I'm sorry. I wasn't a very good husband, was I?"

"No, you weren't."

Bent chuckled. "Tell me how you really feel."

"You want me to lie? Now?"

Bent looked at his hands. "No."

Jean sighed. "The little memories were never enough for you." She said it simply, without malice. "You went through life looking for the big ones, but those are few and far between and when they happen they're as often bad as they are good. If you go through life with a lot of little ones and very few big ones you should count yourself lucky. You never seemed to realize that, even after your father."

Bent nodded. "You're right. I guess I was looking for some great big thing to make up for it. To balance the scales or something. But you just have to go on. You just have to."

He paused, trying to think of how to say what he had to say.

"Abby."

Jean bristled but stayed silent.

"That wasn't about you, you know. It was about me. I could never believe a rich, pretty girl would like me. I guess ever since she went off with Chas I felt like I missed out. She was this perfect thing that I could never have. And I felt so old, Jean. My bones ached and I was so tired. And there were the money worries and the house…When Abby came back I felt like…like I had a second chance. It wasn't even about her. It was about me."

Jean nodded.

"I am sorry."

Jean cleared her throat. "Thank you."

"There's something else, too," Bent said. "Something I never told you."

"What is it?"

And Bent told her. Told her about his father, about his mother saying that he hadn't drowned that day, that he had left them, left because of Bent.

"She said that he couldn't stand being around me anymore. She said I was impossible to love."

Tears spilled down Jean's face. "Oh, Bent... Why did you not tell me?"

"Who would want somebody their own father wouldn't love?"

She turned to him. "Bent, your father fell overboard and drowned."

"That's what Father Fintan says."

"You told Father Fintan and not me?"

"I've known him since I was a kid."

"And Abby?"

Bent paused, then nodded. "You know how it is when you're kids. You tell each other things."

Jean shook her head and cried quietly.

"Anyway," Bent said. "I guess I could never get past it."

"I just wish you had told me," Jean said.

"What good would it have done?"

"I could have told you that it wasn't true. That people do love you. That the kids love you. That I love you."

Bent nodded, looking off into the woods. "I love you, too."

Jean looked at his profile. "It's just not the same as with Abby, is it?"

"Jean..."

"Don't lie to me now, Bent, or try to make me feel better. This may be the last time we ever see each other. Let's clear the books."

Bent looked down, then looked at her sadly and shook his head. "No. Not the same as with Abby. I'm sorry."

Jean nodded and wiped her tears. "It's okay. I've always known. In a way it's a relief to hear you finally admit it. It was never me. I just got there too late. You were already taken."

"I'm sorry," Bent said. "You deserved better. Deserve better. And now you'll be able to get it. Find yourself somebody who will treat you the way I should have. Somebody who will be good to the kids."

Jean nodded. "Time will tell."

Bent's voice broke. "Do you think they'll remember me?"

Jean looked at him. "I'll make sure of it."

She hesitated, then reached out her hand. He took it, intertwined his fingers with hers, and they sat looking out at the woods.

He went to the park. Abby was there alone. There was no sign of the other women.

"Where are the others?"

"They're off haunting their husbands. I wasn't into it."

She was bent over a forsythia, breaking off the edges of branches.

"What are you doing?"

"Cutting the branches of forsythia in the spring forces them into bloom. We could use a bit of color around here."

"Oh. Do you need help?"

"Sure."

Bent took hold of a branch and bent it until it snapped. The sound was satisfying somehow, and he smelled something vaguely like honey.

"This should be done with pruning shears," Abby said, "But…"

When they had finished, she carried the branches over to a mound of debris she had pruned from other trees and shrubs in the park and tossed them onto the pile.

"Do what you can in every season."

Bent looked off toward the town beach. He could just make out the dinghy tied up by the abandoned lifeguard's station.

"You remember the time we sat up half the night in that boat on the beach?" he said.

Abby looked at him and saw that he wasn't just moping, so she allowed herself to enjoy the memory. "Yes. We went to the Willettes' house to try and touch the porch, then that boy Marshall scared me half to death."

Bent thought about it. "He was seeing his dead parents, wasn't he?"

"Yes, I think so."

"Abby?"

"Hmm?"

"I failed you."

Abby turned to him and watched and waited.

Bent took a deep breath. This was going to be hard. "When you pulled up in the car that night with Chas, you looked like a couple, and I felt like this stupid little boy who was foolish enough to think he could have the most wonderful girl in school."

"Because of your father?" Abby said. "Because of what your mother said?"

Bent nodded. "I should have gone with you that night. I should have fought for you. And when you came back when you and Chas separated, I should have gone with you then, too. I should have told Jean the truth. It would have been the best thing for her, too. I've never been a good husband to her because the whole time all I wanted was you."

Abby could tell that it was different this time, him going over their lives, and she stayed quiet and listened.

"We could have worked it out, how to split time with Jack," he continued. "But I didn't do it because I didn't want to be the father who abandoned his son. And because I didn't trust it. I didn't trust that you really did love me. That you could love me. I wasted my whole life. And then when you came back last year and you still wanted me, I straddled the fence for so long because I still couldn't quite believe it. I couldn't quite believe that you could truly love me. That I wasn't impossible to love."

He turned to her then. "If I could change it all I would. The moment I first saw you, it was like bells started ringing, and that was it, I loved you. And I love you now."

Any lingering anger she felt at him melted away. "I love you, too," she said.

They fell into each other's arms and held each other for a long while. And then Bent let her go and took a few steps away and looked out over the water, to imagine a life beyond this and because he wouldn't be able to say what he had to say next if he could see her and touch her.

"You should go."

Abby looked up at him, and she felt her eyes fill with grateful tears. "You *mean* it."

"Yes. Go see your grandmother."

She stepped in close. "Thank you."

They embraced and held each other for the last time, then Abby turned and walked away and vanished into the fog.

Sunset was a full hour later now than it had been at the height of winter. When it finally came, Bent took a last look around their graveyard camp and thought of the time they had spent there. They weren't good memories, exactly. He remembered boredom and restlessness, frustration, loneliness. But he also remembered sitting before a fire with Tell and Machlon, talking, sometimes laughing. In the middle of it all, laughing. They had been his friends, and once he lost Abby and his family they were all he had. He lost Mrs. Rutherford, and Tell and Machlon, and Abby again, and now it was only him. He kicked away the stone circle of the fire pit and spread the ashes with his foot. He crossed the grass to Mrs. Rutherford's grave, said a silent goodbye, took a last look around, and left the graveyard. He didn't bother climbing into the trees to cross the street. There were no cars, and he dashed across, then dipped down the hillside, crossed the tracks and climbed the other side. Here he fell back. Teenage boys took advantage of the warmer evening for a pickup game on the court and Bent knelt in the bushes and watched. The white streetlight bathed the court like a nimbus. The boys dribbled and the hard pock of ball on asphalt echoed and the boys shouted and he could see their breath. And Bent saw himself on the court, and Tell and Machlon and their school friends, saw them and heard them doing the "Locomotion" in the fading light.

A thin voice drifted on the air then, a woman's voice, and one boy froze and cocked his head and waited. The voice came again, and the boy whose name was called popped the ball to another boy, waved and trotted off. The other boys clustered then, one dribbling the ball as they talked. Then the group turned and burst like a supernova and each boy went off toward home.

Bent skirted the court, keeping from the light, then turned left. He stepped onto the porch at Little's and leaned in at the window, peered at the booth where he had taken coffee all those mornings with the others, and farther back, when he had run from home with a nickel given him by his father and bought fireballs and stuffed them in his mouth and tested how long he could hold them in his cheeks. He could feel the burning.

He descended the steps and walked the road, wanting his last walk through his hometown to be the way he always saw it. He reached St Andrew's, climbed the steps and entered.

He stepped into the confessional and waited. Soon the priest slid back the door.

"Go ahead, my child."

"I didn't really come to confess. I'd just like to talk if that's all right, Father."

"Oh, Bent. Yes, of course. I didn't expect you to come. I'm used to seeing you in the graveyard. Good Lord, that sounded terrible, didn't it?"

"I don't know what I want to say, really. I guess I just wanted to see you." They kept silent for a while, then Bent said, "Did you believe in ghosts before all this happened?"

"I suppose I agreed with Mark Twain. He said, 'I don't believe in ghosts, but I'm afraid of them.' Now I don't know what I believe anymore."

"Thomas Aquinas believed that souls could leave the other world and appear to the living," Bent said. "He thought God allowed it either to instruct the living or, if the soul was in hell or purgatory, to frighten them. Into mending their ways, I suppose."

"Yes," the priest said, and was silent for a moment as he considered the question. "A number of early churchmen believed in spirits. Aquinas, as you say. St. Bernard. Augustine thought apparitions were spiritual images, placed in a person's mind by good or bad angels. The apparition had no relation to the dead person's actual body."

Bent looked at his own body, his grey decomposing hands.

"Or to his soul," the priest continued.

Bent sighed and leaned his head against the confessional.

"I'm not very much help, am I?" the priest said.

"It's not that," Bent said. "It's just that I thought the church was meant to provide answers."

"It's been my experience that, at its best, the church is a place where we can come together to wonder together about our questions."

Bent had always wanted things to be settled, wanted to see what was in front of him, next day, next week, next year. Facts. Answers. For years he had searched and never found them, but he'd always believed they were there somewhere. He'd married because that's what you did, and he thought it might bring him peace. But it didn't. He'd had children because it was *next*. It brought him love, but he never gave himself wholly to it, so afraid was he that he would lose it. And now he had, and it was his own fault, and he wished he'd had the courage to love without fear.

"Remember how it used to be?" Bent said. "Before we knew so much, when we thought the dead visited us in our sleep and revealed to us their suffering in purgatory? Before psychologists explained our dreams to us. Are their explanations any more satisfactory? Do we feel less afraid, less lonely? Isn't it comforting, in a way, to think that our dead kin, reprieved for a day to seek out the living and warn them of things to come, that the people they thought to come to were us?"

"Yes," the priest said. The words had clearly struck him. "Yes, it is."

"If I could, I would go to Jack and Ada and tell them how much I love them and miss them. That I wish I could be with them, and how sorry, so sorry I am that I left. I had these two precious, extraordinary beings, and I was so caught up in my own selfishness, I didn't even see what I had. I'd tell them all that, and I would never leave them again."

Bent said nothing more, and the priest could hear he was crying. "Bent?"

Bent leaned his head close to the screen, feeling it all welling up within him. Everything that had happened, what he had become, what he had lost.

"I have to go," he said finally.

"Are you sure? Would you like to come to my office for coffee? Well, you can't drink coffee, I suppose, but just to talk. Where we can see each other. Face to face."

"Thank you, but I can't." He opened the confessional door. "I know you'll look after Jean and the kids, so I don't have to ask."

"Are you all right, Bent?"

Bent stopped. "I will be," he said, and left.

He turned right toward the park. The sky was velvet. It was suppertime, and yellow light glowed in windows, and here and there he saw a family at the dinner table behind gauzy curtains. He heard tires slap on wet pavement behind him and pulled up his coat collar and ducked his head. The car rolled by and moved off down the road.

At the park he turned in. The grass was wet and Bent felt his trouser legs grow damp as he walked. He sat at the picnic table and waited, and after a while the revenants came. Bent walked to the bench where the one he spoke to sat and he sat beside him and looked out at the bay where the revenant watched. They sat quietly for a while, Bent enjoying the nearness of another soul, if not a living one. A dirty crust of snow edged the grass where it dipped down to the sand and the waves trickled over pebbles and quahog holes ticked and popped when the water peeled back.

"I came to say goodbye," Bent said. "I won't be back after tonight."

The revenant, as usual, said nothing. Only stared at the waves.

"Do you not care?"

Nothing.

"Are you not at all curious why?"

Still the revenant didn't speak, just maintained his vigil over the bay. *What in the world was he looking for out there?*

"It's silly, maybe, but after all this time I've begun to think of us as friends," Bent said.

He waited, but the revenant did not speak and Bent became mindful of his dignity. He was dead, but he wouldn't beg. He rose, this time doing as the revenant did, speaking but looking at the sea.

"If you can spare a thought for me, check on my family from time to time? You can do nothing for them, I know, but it will comfort me to know I've sent someone."

The revenant nodded vaguely, though it could have been for some private musing of his own and not to Bent, so Bent made one final try before he left.

"They live on Spring Street. The Fiske house."

The revenant nodded and even smiled a bit. "I know the place. A good old house."

"It is," Bent said. "I had it from my father."

Bent turned and left.

The revenant gazed at the waves, but in his head he heard again the words Bent had just spoken. *The Fiske house. I had it from my father.* Could it be? He turned quickly. "What did you say?"

But Bent had vanished in the trees.

Bent peered in through the window of the sitting room. Through the kitchen doorway he saw the other Bent alone at the dinner table, eating in silence.

Bent moved around to the back of the house, ran, ducking beneath the kitchen windows, stopped at the back door and crouched. He ran over it all again in his head, through all the possible solutions, everything he had thought of and rejected, and tried one last time to think of any other way. He couldn't.

He reached up and gripped the doorknob, then stood and took hold with both hands and turned and pushed hard. The door gave and he burst into the kitchen. The other Bent turned to rise but Bent grabbed hold of his shoulders and spun him about. The chair flipped from beneath the other Bent and skidded away and the thing crashed to the linoleum and Bent was on him, the other's arms pinned beneath his knees and Bent's hands round his throat. He wrenched the other's neck and squeezed, and felt the other's legs kicking behind him, but he wrenched harder, and the legs dropped and the other Bent tried to buck him off. His eyes were big and protruding in the sockets and his face was red as blood. And Bent began to cry, but he kept squeezing. He began to feel dizzy and worried he would pass out, but he shook his head to keep himself alert and squeezed tighter. And soon he felt the other Bent stop bucking, and his eyes died.

And then Bent was above himself and he knew that it had worked. He saw his body blue and strange on the kitchen floor, and he saw their house, so small amid the trees, atop the bluff, above the ocean, upon the Earth. And he saw Jean go through the door of her parents' house, saw Jack and Ada run to greet her, saw her kneel and tell them and hold them to her as they cried. *Daddy*, they screamed. *Daddy*. And he cried because they cried and laughed for their beauty. My poor babies, he thought. They're crying for me. And he wished them long life and hoped for their joy along the way and sat down to wait for them. He waited, too, for his father, who he now knew had not abandoned him, had drowned that day in the Sound. And he waited for Abby, for he knew she would come to him soon.

And he looked down upon the world below and thought, what a pretty blue.

~

Acknowledgements

I am immensely grateful to Elizabeth MacDuffie and Mark Alan Miller for giving this book a home when I had all but given up hope, and for the love, dedication, talent, respect and care with which they have treated the book from the moment it entered their hands. "I was but little happy if I could say how much."

Huge thanks to Jacob Polley and Ian Johnson. What can I say. You are princes among men, the both of you, and I literally could not have written this book without your guidance, your wisdom, and your unflagging support. Thank you, thank you, thank you.

Many thanks to Gerard Woodward for his insightful suggestions on an early draft of the novel, which helped me to mold it into its current form. Thanks as well to Iain Maloney and Tess O'Bamber for their feedback on a later draft, which helped me find the light switch when I was trapped in a dark room.

Thanks to my cousin Amy Nelson, who allowed me to plunder her knowledge of boats and sailing.

Thanks, too, to Velle Espeland for allowing me to use portions of his translation of the medieval Norwegian ballad Draumkvedet, the song Bent learned from his grandmother and sings throughout the story.

I am more grateful than I can express to the School of English at the University of St Andrews for providing me the time and encouragement to think about my writing again as though it were a serious thing, and for the George Buchanan Scholarship, which helped me to write this novel.

Thanks always to my family, for the laughs, the old lady drives and all the rest of the fuckery and shenanigans.

And to Stephen Sacco, my best friend, my co-conspirator, my Wonder Twin Powers activate partner, even though in addition to breaking my vacuum cleaner, he also broke my blender.

About The Author

Christian is also the author of a memoir in essays, *We Are Not Okay*, which the *Los Angeles Review of Books* called 'ineffably important... relentless and courageous and entertaining and upsetting.'
Her stories and essays have appeared in anthologies and literary journals. She has a PhD in Creative Writing from the University of St Andrews. She lives on Earth.

Made in the USA
Middletown, DE
06 October 2023

40122411R00149